The
Promise
Emma
Heatherington

HarperCollins*Publishers*

HarperCollins*Publishers* Ltd
1 London Bridge Street,
London SE1 9GF
www.harpercollins.co.uk

HarperCollins*Publishers*
1st Floor, Watermarque Building, Ringsend Road
Dublin 4, Ireland

First published by HarperCollins*Publishers* 2021
1

A catalogue record for this book is available from the British Library

ISBN: 978-0-00-843514-1

Set in Birka by Palimpsest Book Production Ltd, Falkirk, Stirlingshire

Printed and Bound in the UK using
100% Renewable Electricity at CPI Group (UK) Ltd

MIX
Paper from
responsible sources
FSC C007454

This book is produced from independently certified FSC™ paper
to ensure responsible forest management.

For more information visit: www.harpercollins.co.uk/green

The Promise is dedicated to all survivors of trauma.
May you find the strength and courage to own the
story of your past, and the power to choose what
you become in your future.

Difference is the essence of humanity.

John Hume (1937–2020)
Derry born Nobel Peace Prize Winner.
Taken from the Nobel Lecture, Oslo, December 10, 1998

1.

KATE

'You look pale. You need to eat more.'

My tone is firm and disapproving but she shrugs and looks away as a familiar grip of despair clutches my stomach. She was always thin and small in stature, but every time I come here, she looks sicker and sicker, and I sleep less and less in return with worry.

'It's not as simple as that,' she says, flicking back her wispy brown hair and avoiding my eye, playing with the fine gold chain around her neck. I've never known her without that chain, yet never took the time to ask why it was so special. Someday I'll remember to. 'It's so hard to get used to the food in here but I'll manage. You know what I'm like about my own cooking.'

'Are you hungry?'

'I'm not hungry.'

I don't believe her, so I pile up a mountain of crisps, fruit and a Snickers bar from my oversized straw bag.

'Your favourite,' I whisper.

'It is. Thank you.'

She grips my hand and squeezes it so hard it hurts a little, but I haven't the heart to admit so.

'I'm really enjoying the course,' I say with a burst of enthusiasm, trying to brighten her up a little by shifting the focus from her eating habits in this hellhole to my nursing degree out in the real world. 'I've just another few days before we break for summer, but I've the auxiliary job in the hospital to keep me going until we start again in September.'

'That's nice.'

I casually loosen from her grasp when I can and I play with the visitor's card around my neck, the presence of it against my student's blue uniform feeling as if it might choke me.

She nods and looks away, flicks her hair again, and I know what's coming.

I know she can only absorb so much of what I tell her about real life before she quivers and breaks down in a flurry of panic and guilt and everything in between. She is like a hollow eggshell; a heartbreaking opposite to the fierce campaigner, the vocal activist and the role model I looked up to all my life.

'That's really . . . that's really good to hear, love,' she whispers.

Her lip trembles. Her chin wobbles.

'And I still come home to the girls most weekends when I can,' I remind her, keeping my end of the promise we made and talking so that she doesn't have to. 'We've developed a bit of a routine where I help out with the wee one to give Maureen a break, so nothing to worry about, just like I promised you. Nothing at all.'

She stares so hard at the table that separates us that her eyes might bore a hole in it eventually.

'Thank you,' she says. 'What on earth would we do without you? Thank you, Kate.'

If someone was to sum up my life lately in a sentence it would be just this from her always: *What on earth would we do without you?* I sometimes wish they could do without me more, but I know this isn't going to last for ever and for now we just have to keep going. We have to keep paddling towards the future when this will all be a distant memory and we'll laugh at how good it feels to be normal again.

It's quite cold in here, just as I knew it would be, so I wrap my navy cardigan around me a little more tightly. The room is vast and green like a hospital, but with a distinct air of suffocation and the force of control that seeps from its shiny walls and echoing corridors. She is lost here, in an alien world full of rigid routine, where complex characters from all walks of life move around, some riddled with regret and sorrow for their actions, others dead behind the eyes with denial, stunned with shock and horror at how they ended up here in the first place. Others strut around, their steely complexion fuelled by conviction, ruling the roost as days and months tick by in this bubble-like existence.

'If you can just hold on—'

'But this wasn't meant to happen!' she hisses, wringing her hands and glancing around to see who is watching.

'I know that,' I whisper. 'We all know that. Don't let this place break you, Mum. You're going to be home soon and we can put all this behind us.'

She smiles, but I know it's an empty expression just to please me. She is right. This wasn't meant to happen. There isn't a violent bone in my mother's body but her profile and position made her an easy target for local paramilitaries to hide guns and drugs on her property, determined to keep a conflict going as the rest of us plead for peace.

Years of civil protests on the streets had gained her a reputation for speaking up and speaking out, yes, and her voice for equality and justice through a dirty war drew attention her way and ruffled the feathers of many, but to link her with a political crime she didn't commit that sucked the blood right out of her, leaving her almost soulless and broken for months now was heartbreaking for us all.

The end was near, though. If she could just stay strong for another short while, this would all be over soon.

'Have you seen your dad much?' she asks, changing the subject, her voice shaking now so badly, telling me the big breakdown moment I'm expecting can't be too far away.

Now it's my turn to force a smile and try to stay positive.

'Yes, yes, I have seen him quite a lot lately,' I tell her. 'He's keeping well. He was asking for you.'

She looks away and I see how her eyes glisten at the very mention of him. This is as hard for her as it is for me, I know that.

'He was?'

'He was.'

She inhales. What I can't tell her is just how angry my father is at the dogs on the street who know my mother has been set up. What I can't tell her is how we've argued that he mustn't get involved or he could do something stupid in revenge and end up behind bars too.

Both my parents grew up in an era where shootings and bombings were the norm, where Protestants and Catholics lived at war with each other. While my father has his own strong political beliefs due to his own experiences growing up during The Troubles, he has never in all my years on this planet taken those beliefs into his own hands. I don't want him to start now. He might have his own issues with those he sees as being on the 'other side' and has been cautious of their motives, but to stand up now to the bad boys in our own community who have wronged my mother is a path he dare not go down – for his own safety and for all of ours.

'Did he give you money?' she asks me.

'He always gives me money when I see him,' I reply. 'He's a lot more financially supportive these days. I think he knows he's a lot to catch up on.'

'That's good.'

She takes it as it is, and I can sense her mind scramble as her thoughts build up into the inevitable crescendo. I can tell by her short breaths, by the shake in her voice, by her lack of eye contact, by the way she fidgets with that chain.

I often wonder if it makes her better or worse to see me like this once a month, on the other side of a table with other people lined up like ducks beside us, nodding and talking in stilted hushed tones.

'And your sister?' she asks.

Her eyes fill with tears now.

I know this is killing her, stuck in here so helpless and trapped, unable to do the things she is used to doing around her own home: making sure Shannon gets to school every day without a fuss or an argument, or that my sister Maureen doesn't go off the rails and disappear again like she used to.

'I'm keeping a very close eye on them both,' I say, as though I'm reading off a script, 'and look, before you know it, we'll have all this sorted and you'll be back home again where you belong. It's nearly over. You're so nearly there.'

She nods.

We sit in silence, our eyes skirting the room, finding eye contact with anything but each other.

I hate this part. I dread this moment, these few seconds before she breaks down as the pain of the life she has left behind hits her.

I wait. I know it's coming, and when it does, even though I'm prepared, it just never gets any easier.

An apology is first as usual.

'I'm so sorry, baby!' she says, gulping back a wave of emotion that threatens to choke her and stabs me in the heart at the same time. 'I had no idea the place was being used to hide guns! And I've never touched drugs in my life, you know I haven't! It goes against everything I've always stood for and—'

'I know, Mum. I know,' I whisper. 'Everyone who knows you believes you.'

She looks so tiny and pathetic, so I try my best not to frown or crumble as we repeat the same patterns from before. Her voice gasps and peaks, like a squeal almost, so much so that other visitors and inmates look our way, then shuffle back to their own business. The prison guard shifts from one foot to another and folds his burly arms.

'I'm so sorry to put you all through this, my darling! I'll never, ever let anything like this happen again to our family and—'

'Hush, please. Please don't cry. I already know all of this,' I tell her softly, taking her hand, all the while feeling the stare of a silver-haired woman across from us who is gaping in our direction with her mouth open. 'You don't have to keep saying it, now take a deep breath and try to relax. They've promised us peace and there's great work going on out there. You'll be home sooner than you think. You'll see.'

I grip her hand tighter. I want to fidget, to do something with my hands to occupy my mind so I can hold in my tears and not add to any of her mounting fears that seem so overwhelming every time I come to see her. I close my eyes and breathe, just like I've asked her to do as well. I won't let her down. I can't let her down. I try to remember something, anything to make her feel even just a little bit better.

'I bought Shannon the most beautiful new dress in Belfast this week,' I announce, shifting in my seat to change the energy. 'I got it for her birthday. Oh, it's so pretty and she looks like a real princess, or so she keeps telling us every time she tries it on.'

She lightens up immediately and so easily, like a crying child distracted by a shiny new toy. She closes her eyes tight and tilts back her head so that her eyes face the low ceiling.

'Describe it to me,' she tells me, smiling broadly as she waits. 'Tell me every single detail and I'll picture it all in my mind. Start with the colour and take it from there.'

And so I do as she asks me, and with every word I say about the pretty pink dress and the beautiful chiffon and the way it flows when my niece twirls around to show us as she spins around on the tiles of the kitchen floor, I battle – as I always do – to not cry in here in front of my mother.

'And the little sequins glimmer on the neckline when she stands under the light,' I whisper as tears stream down her face. 'And she sings, and she dances, and she can't believe she is going to be six years old soon. And she misses you so much. We all do, Mummy. It won't be long till you're home. They say it should only be another few months now and we'll be waiting for you with open arms, no matter how long it takes.'

She nods so slowly, soothed in her own world, so I push back my chair and I stand up ever so quietly and leave her there without saying goodbye, lost in thoughts of her precious little granddaughter dancing and singing as she counts down the days to her birthday, while my mother counts down the days to her own freedom.

'Goodbye Kate, my angel girl,' she whispers without opening her eyes. 'You're a good, good person. I'm so very proud of you.'

It's always too painful for her to watch me walk away towards the door so I know she'll keep her eyes shut tight until I do.

My mouth is so dry I can't reply, so I walk without looking back, sensing the silver-haired woman from before is staring at me again. When I hit the fresh air outside I stand against the wall in the summer sunshine, and I cry and cry for what we have become.

I may not be a prisoner like my mother is, but I want to escape this all so badly.

I can't wait to get out of here.

DAVID

'Stop fidgeting, David, for goodness' sake. He'll go berserk later if he catches you.'

I let out a long, deliberate sigh as Mum sits by my side, unable to take her eye off my father in the pulpit as he preaches with fist in mid-air, protesting, at least it seems to me, against absolutely everything that comes his way and I don't think I could possibly be more different to him in every respect.

His powerful, bellowing voice echoes and bounces off the cold stone walls and I stare at the floor, leaning my arms on my knees, but the only thing I'm praying for is that this so-called sermon will be all over soon. It wasn't always like this. I have fond memories of my dad from my younger years before an old aunt left him a substantial sum of money and the adoration of churchgoers went to his head, but sometimes I fear those memories will fade for ever.

'Look at them,' I whisper to my mother whose eyes are now closed in prayer. 'He's got them all eating out of his hands, hasn't he?'

Sarah Edwards, who sits three pews ahead with her new

boyfriend from Glasgow, fills my head with thoughts not belonging in this house of God. Her boyfriend is half my height, probably a third of my weight, but he no doubt has a head full of brains that would double mine so, as much as I ogle, I know there's no way she'd care to even notice me, but it's better than listening to my father's lecture so I lean my head around to try and see more than the back of her head. The man in front of me blocks my view, which is kind of the story of my life.

'It was a heartfelt and passionate sermon as always, Reverend,' I hear one of my father's biggest fans, Julia Sampson, chirp in the churchyard just before she shoots me a look that is anything but Christian considering her husband is standing beside her. 'I particularly related to your passion against changing anything that goes against the word of God. We must say no.'

'No to what exactly?' I ask as I walk towards them. My father's 60-year-old face goes puce at my outburst and I know I'll pay for this when I get home, but I've never been one to stand back and listen to this unreasonable opposition to almost everything from someone like Julia who represents a lot of my father's adoring flock. 'Why is it always no? Why can't you listen to the opinion of others instead of leading with your "do as I say and not as I do" philosophy?'

My dad glares at me, while Julia evidently hasn't listened

to a word I've said. She continues to look at me as if I'm some sort of boy-band pop star, her eyes fluttering uncontrollably with her hand on her bosom. I swear she is nodding in agreement, even though I'm contradicting everything she has just said.

'Don't mind David. He's tired,' my mother whispers, clasping her handbag to her waistline. 'We'll make our way on home, Bob. It's just a mix of late nights and too much TV. He wasn't even listening to you. He was fidgeting as usual.'

She pokes me in the back and directs me away from the gathered fan club towards the car. It's only when we get inside that she bursts out laughing with shock and looks at me with her mouth open wide.

'What on earth has got into you, David Campbell?' she says, unable to hide her surprise at my public outburst. 'You know he won't say a word now over the lovely roast I've prepared! I mean, really, David? In front of those . . . those *people*?'

'Mum, those people are as deluded as he is. They look at him like he's God himself; it's ridiculous. Anyhow, I think I'll skip dinner,' I say as my mother drives us out of the Irish border village where my father's service is held every Sunday and out towards our family home in the countryside, away from reality, away from the TV news and the people that my father preaches to. 'I can't bear to listen to another word of his preaching. I'm sorry, Mum, but it's just the two of you for today.'

My mother shakes her head and clasps the steering wheel, no doubt exhausted by her constant role of playing referee between me and my father.

'He means well, you know he does, David, and he always only wants the best for you. We both do.'

My eyes widen and I shrug it off. I've heard this all before many, many times.

'But I disagree with a lot of what he believes in,' I say to her. 'That's never going to change, Mum. He's incredibly stuck in his ways and you know it.'

She rubs her forehead now and looks me in the eye.

'He's a good man, David. He's a passionate man. And yes, sometimes his views are strict and authoritarian in his approach, but he's given us both a wonderful life and it's not something to be taken for granted. Maybe you should – maybe you should show a little more respect for who he is and what he stands for?'

I stare out through the window as the shades of green countryside blend into one another, counting fences and gates that I've known since the day I was born. I open the collar of my shirt, longing to tear it open and change into my own clothes, which reflect me rather than the person that my father wants me to be. I can't wait to put on my favourite ripped jeans, an old T-shirt, and bang on my drum-kit in the shed, well away from my dad and his cardboard cut-out ideals as to what I should and shouldn't think, act and be.

'I don't like a lot of what he stands for,' I mumble through gritted teeth. 'You can stand by him all you want, Mum, that's your choice, but money and power isn't everything to me like it is to him. I can decide for myself how I see the world. I'm not some plastic doll you both can mould into what you want me to be.'

My mother is gentle and her smile is reassuring as she continues to try and balance out the chalk and cheese family dynamic we have had ever since I was old enough to form my own opinions and make my own friends outside of my dad's inner circle of church groups and Sunday School.

'No, you're not that at all and although I don't want you to hurt each other, David, I am proud of you as much as I am of him,' she whispers softly, then adds with some trep-idation, 'You do know he's going to start on you about the need to go back and finish your degree course any day now.'

I lean my head back, take off my tie and wrap it round my wrist, then I switch the radio channel and I'm delighted when it blasts out Nirvana's 'Smells Like Teen Spirit', my favourite and the very type of track that would make my father fall to his knees in despair. My mum ignores the music and chooses instead to shout over it. 'Have you thought about it at all? Will you go back, do you think? I really wish you—'

'I don't want to be a lawyer! I never did! How many times do I have to tell you both?'

'But it's an awful waste of three years if you don't just

finish the course, and Billy Beattie says he'll give you another chance in his office if you'd just—'

'Stop the car, please.'

'What?'

'I can't stand this any more. Stop the car.'

'David!'

She switches off the radio with swift vigour and the silence it leaves in its wake seems more deafening than the music itself was.

'Stop trying to control me! Both of you!'

She pulls in the car at the side of the lane that leads to our family home, so close to a hedge there's no way I can get out. I take a deep breath, knowing my mother is not the one to blame for all my frustrations and trying to resist the urge to run.

'You know we only want the very best for you, darling,' she tells me again. I push my head back and close my eyes.

'You have no idea what's best for me.'

She starts up the engine again and the car chugs along the bumpy lane to our lavish, inherited family home.

I can't wait to get out of here.

SIX WEEKS LATER

2.

KATE

I can feel our Maureen's eyes burn through me as I put the second spoonful of sugar into my tea, and so I stir it deliberately hard against the mug to drown out the inevitable telling off she is about to give me.

'Don't even start, Mo,' I say with a smile. 'I know what you're going to say.'

I don't need to look around to know she'll be shaking her head and squinting her eyes, her pink face folding up in despair.

'Two sugars? And you who's training to be a nurse?' she says, her voice peppered with envy and with enough of an irresistible 'tut-tut' tone to put me in my place. 'You won't be thin like that for ever, Kate Foley. Wait and see, it will catch up on you one day. I used to be a size ten too, but it doesn't last for ever.'

I spin around with two steaming mugs in my hands and set one down on the worktop beside where she stands, drying the dishes with a tea-towel that I pledge inwardly to put straight in the bin as soon as I have her back turned. I've spent every single hour since I got home this morning cleaning the kitchen, helping her prepare for her daughter's birthday tea party this evening, and she still gives out to me about sugar in my tea.

I notice the mug I give her says 'Little Miss Sunshine', while mine says 'Little Miss Trouble', most definitely the wrong way round. The mugs are almost as old as we are and we chose them for ourselves. I remember the day Mum bought them for us at the market in town and the memory of that day stings inside, making me yearn for those simpler and more innocent times.

Maureen, as hard as she tries, will never be the sunshine type. She's more like an autumn shower, I suppose, but it's never really been her fault. It's the way life goes.

'Are you nervous?' I ask her. 'You always tell me off when you're nervous.'

'I'm not nervous,' she replies. 'I'm not a bit nervous.'

'You are nervous,' I tell her, folding my arms. 'Look, you know he's not worth it, Mo. He's scum and he never was worth more than a second of your time, never mind the worry if he'll bother to show up to his child's birthday party or not.'

Maureen throws down the tea-towel and I eye up the bin, wondering if I could get rid of the greying rag right now as she squeezes the hot mug in her hands.

'If Shannon can't have her nana here on her birthday this year, I can at least hope for her daddy to show up for a change,' Maureen whispers, looking out of the window as she does. 'You may not like him much but, as you keep reminding me, it's only for a couple of hours. I'm sure Sean and I can be civil to one another for the child's sake for that length of time.'

'Of course you can,' I whisper in return, my head tilting to the side as I take in the sight of my big sister, though the thought of Sean McGee or his kind being anywhere near our house makes my stomach burn. The conflict that has torn our country apart for over thirty years might have been officially over since April, but there's an element of the underworld in this rural Ulster market town where we live that still feels the need to rule our streets. Unfortunately, my sister's ex is the leader of a very dark, sinister pack – a pack that no doubt framed our mother by hiding their crap in our garden shed, though we'll probably never be able to prove it. Sean McGee is way too clever for that. He plays my sister like a fiddle and as soon as I turn my back, I know she dances to his tune.

Our Maureen, the most pitiful, sad-looking, pathetic-in-so-many-ways 22-year-old girl I ever did see.

The weight of the world sits on her broad shoulders, the pain of her daily struggle stuck here on her own, day in, day out, with a 6-year-old child and Sean McGee to deal with, the most useless piece of shit, who drifts in and out of their lives when it suits him, terrorizing our housing estate and everyone who comes near it in any way he can. Not to mention the constant stress of our mother, who is paying the price for her well-known views as a 'pro-choice feminist, strongly committed to the struggle for Irish freedom', whose strong but democratic viewpoints made her a sitting duck for cowards who continue to hide behind true crime. The dogs on the street know who set her up, but are too afraid to bark out the truth and prove it.

I try not to imagine what she is doing in there, right now at this very moment, and say a silent prayer for her early release now that we've peace at last. I blank out the stories I've heard of strip-searches, of bullying and other obscenities, thoughts that consume my mind every night as I lie in the dark, riddled with anxiety for her. Even trying not to imagine it makes me sick to my stomach, but I can't let Maureen see how worried I am every minute of every day. I will never let her see that.

'Will you do my hair in a bit?' Maureen asks me, touching the back of her fluffy, fuzzy brown bob that lacks shape and beauty since she almost gave up on the world a few years ago. 'I may as well make an effort for my daughter's sixth birthday, I suppose. I might even have my photo taken to mark the occasion when you're here to take it.'

I brighten up instantly. It's the most positive thing I've heard her say in months, but then again, it's the most positive thing I've heard at all in this house in the past year since . . .

'Mum won't be gone for ever, Maureen,' I remind her. 'And soon it will be you, her and Shannon here like it used to be, and you'll be giving out to her over putting sugar in her tea, and giving out to me for not partying enough down in Belfast while I'm still young and irresponsible enough to do so. I get it from her, you know.'

'What? Being *responsible*?' Maureen says with a raised eyebrow and just a touch of sarcasm.

'Yes, she can be very responsible when she needs to be. She just has strong beliefs and you can't fault that,' I say, tilting up my chin. 'I was talking about her sweet tooth if you must know, and the fact that she's still got a figure to die for.'

Maureen fixes her size eighteen black cotton dress and I close my eyes, instantly regretting any reference to weight in her company.

'Prison food is a good way of keeping slim, I suppose,' she retorts, staring at the sink before bursting into tears. 'She'll hardly . . . she'll hardly put on a lot of weight in there, will she? Oh Kate! I'm so worried for her.'

I put down my Little Miss Trouble mug and walk towards my big sister, pulling her into a tight hug where we both collapse into each other's shoulders and shed tears as the hum of a neighbour's lawnmower and the sound of Shannon singing spills down the stairs of our tiny childhood terraced home.

'Mum's going to be fine, we'll all be fine,' I say, pushing

Maureen's fuzzy curls behind her ears and staring up into her emerald eyes. 'Now, today is going to be a good day and it's all about Shannon, so I'm going to take her to town and spoil her rotten while you soak in a nice long bath. We'll make the best of today, no matter about Sean McGee and his grand appearance or lack of it. We'll do our girl proud, yeah? I'll fix your hair really nice when we come back. I'll do your make-up too if you want?'

She sniffles and nods, tears spilling from behind her glasses and down her flushed cheeks.

'You don't need to spend your student loan on Shannon, Kate,' she stutters, wiping her eyes under her steamed-up glasses. 'She isn't used to a fuss, birthday or no birthday.'

'Well, she's having a fuss made of her today and I won't be told any different.'

Maureen bites her lip and we hold each other's gaze for a few seconds. There may be only two years between us but there's a world of difference with the way we live our young adult lives. She is simple and fragile, vulnerable and easily led. She tried so hard to stay out of trouble but she always ended up in the wrong crowd. I, in turn, am known as the strong, focused, sensible student, determined to make a better life away from the claustrophobic confinements of these pebble-dash terraced houses, where the neighbours don't need to ask what you had for breakfast because they can see so much through your window from their own.

'You'll make a really good nurse one day, Kate,' Maureen

tells me, her green eyes drowning in pain as she nods her head. 'You deserve to get out of here and make a name for yourself. I'm so proud of you already.'

I smile and she does too.

'And I'm proud of you too, Mo,' I tell her gently. 'We're a great team and always will be, no matter where I end up when I graduate or whatever life throws at us. Now, I'll go get the birthday girl. Enjoy your soak and for goodness' sake don't be worrying about a thing about today. This will be the best birthday ever, just you wait and see.'

DAVID

'He is testing us! He is testing us!'

'Flee the evil desires of youth!' I say to my workmate and best friend Aaron. He is brushing the supermarket floor behind me with a great vigour that only a Saturday feeling can bring, while he copies my father's gruff voice and makes fun of me for ogling after Sarah Edwards.

Sarah, the red-haired trainee doctor who first stole my heart in primary school and whom I last saw in church six weeks ago, is leaving through the shop's exit with her Scottish boyfriend, now wearing a pair of shorts that would give any 21-year-old heterosexual young man like me a nose bleed.

'Do you think she'd fancy you more if you quoted God's

word as you blatantly stare at her bare legs?' Aaron teases. 'I bet she's like every other girl in this town and is just gagging to go out with a vicar's hunky son if you ask the right questions.'

I don't bother correcting my friend that my father's actual job title is 'church minister' and not 'vicar', and focus instead on the mounting queue that is building at the corner shop counter where I've spent what feels like every moment of this long, hot summer and, as my father keeps reminding me, I am probably going to spend the autumn and winter here too if I don't up my game on the career front.

It's almost three in the afternoon and I long for my break, where I plan to saunter up the street and window-shop, daydreaming for a while away from the hubbub of a Saturday shift of selling mainly ice cream, cigarettes, scratch cards and lotto tickets to revellers whose eyes light up as I hand them their weekly flutter, dreaming for a fleeting second of a life that's different.

'So, what do you say then? Beers tonight? I heard Sarah say to her friend she's—'

'For sure!' I answer too quickly, trying to shut Aaron up as I deal with one of my least favourite customers, Julia Sampson, who as usual can't decide whether she wants a vanilla ice cream or strawberry, as a short queue forms behind her.

'You decide, David, darling,' she says, leaning across the counter at an angle that leaves little to the imagination in her summer dress. 'I think you're good at making decisions, aren't you?'

I gulp and feel my cheeks burn as she looks me up and down seductively. The lady is almost old enough to be mother, or at least my younger aunt, but that doesn't make her ever want to change her behaviour. It's the same thing every time I see her, even at church, and it makes me very uncomfortable to know her husband is waiting in the car with their two very spoilt kids waiting on ice cream.

'Er, strawberry is good, I think?' I say rubbing my chin, eager to get her out of my way. The heat from the street outside steams off the skin of every customer, sweaty and damp from the humid August day, and my excitement from this morning returns, reminding me of a whole new world of freedom that now sits at my fingertips.

'Strawberry it is. Oh, and congratulations, by the way,' says Mrs Sampson, allowing her fingers to rest on my palm as she lays a ten-pound note in my hand. 'Your father told me your good news earlier. I just had to come in to congratulate you in person.'

I feel the roof of my mouth go dry and the shop floor threatens to come up to meet me. It's really heating up and I'm sure I've a river of damp sweat running down my spine, a grey line of patches on my white T-shirt.

'Thank you,' I whisper before fetching her ice cream, and she tiptoes away in her high wedges and flowing white dress, leaving me to breathe in her sickeningly sweet perfume for a second before I deal with the next person in line.

'News of what exactly?' asks Aaron, who has now taken up position at the adjacent till at the same counter. 'What's she congratulating you about?'

'Who?'

'Your fancy woman, Mrs Robinson the ice-cream vamp?' he says, laughing as he deals with a customer return, something he could do with his eyes closed. I laugh in return at his reference to the famous character from *The Graduate*, the sultry Mrs Robinson who woos her young student, and feel my cheeks burn again. 'You're like a magnet, man. I swear, I only wish I had half your charm. Is it the vicar's son thing or is it the rugby-boy physique that gets you all the attention?'

'It's my puppy-dog eyes,' I joke in return. 'I passed my driving test this morning if you must know – not that my father will ever in his life let me drive his precious car – so that's my big news. Better late than never, yes, before you say it yourself.'

'Way to go! You dark horse!' says Aaron, stepping across to give me a high-five. 'Ladies and gentlemen, our shop's very own poster boy David Campbell has passed his driving test at the grand age of twenty-one, just three years after his first attempt! Now, how about giving him a round of applause?'

I shake my head and look at the floor, then close my eyes

as the small audience of customers, about five or six people in front of us, burst into a very enthusiastic cheer led by Aaron, who I swear will make it one day in theatre, just as he aims to do when he finishes his last year at university. He's annoyingly observant, highly articulate and never misses a moment to take centre of attention, even when pretending to give adulation to others. I may be the eye-candy, or so they say, of this little town-centre corner shop, but Aaron has the charm and the comedic nature to make little old ladies swoon and young children want to be entertained from behind the counter, so it's no surprise when the next little one who comes in goes straight to his side of things to be served.

'Have whatever you want, Shannon. It's not every day it's your birthday, so choose an ice cream and whatever else you would like.'

Aaron goes into full performance mode when he hears it's the child's birthday, but it's the person accompanying her who has my full attention. I've never seen her in here before, but there's something vaguely familiar about her that I can't place. She has highlighted brown hair that falls around her fine face, she's delicate and pretty with a multicoloured neck scarf that brings out the turquoise shade of her striking cat's eyes. Her flat biblical sandals, turned-up dark blue baggy jeans and white shirt tucked in is casual and cool, if rather too warm for this weather, but she looks unflustered and calm, unlike so many who have come in here today.

'A balloon!' says the little girl. 'Can I have one? Please? The Minnie Mouse one!'

She glances my way briefly. Our eyes meet and she smiles.

'Go on then. We'll have a bubble-gum ice cream and a balloon as well, please.'

I swallow hard. I realize I'm staring but I can't help it. She sounds local, as in she must be from the town itself and not from the countryside like me, where our accents are rounder and broader, and I wonder how I've never seen her before even though she looks so—

'Everything OK?' she asks me, catching me looking her way.

'What? Sorry!' I say, snapping out of my daydream, feeling my face go pink, which adds to my embarrassment at being caught. 'Yes, yes, fine. How old is the birthday girl today?'

'Six!' says the little girl, her freckled nose crunching up as Aaron hands her a circle-shaped helium-filled Minnie Mouse balloon in one hand and a sticky blue ice cream in the other. 'I'm having a party at my house, but no boys are allowed, except my daddy of course.'

The older girl tucks her hair behind her ear as she watches me, then puts a protective hand on the wee one's shoulder.

'Ah, that's a pity,' I reply, pretending to be terribly disappointed. 'Well, you have a lovely day and I hope you get lots of presents.'

'She will,' says her minder with a smile and off they go,

her eye catching mine one last time on the way past. 'Nice T-shirt, by the way.'

Her compliment takes me by surprise, and my gaze follows them towards the door, not in the jaw-dropping, lustful way I looked at Sarah Edwards earlier, but still in a way that makes Aaron raise an eyebrow when I turn to face him again.

'What?' I ask him, thankful my blushing has subsided.

'Nice T-shirt? Don't tell me you know *her* too?' he asks me, his usually slanted eyes turning wide in wonder. 'Is there anyone in this town who doesn't come in here just to see you in the flesh, David Campbell? Is there any woman on the planet who doesn't want to fall at your feet?'

'No, I don't know her at all actually,' I tell him. 'And she certainly wasn't falling at my feet just because she liked my T-shirt. I just feel like I've seen her before, but I can't think where. I don't know her.'

'She's out of your league anyhow, sunshine, if you don't mind me saying so,' Aaron says, watching her disappear through the automated doors and out onto the street where she crosses the road at the traffic lights. 'She looks way too intelligent and I think she fancied me, actually, which is a welcome first. Chicks do dig gingers sometimes, believe it or not. They aren't all into smouldering, brooding types, you know.'

It's nearly three, which means Aaron's shift is unfortunately nearly over, but the good news is that it's almost time for my break at last. I burst out laughing at Aaron's brooding remark and start totting up my till with the girl's smiling face still on my mind. For some reason I know it's going to stay there for a while, as if the clocks have stopped in my mind with her face on repeat. Maybe she'll come back in soon.

I hope she does.

3.

KATE

'What do you like best, babies or horses?'
Shannon's little hand holds onto mine tightly as she skips along beside me, asking the usual ream of steady, never-ending, random questions that only a 6-year-old can conjure up. It follows a debate as to why we were born in the first place, do leprechauns really exist, and can lava melt a river? I wonder sometimes how my sister keeps up with this all on a daily basis, but at the same time I find it highly entertaining and very insightful to get a glimpse into her young, innocent mind.

'I think I like horses better sometimes but then I saw my friend's baby sister the other day and she looked really cute, but she cries all the time,' she continues. 'What do you think, Kate? Babies or horses? You can only pick one.'

The ice cream from just minutes ago has already been devoured, and after a quick swipe with some wet wipes around her mouth, her fingers and hands, and of course along the front of her T-shirt, any evidence of the hideous blue bubble-gum-flavoured dripping mess is gone.

She holds the red circular plastic weight attached to her precious Minnie Mouse balloon as tightly as a vice in her left hand, and its lengthy ribbon threatens to catch on the arm or shopping bag of every passer-by, meaning my concentration on her very important question is diluted, but I do my best to answer.

Babies or horses? Babies or horses?

'Babies, for sure,' I tell her eventually. 'I mean, horses are lovely, but there's nothing like a newborn baby, even if they do cry a lot. Babies are the nicest thing ever. That's what I think anyhow.'

She seems pleased with my answer, but it triggers another question from her over-active mind of course.

'Was I a very cute baby?' she asks, her lilac sparkly trainers scuffing the pavement as she skips along beside me. I can't believe how her head skims past my waist already, her limbs stretching and her face changing slightly every time I see her with every single weekend that passes by. 'My mummy says I was the cutest baby in the whole country, but what do you think, Kate? Was I really?'

'You weren't just the cutest baby in the *country*. You were the cutest *and* the best-behaved baby in the whole *world*, Shannon Mary Foley,' I tell her, apologizing again to a stranger as the balloon catches their arm on their way past, 'and don't you ever forget it.'

'Good. So, do you like hard chairs or soft chairs best?' she asks next, and my eyes widen as my face breaks into the brightest smile.

'Tell me which you like best first,' I reply. We have one more shop to visit for some party poppers and party-bag treats and then we're done, but I don't want our day together to end just yet.

'I think I like soft chairs best.'

'Me too,' I say to her, steering her out of the way of a passer-by, but stopping abruptly as the string of her balloon catches in the handle of a pushchair.

'Which do you like best?' she asks next. 'Real babies or doll babies?'

'Real babies,' I answer this time straight away as I detangle the ribbon with the help of the very patient young mummy beside me. 'Definitely real babies.'

'Me too,' says Shannon. 'It's my birthday today.'

'Happy Birthday,' says the lady with the pram. 'I hope you have the best day ever.'

DAVID

The sandwich in my hand is disappearing as if I'm inhaling it and I don't care that it's limp and soggy at all. In fact, I didn't realize how starving I was until I left the shop and hit the fresh air, but my hunger is averted momentarily by the sight of the glistening, brand-new, azure-coloured Ludwig drum-kit in the window before us.

'If I don't go back to university after the summer holidays, my parents will just have to suck it up. I hate it, they know I do,' I say to Aaron as I stare in the window, our reflection catching my eye beyond the powerhouse drum machine. Aaron, so tall and lanky, with shoulder-length auburn hair and a pale, pointed nose, sometimes reminds me of a bird, I realize. He is handsome though. He is a handsome bird, like a golden pheasant, not common like your everyday blackbird or crow. Aaron is exotic-looking. Yes, that's the word. Exotic.

I'm bulky and muscular in comparison to his slender physique. I reach up to his shoulders, just about, and *I'm* skimming six one, making Aaron possibly the tallest person I know right now. My unruly dark hair is sticking up in a way I hadn't noticed before I left the house this morning, but I'll fix it later when I get back to work. No point worrying about such trivial things when the clock is already clicking on my thirty-minute break of my six-hour shift.

'You know what I think, David?' he asks me, and I reply even though I already know what he thinks.

'What do you think? Tell me, oh wise one.'

'I think that life is short, so if you've got the change in your pocket, buy the lotto ticket every time,' he says, just as I predicted that he would. It's Aaron's answer to almost every dilemma in life. 'Yes, that's my motto and I'm sticking to it. Take a chance and buy the lotto ticket, every time.'

'I mean I'm twenty-one years old for crying out loud,' I continue on my own wave of ranting while chewing the last mouthful of my soggy salad sandwich. 'I've loads of time to decide what I want to do with myself, haven't I? Why should I be pigeonholed into completing a course that makes my head spin? Why?'

Aaron, who has absolutely no interest in musical instruments and who is more interested in what boldness we can get up to tonight when we get to the pub, looks around him while crunching into an apple. There's no one in this whole universe eats as loudly as Aaron Dempsey and I hit him a playful nudge in the arm when he doesn't answer me.

'Sorry, sorry, university what?' he replies, wiping the juice of the apple from the side of his mouth with his sleeve. 'Look, no harm to your desperate dilemma, David, but at least your parents care what you do, yeah?'

'You think?'

'Yeah, I think,' he replies as we saunter along the pavement, away from my drum-kit of dreams. 'I definitely think. Put it like this. Every time I mention my acting ambitions at home I can see my ma's eyes glaze over and she says something totally irrelevant like asking me what I want for dinner or she tells me to go and put the bins out. I'd love her to be just a *wee* bit pushy, ye know. Just a wee tiny bit of interest would go a long way.'

We walk and chat, window-shopping as we go along and stopping only to admire clothes in shops we could never afford even if we clubbed our wages together, or to contemplate more food or snacks for me as I've to go back to the shop to finish my shift, while Aaron goes home to prepare for our big night out on the town.

'It's constant pressure, I swear it is,' I tell him, already dreading going home to the inevitable interrogation that awaits but also excited about our antics later when we get to let our hair down in town. 'Like, don't get me wrong. I love going to Belfast and getting away from them for five whole days, wrecking around in student accommodation before coming back on the weekends, but—'

'Ow! Watch where you're going! Ow!'

A man who seems to be in a frantic hurry bumps into Aaron not once but twice and mumbles something, drawing our eyes further down the street to a sight that stops us in our tracks and puts my moaning firmly where it probably belongs.

It's Saturday afternoon and it's always busy in town on a Saturday, but this is a different type of busy in the near distance.

People are coming towards us, in trickles at first, but within what feels like three seconds it's like a small stampede, and before long it feels as though we're on a one-way street going in the wrong direction for reasons we don't understand.

'What's going on?' I ask someone. 'What's happening?'

I look at Aaron. He stops. He has gone paler than usual.

'Run!' they tell us as they flurry past. 'Just run! This way!'

But run where? I'm not running. I've no idea where they're telling me to run to.

A girl around my own age bumps into me and spills hot coffee over us both and I gasp as it scalds my chest through my T-shirt, but it's the desperation in her face that alarms me most. I look around for Aaron, but he's gone, so I cop on at last and I do as I'm told.

I run.

I have no idea why and I've no idea where I'm running to, but I run.

KATE

People are pushing past us and I don't know what's happening. I'm knocked to the side and I lose my grasp on Shannon's hand as my stomach churns with bile at fear of the unknown. I can't lose her! Mo will kill me! It's her birthday! Oh my God I feel so sick. What on earth is going on?

'Shannon!' I cry out, my shoulders bumping against men, women and children coming towards me. 'Shannon, where are you?'

'Go that way!' someone screams in my face. 'There's a bomb about to go off! Quickly! Go that way!'

A bomb? How can there be a bomb? There must be some mistake. There can't be a bomb!

'Shannon!' I scream, my hands holding my face as the force of their bodies spins me around. I start to cry uncontrollably. How can there be a bomb? My God, please let me find her.

I look upwards into the blue sky to see the ribbon and balloon my niece was carrying float aimlessly upwards and out of reach, and I stretch out my arm to save it for her, knowing it's impossible to do so and then it's gone.

'Shannon!' I cry out again. 'Where are you, baby? Can you hear me?'

People scramble past and I shuffle and wobble at first, then I follow them like I'm caught up in a herd of frightened deer, my eyes skimming unknown faces. I crouch down in the crowd, trying to control my panic and to pick out her bright pink T-shirt amongst the fleeing figures. Terror rises, threatening to suffocate me. I can barely breathe. Where is she?

'Shannon!'

I'm so scared. But then I see her nearby. She gazes around, fat tears falling down her pretty face. If anything, or anyone hurts her—

An almighty, thunderous crash explodes through the air.

The noise is furious, and I fall to the ground as the sound of the deafening blast rings in my ears. Something stabs me deeply in the leg before I'm thrown into a shop window, shards of glass falling down round me like rain. A gush of water forces a torrent, bringing a wash of red blood past me. It's like an earthquake – no, worse. It's like a volcano erupting – no, worse. It's enough to have blasted my whole body into mid-air before I land with an almighty, excruciating thud inside a fog of smoke that fills my nostrils and stings my eyes.

The world has gone grey around me; everything is in slow motion. My senses are numbed for what feels like minutes but is probably only seconds – I can't see in the darkness, I can't hear anything, only silence. I try to move but I can't. I call out for Shannon, but I can't even hear my own voice.

The silence continues as a blanket of smog tumbles from the hill in front of me. It's so eerie and black as my head spins, and the smell of burning flesh awakens my senses, making me choke and gag, scalding my nostrils and throat. I feel sick. I think I'm going to be sick.

Long, drawn-out, demonic moans surround me and are soon replaced by deafening screams that pierce my ears but then I realize that I too am screaming. My God, I'm screaming and then I'm crying in silence again, then I'm screaming again until I break down into a pathetic sob that can go nowhere against the ear-splitting, riotous roaring around me.

'Shannon! I'm here, my darling! I'm over here!' I sob

helplessly, lying on the ground. 'Please God, please let me find her! Shannon!'

DAVID

I limp along the street, holding myself up in doorway after doorway. Bodies and body parts are strewn around me, tripping me up and making me weak at the sight of the brutality that surrounds me. This can't be real. It's too horrific, it's apocalyptic and dark, and fear makes me feel as if I'm going to puke.

The smell of burning flesh scalds my nostrils and waves of dizziness make every movement I see blur into slow motion; sounds of unearthly groans and whimpering like the stuff of nightmares and scary movies fill my ears.

An old man lies trapped under a heavy pillar just out of my reach, his brown coat drenched in dark blood and his eyes rolling back in his head. I hobble towards him, sure that I recognize him.

'Don't stop,' he whispers to me as I fall to my knees by his side. 'Don't stop for me, son. Save yourself. Get help.'

His voice is shaking and low, but I can just about make out what he is saying. I shake my head frantically. I do recognize him! Yes, he comes into the shop all the time! He made a joke about the cost of a morning coffee in the café up the street and how he was going to visit his wife in hospital.

'You're going to be OK,' I tell him, wiping what I hope are tears from my face but when I glance at my hand I realize it's my own blood. 'You're going to visit your wife like you said you were. This isn't real. It can't be. We have to get help. They're coming, I know they are, so just you wait and see. Listen. Can you hear them? It's sirens. Help is coming.'

His weary eyes catch mine and his hand reaches towards me before flopping to his side in defeat.

'*No!* No, please *no!*'

I look away and close my eyes tight, doing my best to distance my mind from what can't be unseen. I just can't watch as the last seconds of this elderly man's life are sucked away from him. He had plans for today! He was going to visit his wife!

'I'm so sorry!' I scream into nowhere. 'I'm so, so sorry!'

I sob into the darkness as I pull myself up from my knees, stumbling with every heavy step, not knowing where to go next. Others do the same, climbing up the hill in slow motion like dust-covered zombies, calling out names and clutching onto the thread of life as best they can.

I can barely walk now. It makes me sick with anger to realize I can't help anyone else no matter how I try. I should have helped that man! I should have saved him!

'Help!' I cry out, as loudly as I can, to nothing and nowhere. 'Somebody help us! Please!'

The cries of the wounded screech in my ears and the urgency of the sirens I heard before still squeal in the distance, coming closer and closer, but it's taking so long for them to get this far.

I can't look down. I know my arm is ripped open from my shoulder to my elbow, but I must keep going. I don't know where, but I keep moving for as long as I can and then I see her, holding tight onto what's left of a lamppost, so alone and afraid, her face blackened and charred and her hands patched in red, the colour clashing with the hot pink T-shirt I recognize from earlier.

It's the birthday girl from the shop before, the little girl who had the balloon and the blue ice cream, but she's almost unrecognizable and I'm not sure if it's my eyes or the fact that she's covered, like most of us, in thick dust. I reach my arm out towards her but the force of the water that gushes down the street beside us knocks her off her feet and she goes with it, thrusting her into a doorway where she lies, pinned to the concrete wall, her eyes wide and so frightened. I have to follow her. I can't leave her alone.

'I'm coming for you now! It's OK!' I shout to her. My arm is agony, stabbing pains shooting up into my neck, but I can't just leave her alone. I need to get to her. I couldn't help the man before, but maybe I can help this little girl and that will mean something.

'*Shannon!*'

'I'm on my way now! Don't be scared.'

'*Shannon!*'

We both get to her at the exact same time and collapse down beside her. Everywhere I look I see death and I smell fear. But this little girl. She's like a ray of hope and I need to focus on that. We still have hope.

'Thank God! Baby, are you OK?' The girl from earlier with the rolled-up jeans and the white shirt – now a mix of black dust and red blood – sits beside us. She grasps the little girl, holding her close. 'I found you! My darling girl! My sweet baby girl!'

She kisses the little girl's forehead frantically, holding her tight, checking her over and over to make sure she isn't hurt.

'My balloon!' the little girl weeps. 'I'm sorry, Kate! I let go of my balloon!'

Kate's striking eyes look into mine as she cradles the child's head to her chest, rubbing her matted hair as the sirens scream louder towards us. Thick tears stream down her face leaving flesh-coloured lines in the black dust that smothers us all, like a river of hope that there's life beyond this madness.

'Are you all right?' I ask her, barely recognizing my own voice. I can't stop shaking. 'We can wait here together until some help comes. I won't leave you, I promise.'

She shakes her head quickly.

'I'm not all right,' she whispers and she reaches out her free hand to me and I take it and we sit there, the three of us, huddled together in the doorway as scenes of a battle-field unfold around us. Her hand is hot and sticky, and I glance down to see that the stickiness is blood – her blood and mine mixed together, gluing our hands so we don't let go. I won't let go.

'My leg!' she whispers to me, rocking slightly as she does so. 'I think I've broken my leg.'

I glance at her leg and then I look at her face, her head shaking with a nervous twitch, her eyes pleading with me for this whole experience not to be true.

'I want my mummy!' yells the little girl.

'We'll get home to Mummy soon, I promise, Shannon,' Kate tells the little girl. 'We'll get help soon.'

'You are so brave,' I whisper softly to Shannon. 'You are so, so brave, and you'll be home soon in time for your party with no boys allowed except your daddy. We're in this together now. Don't worry. You're not alone, Shannon.'

I glance at Kate, trying my best not to let the horror of this all sink in.

'Thank you for saying that,' she whispers, her face etched with pain and despair. Her eyes meet mine as her chest heaves up and down. She smiles in appreciation at me just a little, a bit like she did earlier when she was leaving the shop.

I keep holding her hand. I don't ever want to let go.

KATE

There's no time for formalities or introductions in this tiny shelter, no space to breathe or to ask any questions as to what we are experiencing right now.

It's a bloodied blur, it's carnage, it's a war zone, and the only thing that keeps me sane right now is the knowledge that we are at least still alive. I dare not look left onto the street opposite the doorway we are sheltered in – me, Shannon and the boy from the ice-cream shop.

'Let me help you,' I say to him. His hand is still clutched in mine. His upper arm is sliced wide open, a huge weltering wound, and I know he hasn't even glanced at it yet, but I see his skin going paler and paler and I know I need to help him.

I quickly check Shannon for serious injuries, but I know already that she seems physically OK apart from her hands and knees that are grazed and bloodied from where she must have hit the ground, but miraculously she isn't in huge pain. But he is white, with shock beneath the soot that covers his face. I don't need to see his skin to know this.

'Just keep breathing nice and steadily and don't look,' I tell him. 'It's going to be fine. We're all going to be fine.'

I know of course that nothing of what we are experiencing right now is fine. The street to my left is like a bloodbath.

I hope I'll never witness anything like this in my whole

lifetime again, no matter how long I work in the medical profession I'm training for.

'Is it really bad?' he asks, staring into my eyes as I loosen my neck scarf and fix it around his arm, tying it tightly to stop the bleeding at least for now.

'This will help,' I whisper, but I can barely hear my own voice over the racket around us. People are screaming out names of loved ones, others are trying to help each other as they too howl in pain at the same time, sirens squeal in the distance and the walking wounded groan and moan in despair as they wander aimlessly hoping for assistance.

As I'm fixing the makeshift bandage around his arm, despite the agony he must be feeling, he keeps focusing on my face and we both keep talking, which is a very welcome distraction to the surreal events around us.

'Ask me something,' I say, determined to keep him conscious. He is bleeding a lot and I'm afraid he might faint soon. 'Ask me anything. First thing that comes into your head.'

He blinks his eyes ever so slowly.

'Why are you so beautiful?'

'You charmer,' I say. 'Ask me something else.'

'What's your favourite song?' he asks me, his voice slightly delirious. His question, however random, does what I assume he intends it to and takes all our minds off the hideous job at hand as I wrap my scarf around his arm one last time.

'I . . . I'm loving the new Savage Garden song,' I say, trying to remember it in my head.

'She plays it all the time,' says Shannon's little voice by my side.

'And you, birthday girl?' David asks Shannon. His breathing is slowing down. I really hope we get proper help soon.

'I can't think,' she says, her words so tiny against the noise in the air.

'Of course, you can,' says the ice-cream shop boy. 'I bet you like, what's his name . . .?'

Shannon's voice rises slightly.

'I just like boy bands,' she says, her tone showing me she is still very much with us, whereas I fear he is not going to be for long. 'I like Backstreet Boys.'

His breathing is becoming shorter and more rapid. I'm doing my best to stay calm, but my leg is in sheer agony. It feels as though it's full of glass.

'You're doing really well,' I tell him. 'So well. You're going to be fine. Just keep breathing. It's going to be OK.'

'You deserve . . . you deserve the best birthday party,' he tells Shannon, his own voice fading in comparison to hers. 'Do you like dancing?'

He looks my way, but his eyes begin to roll back a bit, so I take over.

'We love dancing,' I tell him, doing my best not to cry. I've put everything I can think of into fixing the scarf to

49

his arm but now I'm so scared. I'm losing him. 'We'll go dancing and we'll all go to the beach one day. I bet you love the beach?'

'I do,' he says. 'Keep talking,'

'And the amusements up at Barry's and we'll go to Donegal and go horse-riding,' I continue, hardly even knowing what I'm talking about. 'And you can come to Shannon's party even though no boys are allowed. Is that OK, Shannon?'

'That's OK,' she whispers.

She's so frightened too.

'I feel so faint,' he says. 'Don't leave me.'

'I won't. I promise I won't leave you. What's your name?' I ask him, trying my best to blank out the screams from the street that threaten to either smother us or distract us.

'David,' he says. 'David Campbell.' I take his hand and it's shaking so much it takes a moment to steady it. 'You're Kate.'

'Yes,' I say, nodding and holding his eyes with mine. Shannon grips my arm tighter. She is stuck to my side, clinging to me like a vine. 'You OK, baby?'

'I want Mummy.'

'Keep talking, please,' says David. His eyes roll in his head and I need to keep him with me. 'Please keep talking to me. Please don't let go.'

'I won't.'

The screams are getting louder now, and the horror is

suffocating me, but I need to stay present and calm as we wait for help.

'You said you liked my T-shirt,' he whispers, managing the faintest side smile as his eyes close. 'Were you flirting with me?'

My leg throbs and I'm starting to fade myself, but I know we both need to keep each other's minds busy for just a bit longer.

He opens one eye a little and reaches for my hand again. I hold it and close my eyes too.

'I think I was,' I admit to him, wondering how something so simple and innocent and age-appropriate for us both has ended up like this. 'You seem like a nice person, David. And I did like your T-shirt.'

He smiles properly this time between shortening breaths. His dark hair is sticky and matted with blood and I see a tear fall down his cheek. Oh God, please let him be OK! I don't know what else to do!

'You're a nice person too, Kate,' he whispers, shaking almost uncontrollably now and then – with a rustle of movement and some swift, direct voices – we are suddenly being helped from the doorway and panic rises inside me.

'No!' I scream. 'No, she has to come with me!'

'Kate!'

I watch them bundle my little niece into the back of a makeshift ambulance, then to my relief they come back for me. Assessing my injuries, they strap me to what looks like a door or shelf acting as a stretcher before they take David in the opposite direction to another waiting ambulance. Every movement, every jolt makes me yelp in pain, but as they bob me along the pavement through the carnage and despair, I catch David's eyes one last time before we go our separate ways.

'I'll find you, I promise,' I call after him. 'I'll find you again, David!'

'Please do,' he mouths to me before his head sweeps backwards and his once white T-shirt, so bloodied, charred and torn, is the last thing I see before my own world goes pitch black.

It is over.

This whole living nightmare of today is over for us.

At least, it is for now.

2008

Ten Years Later

4.

KATE

I fix my silver hoop earring in the bathroom mirror of my Dublin apartment and Sam, fresh from the shower, slips his arms around my waist, kisses the skin on my neck and sends a shiver right through me. I savour how he snuggles into me, making me feel like the luckiest girl in the whole world.

Next Wednesday, it's going to be three years to the day since we first met. Sam McGarry, a news journalist with exotic Mediterranean looks, caught my eye in the hospital canteen one sunny August afternoon when he was in with us to cover a story on how the looming recession was affecting the health service, and once our eyes locked, the rest was history.

He asked a few questions, like every good journalist does, sent me flowers a few days later, invited me for dinner, and it's been happily ever after since then.

His nonstop inquisitive nature keeps me on my toes and

makes me marvel at his vast knowledge of everything from current affairs to pop culture, and maybe I'm barking up the wrong tree, but I've a secret funny feeling by his unusually quiet behaviour lately that he may be planning something very special for next week – I wouldn't dare say it aloud to anyone, but I think he might be planning a proposal.

'Are you sure you don't want me to come with you today?' he asks, catching my eye over my shoulder in the mirror. 'I could cancel the meeting, even at short notice. I don't mind. Honestly.'

His caring side also never ceases to amaze me.

'I'm sure,' I tell him, turning to face him. I run my finger down the side of his face and then lean in to kiss him goodbye. He smells manly, fresh and clean, and I'm tempted to change my mind and stay here in the safety of my cocoon with him, one hundred miles from home in a city where hardly anyone knows my history and connection to the memorial service today. 'I'll have our Maureen and Shannon by my side – but thank you. It means a lot you'd do that for me.'

My train leaves from Dublin's Connolly Station in about forty minutes, and I can walk there in fifteen from my apartment, so I'd better get going. Today is a day I've been contemplating for a long time but deep down I know I need to do this. I'm looking at it as another layer of armour, another milestone, another element of closure for the horror of that day that sometimes seems so long ago, but at other times feels as if it happened only yesterday.

Almost an hour later I sit on the train, thankful for the empty seat across from me so I can while away the time on the two-hour journey north alone and prepare myself for the emotions that today's short event will bring. It's important that I go. I know it is on so many levels. I need to show solidarity for the people of my home town and, most of all, I need to acknowledge how far I've come since the day that almost ruined my life.

I say almost because I refuse to give it that power.

'Name your trauma,' I was told in one of my numerous counselling sessions over the past decade. 'Give it your own name so you can visualize it as a thing and rise above it. Never, ever give it the power to destroy you.'

And so, I named it 'Terror'. It's the best word I can come up with to describe what we all went through on that horrific Saturday afternoon in the worst massacre in our country's modern history. Terror.

As the train rattles along the coastline out of the city, I close my eyes and reflect on all that has happened since. A year out of university to recover physically after my leg was smashed from knee to ankle; my mother's early and welcome release from prison, which was like someone wrapping a blanket of comfort around my broken heart and fragile mind; my eventual graduation as a nurse, which made the local newspapers as a good news story linked to such an atrocity, and a move to Dublin to work in a hospital where I've met so many good friends and, of course, Sam.

'I'm thinking of you, gorgeous. Stay strong,' he texts me, which makes me smile as I lean my head against the window on the train. My overnight bag, which sits at my feet, contains a birthday card and a phoenix necklace gift for Shannon, who turns sixteen today. My sweet, brave, beautiful niece who has risen from the ashes in so many ways, turning her pain into art as she paints her way towards becoming, I've no doubt, a much-sought-after artist when her grammar-school education finishes.

And as I make this journey home to see them all, I wonder – as I so often do – whatever became of the boy in the white T-shirt, David Campbell, or the 'ice-cream shop boy' as Shannon has so fondly referred to him since. I picture his face in the shop that day, blushing when I caught him staring my way and then the look of fear that engulfed him only minutes later as we sat together in that bloodied doorway, soothing our desperate, terrified minds as best we both could.

I did try to look for him afterwards, of course. In fact, as soon as my leg had healed properly, and as soon as I was mentally prepared to look him up, I went to his house, which I easily found out was five miles out of town, but the response I got that day almost destroyed me all over again. Nothing could have prepared me for it.

'So, you're the famous Kate?' his father, who introduced

himself as Reverend Campbell, had said when he greeted me at the huge shiny red door of the magnificent manor.

The driveway to their family home was a breathtaking, winding lane of pale pink gravel, framed to the sides with neat flowerbeds filled with delicate white roses and neatly trimmed miniature hedges. The house itself was jaw dropping and ivy clad, overlooking acres of land, and I could see a tennis court in the background, tucked behind a separate cute yellow rose garden with a water feature at its centre.

Reverend Campbell was a smaller man than I had expected him to be, given David's tall and strong stature. I'd known of him to be controversial yet well respected, and although my mother sniffed when she heard of my enigmatic 'friend' David's connection to him, she knew her own personal opinion would never stop me from trying to track David down as I'd promised to. Reverend Campbell wore dark rimmed glasses that sat so close to the end of his nose they might fall off, and he immediately invited me into a large parlour and sat me down, explaining that David had gone to stay with a friend in Scotland for a few days. He had to do that quite often. He had to get away from it all.

'I'd really like to chat to him again, just to – you know – talk things through,' I explained, feeling my breathing go shallow as old familiar emotions crept up on me. 'It's hard to describe to anyone who wasn't there at the time, I suppose, but we shared a very frightening moment and he really helped me and my niece, so I'd like to thank him properly in person. And to see if he's OK of course.'

He paused, took a deep breath and then sternly locked eyes with me.

'David doesn't talk much about what happened,' he replied. 'I don't push him to.'

'OK . . . of course. I understand that.'

I hadn't spoken a lot about it myself, not to many people outside my own family, but I'd had plenty of professional help and I have to say Maureen and my mother had looked after Shannon and me like eggs that might crack at any moment, making sure we had space when we needed it and a shoulder to cry on when the time was right.

'He doesn't talk about it much to *me*, I should say,' Reverend Campbell explained further. 'Not to me, no, but he did mention your name once. In fact, he called out for you one night in his sleep, I believe – in a nightmare, one of many – and his mother told me you'd helped each other. It's nice of you to look him up. Who knows, it might do you both good to have a chat and you know . . . reconnect?'

I remember how my heart leapt a little when I heard this, because the same thing had happened to me on occasion where I'd wake up in the middle of the night, sweat dripping down my face and my nightwear stuck to my skin as my own mother sponged me down. I'd call for David and for Shannon in my nightmares, and it floored me to think that he had done the same.

'Yes, I'd really like to – I'd really like to reconnect with him. I promised I'd find him again.'

'How lovely,' he replied. 'It's important to keep our promises.'

I swallowed back tears and took a deep breath to try and compose the emotion of being so close to David again. I was standing in his home where he'd lived and breathed and cried, and I couldn't believe I'd found him.

'So, I was hoping,' I said with a quiver, 'I was hoping maybe you could give him my number? And if he doesn't – if it's too painful for him to talk to me, I totally under-stand, but I just had to come here today for my own closure, and in the hope it might help David too. He's a special person, Reverend Campbell, but then you probably know that already.'

He nodded, acknowledging the compliment towards his own son.

'He's a good lad, I suppose, in his own way.'

I handed him a piece of pink lined paper from a notebook I carried around on a permanent basis, another tip from my counsellor, who encouraged me to write down my fears. He took it from me and smiled.

'How is he?' I asked. 'You know, how has he been since?'

David's father contemplated his answer very carefully.

'He is struggling,' he told me with eyes that, despite his kind words, seemed numb to reality. He took the piece of paper from my hand. 'He is struggling in a way that only you unfortunate souls who were there that day will ever truly understand. We're finding him all the help we can, but he has shut himself off a lot from reality and he is very, very angry.'

I nodded.

'And you?' he asked.

I shrugged my shoulders. It would be my twenty-first birthday in a few days and I too felt so angry at how every milestone and celebration I'd have from now on would be tinged with sadness, ruined by the memories and flashbacks that I feared would never go away.

'I'm struggling too,' I told him, looking at the floor. The tiles, black and white and shiny, had little streaks of lilac running through them. I'd never seen such grandeur before in real life, and couldn't help but try and calculate in my head how many times our house in town would fit inside this one. 'And I'm very angry still. I would love to talk to David. Maybe we could help each other, just like we did before.'

I noticed his hands were shaking at that moment as he stared at my handwriting on the pink piece of paper and, all of a sudden, the good energy we had shared was sucked from the room. My heart thumped in my chest when he looked up at me, his previous jolly, welcoming and friendly expression gone and a look of disdain replacing the former enthusiasm on his face.

He cleared his throat.

'You name is Kate *Foley*?' he said, as if it was a question, even though my name was written in deliberately plain capital letters in front of him. 'Kate Foley.'

'Yes,' I replied. 'Kate Foley.'

'From where exactly, Miss Foley?'

'I'm from – I'm from the Green Park estate, you know, up by—'

'Yes, I know exactly where it is,' he said, handing me back my phone number. 'Your mother is Annie Foley, yes?'

He gestured at me quickly to stand up, telling me my time here was up, then he put his hand on my shoulder and gently steered me towards the door. As I walked, I looked at the floor and bit the side of my cheek, feeling tears spring to my eyes. Then I stopped. I turned and looked him right in the eye.

'Yes, my mother is Annie Foley. That is correct.'

He raised his eyebrows and sniggered in sheer disbelief and shook his head. I wasn't going to allow him to steer me any further. I knew what was coming and I would face him head on.

'Are you a troublemaker like your mother?' he sneered at me, and I took a step backwards, as though he had punched me in the throat. 'I've spent many years denouncing the likes of your mother in my church. She and I have quite a turbulent history, one might say.'

'How dare you!'

'Look, Miss Foley,' he said, looking right at me. 'I know you'd like to see my son and I hope you don't take this personally, but I'm requesting that . . . in fact I'm telling you . . . please don't call here again.'

The tears threatened to burst from my eyes and I momentarily lost my breath.

'What?' I asked him. 'You know nothing about me, and you know nothing about my mother!'

'I know a lot more about your connections than you may think I do,' he said firmly. 'I believe you are friends with a local, er, *thug* called Sean McGee?'

My heart leapt. 'He is not my friend,' I choked, my eyes widening.

'He's your niece's father. Now, I'll see you to the door and I'll repeat: don't ever try to contact David again. I'm sure when you think about it properly, you'll understand why.'

I marched out of the house on autopilot, gripping the scrunched-up piece of paper in the sweaty palm of my hand, and threw it onto the passenger seat of my car, doing my best not to cry when I was still within his sight.

His arrogance and his unfair judgement of me stung so deeply I wanted to scream in his face, but I knew that would only prove his conviction that someone like me – from my end of town, with my dubious family background – would never be good enough to speak to his son.

The tyres of my car spun on the gravel as I left the driveway of their magnificent home, feeling as if I was dirt on Reverend Campbell's shoe. When I got home I went straight to bed, slamming the door and ignoring my mother's questions of concern.

'I'll go back there with you,' she told me defiantly. 'I'll go right back there and give that man a few home truths! He has always had it against me but how dare he judge you? How dare *anyone* judge you? He has no idea what he is talking about! No one does!'

'Just leave it, Mum,' I told her, afraid I'd never find my breath properly again. 'Just leave it, please, and just leave me alone.'

I spent the next few weeks – maybe even months – in that room, spiralling backwards in my depression, unable to leave the house, not even on my twenty-first birthday when I should have been out celebrating like normal girls my age.

Nothing in my life has been normal since, of course, and now, as I sit on this train heading back there, I hope I never am made to feel as low as that ever again.

But despite his father, despite that terrible day and despite the sleepless nights I spent reliving everything so horrible about that particular year of my life, I still think of David Campbell like a shining light in the dark, even today. I still dream about him, I still remember the promise I made to find him, and I still long for a day that – when the time is right – our paths will cross again.

I wonder if that right time will be today.

DAVID

I am ready for this.

At least, I am physically, though my mind isn't so sure; my head races with flashbacks and memories, just like it always does when I spend time at my family home or when I remember the bomb and the horror I've lived with since.

My childhood bedroom has been redecorated many times since I left home, its floral bedspread and matching curtains typical of my mother's attempts to keep the Old Rectory's traditional style, but its unfamiliar decor doesn't prevent me thinking about times gone by.

I've come to accept that my life is made up of two very distinctive parts. Life before the bomb and life after the bomb, and sometimes, although I've moved on and progressed immensely, I like to allow myself time to drift back to those carefree days beforehand when none of us had any idea of how our lives would change.

Most of those memories are of my deep friendship with Aaron and just thinking of him comforts me deeply. I remember the first day we met, when I started working in the shop; his geeky, lanky demeanour was a stark contrast to my more athletic physique but we clicked over a love of rock music and a desire to philosophize and challenge the norm. He was Catholic, I was Protestant, and we loved that we crossed that divide so seamlessly, just how it should be, from day one. In fact, I don't think we ever said those words out loud. We were friends, we made each other laugh a lot and that was all that mattered.

'Pints?' he suggested to me one afternoon when our shift ended simultaneously just a week into the job. I remember the sparkle in his green eyes as he suggested an unplanned afternoon in a beer garden, the look of 'divilment' as my teachers would have described it, luring me into a world so far removed from the rigid routine my father loved to subject me to.

I left work with a breeze behind me, mesmerized by his happy-go-lucky ways. I loved how every story he told was delivered with so much enthusiasm. We talked that day about everything from his love of listening to music turned up really loud to my love of playing the drums in our garden shed. He told me of the time he bungee-jumped in Belfast when hungover aged just fifteen, and when he broke his leg in a motorbike accident the very next day, almost breaking his mother's heart. He was wild, he was carefree, he was upfront and honest, and he was soon my very best friend.

What I'd give to hear his heart-warming laugh again today. What I'd give to be planning a beer with him this evening in that same garden. What I'd give to be able to visit him now, and I'd laugh and he'd laugh and we'd plan our next post-work shenanigans, where we'd convey how much we loved each other through a pat on the back and a swig from a bottle of beer. What I'd give to hear his stories just one more time.

That will never happen, though. Just a year after the bomb, Aaron's mother found him cold in bed with a note saying he couldn't suffer the darkness that engulfed him any more. Like me, he'd seen too much that day. Unlike me, he hadn't found a way to cope with it all. Where I was sent off to friends in Scotland, to therapists, to anyone my parents felt could help me vent off my anger and pain, Aaron took to his bedroom and shut the whole world out until the day came when he decided he'd shut it out for ever.

Aaron, the tall, ginger, apple-crunching, entertaining, funny, handsome and most wholesome person I have ever met is gone for ever. His experience on the day of the bomb, what he saw, what he witnessed, never left him, so he left us instead.

Tears sting my eyes and nerves grip my stomach. I have second thoughts about attending today's memorial, but there's no going back now. I have to do this for so many reasons, but no one in my life could understand them. Not my parents, not my fiancée Lesley, only me.

And then I think of Kate – the mysterious Kate who I spent only minutes with, yet it felt like a lifetime – and I wonder why we never did manage to find each other as promised, for comfort, for friendship, and to see if the bond we'd once felt was bigger than the trauma we shared.

Kate and Shannon. Two names that will stay with me until the day I die. I've thought about Kate a lot since then, of course, and I still do.

Not long after the explosion, before I left home, I took to driving around the whole town night after night and day after day, hoping to catch a glimpse of her by accident. I'd picture the scene in my head, imagining where I'd see her, perhaps walking a dog along the pavement, or coming out of a shop with her mind busy, or riding a bike along the road. Our eyes would lock and we'd both smile and maybe even cry a little. We'd hug. We'd hold hands again. We'd heal. We'd be friends like no other because no one else could ever understand the anger and sorrow we'd lived with since. She was the only other person I know who experienced what I did that day. Well, the only person other than Aaron, and Aaron is gone for ever.

Lesley enters the room, interrupting my daydream. She looks beautiful in her long, figure-hugging navy dress and if she doesn't want to be here, as I've suspected since we arrived this morning, she is hiding it well. Her smile reassures me that I'm doing the right thing by going today. We talked about it a lot lately, and even though she could never possibly understand the depth of the trauma I experienced ten years ago, she knows it's important to me to come and pay my respects to other victims and attempt once more to close a chapter of my life that has haunted me for a very long time now.

'We'd better get going, honey,' she says, brushing the shoulders of my jacket down as she speaks in her beautiful Welsh accent. 'I'll go start the car.'

'I'll be right there,' I tell her, straightening my tie in the mirror in my bedroom. I wasn't sure what today's dress code would be, but I thought it important to look smart in honour of those who lost their lives and those who were seriously injured.

Lesley leaves me to it, so I take my time and then I follow her downstairs, so glad that my father has taken Mum to a hospital appointment which means they've gone before we leave. As I walk to the door I do my best to erase Kate's face from my mind. I never did find out her surname, but I didn't need to know that minor detail to remember her so vividly. I step outside into the summer sunshine, wiping my eyes with the back of my hand, and open the car door, taking a deep breath and blowing out the negative energy that always fills me when I come to this house. I don't think I ever realized how big it was during my childhood, or how much living in such a palatial manor made me so different to many of my peers. Back then it was just my home and I knew no different, but now it stinks of contradiction, grandeur and a two-faced life I'm glad I left behind.

'You sure you want to do this, David?' Lesley asks when I get into the passenger seat of the car we hired this morning at Belfast Airport.

'Yes, I'm sure.'

'It's just – well, I don't often agree with your father, but he believes it's going to open up old wounds that—'

'Please don't quote my father, Lesley,' I beg of her. 'Please,

I've made my decision. I want to be here today. I have to do this. I want to.'

I stare ahead as my thoughts are filled once more with Kate and the possibility she might be here today. I think back to the aftermath of the explosion and feel her hand in mine again, so sticky and fine, as we held each other together – almost literally – and I realize how much it would mean to just see her one more time.

I've never told Lesley about Kate.

I've never told any of my girlfriends about her or how we helped each other in the most tragic, surreal moments of my life. I don't know why, but I could never bring myself to talk about her to anyone really, apart from to my mother when I'd woken from a bad dream having called out her name – and to Aaron of course. I'd told Aaron all about her just before he died, not that he was in any fit state to listen.

I've had many girlfriends in England, some of whom I spilled my guts out to so much, revealing my trauma about losing Aaron and my emotions about the bomb itself, that they'd run a mile. Others, like Lesley, had very little idea what went on sometimes in my muddled-up mind although I did open up to Lesley over time. With her father's military background, she knew the effects of post-traumatic stress and did her best to listen even if she never really could fully understand what I was going through.

But I never told any of them about Kate. No matter who

had shared my heart, my time or my bed in the last ten years, I never did tell them about the woman who helped me through that day.

Maybe I've been afraid that, by doing so, I'd realize that I have never stopped looking for her. Somewhere, in the back of my mind, I have always been searching, even in places where I knew she couldn't possibly be. I'd look for her on buses, on trains, on beaches in foreign countries when on holiday, I'd scour the streets of my home town when I'd visit. Sometimes I would think I'd seen her, but then I'd realize it was just my mind playing tricks on me.

I can't tell anyone, I can't even tell Lesley, but I've never stopped thinking about her.

And I know I never will.

5.

KATE

'You look very pretty. You suit your hair like that,' Shannon tells me as soon as I walk in through the door of my childhood home, almost three hours after I left my life with Sam back in Dublin.

I kiss her forehead, not having to lean down as far as I used to have to, then look down at my yellow summer dress and tuck my shortened, darker hair behind my ears as I follow her down the narrow hallway.

The woodchip wallpaper that graced the walls for so many years has been long ago replaced by much nicer floral decor, and the floor beneath me that was once topped with lino now has much more pleasant laminate wood, a big step up and a sign of life going in the right direction for all those who live here, at least on the surface.

'Why thank you, darling niece,' I say in return. 'Happy birthday, my favourite girl! How are you feeling? Sweet sixteen! Ah Shannon, I can't believe it!'

'I feel exactly like how I felt yesterday and the day before,' she jokes as I follow her to the kitchen, towards the sound of the news on the radio. 'But maybe now I'll be allowed to stay out a bit later than eleven on weekends!'

My mother turns to greet me from the sink where she is, as usual, in the middle of preparing a delicious dinner for us to enjoy later.

'Don't tell me, steak and kidney pie?' I ask, my stomach growling at the very thought of it. Mum is an exceptional cook and she loves to get me home so she can show off some of our old favourite dishes, especially on an occasion like a birthday. 'Please say mash, veg and your famous gravy?'

Since her time inside, which thankfully feels like a world away, she has turned her hand to cooking, baking and community work, and maybe even a little bit of romance with a man we refer to as 'the lovely Liam'.

'I must be very predictable,' she jokes, wiping her hands on her apron and turning to greet me. We hug awkwardly and she quickly goes back to her station, preferring as always to keep her mind and herself busy than engage in idle small talk or physical gestures.

'Predictable is good sometimes,' I say to her. 'How's work been? And how's the lovely Liam?'

At the mention of Liam, she shakes her head in a swift little trait she has that makes her brown hair move. Liam is a very dashing local youth worker whom she talks about all the time.

'Work is thriving, and Liam is indeed very lovely,' she tells me. 'But not in the romantic fashion you are hoping for.'

'Still, he sounds promising!' I tell her, trying to encourage her a little. She deserves some love in her life at last. Gone are the days when she'd wait and pray for my sister Maureen's dad to come out of the pub for long enough to financially support her, or for my own father a few years later to do the same.

She looks like a different person these days than the woman I used to visit in prison ten years ago. She is rounder, fresher in the face, and she appears a lot younger than her fifty-two years. I feel sorry for her still, but only in the sense that she wasted so many months in a place she should never have been, serving time for a crime for which she had been entirely framed by those who still know the truth to this day. People like Sean McGee and his tribe, who continue their campaign in an underworld I'm glad to be away from. But my mother's time in prison has made her stronger, steelier and more admirable, as she has battled against prejudice and judgement from a lot of people who know nothing of her story and couldn't be bothered to take the time to listen to the truth. She is my mother and I will always love her and defend her deeply.

'Nana's mad in the head about the lovely Liam, Kate,' chirps Shannon. 'He phones her over the weekend, but it's purely platonic of course! Just good friends, you know?'

'Sounds like it,' I say with a wink. I check the time. It's almost time to go. 'Where's Mo?'

'Doing her hair upstairs, or should I say, *trying* to do her hair upstairs,' says Shannon, rolling her eyes in a way only a teenage girl can. 'She has no clue. Please go and help her, Kate. She won't let me anywhere near her mop of curls and says I'm obsessed with hair straighteners, which may be actually true.'

Going by Shannon's poker-straight long blonde hair and heavy side fringe, I can see my sister definitely has a point. Shannon's eye make-up is heavy too and she still wears braces on her teeth, but to me she will always radiate beauty and survival and her school grades are on the up, telling us that she has a very bright future.

'I can't believe I'm the mother of a sixteen-year-old!' Mo says when I come to her beauty regime rescue. 'How on earth did that happen, Kate? And how come she's so bloody sensible, not that I'm complaining. I was pregnant when I was her age! I sometimes think she's more like you than she is me. In fact, I don't think it. I know it, thank goodness.'

We need to get going, so I quickly fix Mo's curls so that they frame her pretty face, say goodbye to Mum who has opted to stay at home and prepare the birthday dinner rather than face the crowds and no doubt the cameras that will be at today's memorial, and we walk the short route into town together, where it's predicted that thousands will travel to pay their respects on this ten-year anniversary.

'Do you think we'll ever see him again?' Shannon asks me as we join the expanding crowd of people, gathered around a purpose-built stage in the town centre, where a specially commissioned sculpture is set to be revealed. Dignitaries from all over Ireland and afar, representing most walks of life, can be spotted in the distance as TV cameras and press photographers scramble for their reaction.

I don't need to ask Shannon who she is talking about. I already know of course. She's talking about the 'ice-cream shop boy'.

'I'd love to see him again, darling, but I don't think we'll see him today, even if he is here, not in these crowds anyhow,' I reply, scrunching my nose up as I scan the masses of people. 'I hope wherever he is that he's happy and well.'

'I do too,' she says, clutching my hand, and then taking her mother's with the other. 'I'll never forget him.'

There's a weight in my stomach at the enormity of standing here again, and when the speeches begin in memoriam to those who lost their lives and to the many, many victims who were injured, I can't help but sob from my very core as memories come flooding back, making me weak and feeling like I'm 20 years old again and not the confident, city-living 30-year-old who deals with trauma on so many levels in my job on any given day.

'Oh, David,' I find myself whispering, and I can feel Shannon's eyes on me as the crowds close in. His face is in my mind when I close my eyes, and his face is on every person who stands around me when I open them.

I know that I long to see him again more than I ever realized. I don't know why I want to, but I just do.

I have such a strong feeling he is here somewhere, and I wonder if he could possibly feel the same as I do.

For some reason, I think he might.

DAVID

'How're you feeling? Remember what we said when we decided to come here. We can leave at any time you feel like it. You don't have to stay.'

Lesley's singsong voice lilts in my ear as I stare at the ground, doing my best not to let this all totally overwhelm me.

I've asked her so many times not to fuss, but every time I look her way she is staring at me as if she could possibly help me at all right now. She could never fully help me. No matter how empathetic she might be, she wasn't there to witness what I did that day.

There are so many people, and those who speak and address us up on the platform could be reciting nursery rhymes for all I can tell. I can barely look up in their direction, never mind absorb what it is they have to say.

Shiny new shop fronts whose names I don't recognize

line the streets in front and behind me from where we stand. Newly laid cobbled pavements lie under my feet. Everything is in full working order again here, but the mood is different and of course it will never be the same again. It's not the place I know any more. Nothing is the same.

The corner shop where Aaron and I spent carefree days working and joking together was never rebuilt as it once was, and a shoe shop now operates from beneath brand-new walls on the same site. My stomach leaps when I think of him, but I'm not ready to show it here. I'll do that in my own time. I don't want to break down today.

'I'm OK so far, Les, thank you,' I whisper to my fiancée, knowing she means well by checking. She glances around to look at me, but I know if I catch her eye at all, I'll go to pieces. I have never reacted well to people feeling sorry for me. Maybe it's because I had always been used to my father's tough love, but the very moment someone sympathizes or tries to understand how I feel deep inside about what happened, I tense up and walk away. I can feel it happening now. It's not Lesley's fault. It's no one's fault. She means well but if she asks me if I'm OK again I might have to leave her and be alone to compose myself.

The growing crowd is becoming very claustrophobic and the stupidly unnecessary shirt and tie I wear is choking me. I wish I'd dressed down a bit. I don't see anyone I know or recognize, but I try to cop on and stop feeling sorry for myself by realizing that amongst these masses of people are hundreds who have their own version, their own suffering, their own trauma to deal with day in and day out of their lives. It's not just me who feels like this, and the thought of that alone, although comforting in a way, is also very hard to absorb. We are all victims – we are all someone's father, mother, son, daughter, husband, wife, sister, brother, cousin or friend. Everyone remembers their own side of the story. Everyone remembers exactly where they were in town or at least where they were further afield when they heard the news.

'I'll never forget when the phone rang that day,' I hear a lady say beside me to her friend. 'My blood ran cold. I just knew it was bad, but no one thought it would be *that* bad.'

Everywhere around me shares different versions of the same story.

Most people stayed here in town afterwards and picked up their lives as best they could over the years. Some, like me, chose to run away and start all over again, hoping the nightmare would stay put, but the horror followed me of course. I've learned over time how there is simply no way of escaping your own mind and memories. You can run from them, but you can't hide, no matter how far away you try to go.

'Here, have a sip of this,' whispers Lesley again, handing me an open bottle of water. I wipe beads of sweat from my brow with a handkerchief. 'You look like you might need it.'

She leads me over to a small bench on the street and we sit there together as a host of formalities go on around us. My skin begins to feel prickly. I don't know what I thought I'd achieve by coming here or how I might benefit, and I begin to think that maybe my father was right. Maybe this is just a way of reliving the horror again, of opening up old wounds. Maybe I should have focused on how far I'd come rather than take this step back in time again. Maybe I should leave.

'Can I get you anything?' Lesley asks me. 'I need something to cool me down a bit. Would you like an ice cream?'

I shake my head. We are at the very back of a crowd of thousands and the heat and atmosphere is somewhat stifling.

'No, I don't want ice cream.'

I don't know what I want right now, but it's far from an ice cream. Her very suggestion reminds me once more that my mind and hers are on opposite planets sometimes, plus it brings my mind back to the shop I used to work in with Aaron and my hands begin to shake.

Do I want to stay? Do I want to go? I feel like I'm in some strange place of limbo, like a fog; like my body is here but my mind isn't, or maybe it's the other way about.

Lesley slips into a shop behind us and comes back out minutes later with an ice cream for herself. I catch her in the corner of my eye, doing my best not to begrudge her for not having lived through what I have and for being able to think of something as simple as an ice cream right now. She sits there, looking around her, oblivious to my feelings, and my father's face comes into my head.

None of them has a clue. They don't know. How could they? They weren't there. They have absolutely no idea of the torment that I live with on a daily basis. Her complacency as she sits there like a fish out of water reminds me so much of my father and his lack of support over the past ten years. He should be by my side today. He should be showing his face and supporting our community instead of hiding away and pretending it never happened. He was never there when I needed him, yet he felt it his place to preach to his followers about the evil behind the act. If he'd spent more time helping his community heal instead of focusing on the hatred in his heart, it would have been much more helpful.

And all Lesley can suggest is a bloody ice cream. She too is so far removed from all of this. She just doesn't get it at all.

'Lesley, I need to take a walk,' I say, and she stands up immediately to join me. She sits back down again when she sees my face. 'Alone.'

'Oh.'

'I'm sorry, but do you mind?' I ask, even though I don't mean it as a question. 'I just need to try and absorb all of this. Wait here if you want? I won't be long.'

I leave her there before she can answer, unable to feel any

guilt or sorrow for doing so, even though she made this trip to be by my side. I just need some time out. I actually don't know where I'm walking to, but within minutes I find myself standing at the doorway where Kate, Shannon and I sheltered together, staring at it with tears dripping down my face.

I hear the screams again, I smell the burning, I feel the trembling air, I taste the soot on my tongue, and I see black and red and grey everywhere.

I think of Aaron and how he couldn't bear to live with the mental scars it left rooted on his fragile mind and my hand goes to my mouth as I try to smother the heaving sobs that come from deep within me.

I try to remember the colour of the door as it was then, but I can't. It's blue now, and wind chimes hang on the other side of the glass. Little trinkets with inspirational quotes and dream catchers of all colours stand in neat displays where people browse around, so far from the history of this very place, where the three of us held each other and waited for someone to come to our rescue.

I gather myself and turn to go back to Lesley, to run away from this all again and, just as I do, I see her.

Oh my God, I see her.

6.

KATE

'David? David Campbell, is that you?'

Just seconds ago, I'd found myself wandering away from the huge crowd, when the emotion of what was being said on stage became too much for me. I made an excuse to my family that I needed some water and then, as if on autopilot, I walked until I came to this doorway. David was staring through the window.

'Wow,' he says, squinting in disbelief. 'Kate?'

He smiles, wide eyed now. I do the same in return.

'I can't believe this,' I whisper. 'How have you been?'

I knew him instantly and the rush of emotion that fills me as I look at him now is like nothing I've ever felt before.

He looks distracted and exhausted, though the past ten years have been kind to him overall – well, physically at least. He is still so handsome in his features, his dark hair and blue eyes, his cheekbones that define his beautiful face now lined with a very sexy dark stubble – the striking face and strong physique that first caught my eye and made me do a double take in the ice-cream shop where he worked back then.

But even though I ask him the question, before I hear his reply I see already a storm in his brooding eyes that tells me it isn't just today that has triggered his trauma. I know simply by looking into David's eyes that he has held onto a lot of bitterness and anger that I – thankfully – have learned over time, and with a lot of work, not to let go of totally but to manage as best I can.

'I . . . I've been OK,' he says. 'I still have flashbacks to that day, but I've done my best to cope with them. I've had a lot of counselling, which helped me, but—'

David pauses and breathes. I want to reach out to him physically when the pain overcomes him here where we stand as a whirlwind of activity goes on around us. For both of us right now the clocks have stopped and the world has stood still.

'It changed me a lot – the bomb,' he continues. I feel a shiver run through me. We are strangers in so many ways, our lives and backgrounds so many worlds apart . . . and yet it seems to me we are looking at each other as if we've both finally found the missing piece of a puzzle for which we've been looking for ever. 'It took me a long time to accept it all . . . and just by being here now I . . .'

I wait to let him finish.

'I can't sometimes . . . anyhow, I live in England now,' he

says, as if he's trying to shake off what is really going through his mind. 'I guess you could say I ran away from all of this, or at least I tried to. It never really goes away, does it?'

I nod and swallow, understanding exactly how he feels, and I can see that his terror still surrounds him and follows him, no matter how fast or how far he runs.

'I ran away too, but just to Dublin,' I tell him.

'Dublin,' he repeats, smiling softly. 'It's a great city.'

We both take a step closer to each other, a need to be nearer physically that demands no explanation.

'I've been there since I graduated. I work in a hospital now.'

We almost touch, but we don't. I look at his hands, which once held mine so tightly as we waited in this doorway, and I long to reach out, but I don't.

'In the strangest ways,' I explain further, 'it helps me to help other people and makes me realize I'm not the only victim in the world. Maybe doing something positive for other people has saved me. I love it there.'

Our eyes are locked and the blur of what is going on further down the street, a whirr of speeches and applause, leaves a constant hum in the background. It's as though we have found this cocoon again together, our little shelter from the world, and nothing else matters.

'You helped me so much that day. I always knew you'd do something special,' he says softly. His eyes sparkle when he speaks, like he is drinking me in, and I too am hypnotized by his presence. I feel his strong, manly body beside me like energy, so forceful and powerful. 'I trained with the Air Force in England to gain some focus and discipline but I realized I'd only buried my internal issues. They couldn't support me any further and I ended up leaving to get away from bombs and bullets for good. I – I retrained to be a teacher. I teach science to teenagers now.'

'The Air Force,' I repeat, unable to disguise my shock but doing my best to, all the same. 'So you were a pilot? In the Forces?'

He shrugs humbly, but his words choke me. He certainly looks like a handsome military pilot, but his revelation takes my breath away for different reasons and I don't know whether to run away from him or run to him. I was brought up to believe in Irish unity and denounce British rule, while he has gone on to work in the military, which people of my beliefs see as the enemy. We couldn't be more different if we tried.

'Yes, a pilot, but it made me realize, even though I should have already known, that bombs and bullets are definitely not for me. I failed psychology tests as the past caught up with me again. I had to leave.'

A silence follows, and the fact that there are worlds between us hits me once more like a slap on the face. He joined the *Air Force*. In Britain. It's a world away from anything I've ever known or ever could know, and spells out the huge differences in the way we both grew up, despite living in the same town.

I immediately recall the look of disgust on his father's face that day when I went to look for him. He's the son of a church minister, from a very privileged Protestant background, and now an ex-RAF pilot, whereas I'm from a sprawling housing estate, with a Catholic upbringing and political beliefs that doubtless couldn't be more polar opposite. Our two very different communities are divided by blood-red lines that have remained indelibly fixed for hundreds of years before us – my side of town is made up of people who are Irish and proud of it. The people on his side of town are bound to a union with Great Britain, leaving us separated by a history that runs like a deep dagger wound between us, yet I still can't help but feel there is this connection, this simmering bond between us that defies all of that.

We are beyond history, we are beyond a bomb. Because of that day and the brief time we spent together, despite those differences, we are bound together in a way that no one else could ever understand and it scares me a little.

'Are you married?' I ask him, feeling my stomach flip as I say it out loud. I look at his hand as I ask, noticing there isn't a ring but that's not entirely unusual.

He shuffles at my question, and I see and feel the deep pain that surrounds him. Unlike me, he doesn't seem to hide it so well. There's a silence in his voice and heaviness in his heart that I've learned to spot in others through years of training in the aftermath of personal trauma.

He pauses, as if he has to think of his answer. I laugh a little, trying to let him know it isn't a trick question.

'Sorry, yes. I mean no, but I'm getting married next year to Lesley,' he says as he laughs back, though his eyes, I believe, tell a slightly different story. 'She's from Wales but she's here today. In fact, she's down there, waiting for me, with absolutely no idea of what that day was really like right here ten years ago. I guess she's lucky that way.'

His eyes skirt away and then back to mine. He fidgets a bit but his eye contact is intense once again and it draws me in.

'I understand what you mean,' I tell him. 'I know exactly how you feel.'

My lip trembles as the memories of that day wash through me.

'It's so, so good to see you again,' I tell him and, at that, out of the blue, he leans towards me and puts his arms around me, holding me so tight to his chest I can hear his heart beat. He smells so good and I close my eyes as we stay like this, clinging to one another until a lady tries to enter the shop and we come back to reality. I wipe my tears as we move to let the woman past. She looks at us knowingly. There's a level of empathy in the air today with everyone in this town. So many memories being relived, so many tales of survival and of hope, and so many heads bowed in sorrow at those who aren't lucky enough to be standing strong ten years on.

'I think about you all the time, you know,' he says hurriedly in a whisper. His hands are distracted, as if he wants to reach out to me physically again. 'I've never stopped thinking about you, Kate, wondering how your life turned out, or how you've been.'

His words almost take my breath away, and he looks as if he is so relieved to finally get to say them. All this time, all those months and years that have passed and he has never forgotten me, just like I have never forgotten him.

'I think about you too, David,' I tell him. My knees are weak and I feel a little dizzy as we stand together on the cobbled pavement. He looks so pained in his expression, as if he really, really cares, but that it hurts him just to be here and to see me again, even though we've both thought of it so often. 'But yes, I'm really good, thanks. I've a boyfriend called Sam who lives with me in Dublin. I have a nice life there. We are very happy.'

'That's so good to hear,' he whispers. 'How's Shannon? It's her birthday again today?'

He tilts his head to the side as if he is asking about his own child.

'It is, yes. She is amazing,' I tell him, unable to contain a beaming smile now. 'She is the bravest girl, just as you told her she was that day. She's a ray of hope every single day.'

The applause from the streets beneath the hill where we stand grows louder, and we both turn towards it briefly.

'Look, I probably should get back to Lesley,' David says,

glancing over my shoulder towards the crowds, and my heart sinks a little. I can tell by the agony in his eyes that he might feel the same. 'I could talk to you all day but she'll be worried if I'm gone for much longer. Can we keep in touch, Kate? I'd love if we could.'

He reaches into his jacket pocket and hands me a business card, crisp and new, where his name is stamped in the corner. I play with it in my hand, looking at his name in print, and the enormity of meeting him again hits me once more.

He tilts his head and looks at me as if in confession, an aching smile etched on his gorgeous face. He breathes in, as though he is trying to force out what he wants to say next.

'You know I used to drive around this whole town, into every housing development, and around every corner of the countryside, hoping to bump into you,' he tells me with a faint smile. He pushes his hair back and bites his lip at his hurried admission, laughing shyly now. 'I told myself that if I met you, I'd bite the bullet and ask you out on a date. I'd take a chance and just go for it.'

I can't hide my surprise. 'You did?'

'I did.'

He smiles more, his eyes brightening, but he has no idea how much it pains me to think we were both looking all this time, if not always physically, at least in our own minds.

'And you would have asked me out on a date?' I repeat.

He glances around and unbuttons his shirt at the top as the heat from the street rises. I do my best not to stare.

'I wanted to ask you out for sure,' he says with the same side smile I remember so clearly from before. 'I fancied you a lot back then.'

I lick my lips and look away, and when I look back at him our eyes meet; we stand in silence for what feels like for ever.

'I wanted to find you so badly, Kate,' he continues more seriously now; then, as quickly as he says it, he snaps out of his daze. 'Anyhow, you could drop me a line or give me a call and maybe we could meet up again, properly, away from here.'

I can't help but feel a bit lost in this quite surreal moment. It's like today, at this moment, in this place, this was meant to happen, but then I recall his father's words, his hurried, definite tone, his warning to me, and at that moment the reality of the world we live in hits me hard.

How could an ex-RAF pilot and the daughter of a Republican family be friends? I didn't think it would be possible. We had grown up amid a fierce, bloody conflict that had lasted more than thirty years, from the 1960s to the late 1990s. Until the peace agreement, it was all our parents and we had ever known, living through sectarian shootings, bombs, street riots, reprisal attacks. So, despite that incredibly traumatic shared moment, when it comes down to it David and I are two people from opposite ends of a war that still seeps through the bones of those who lived through it.

I hand the business card back to him. I shake my head and my face creases with disappointment.

'It's not me or you, David, but I don't think we can be friends, sorry,' I tell him. 'Your father disapproves of my mother, my family. We're on opposite sides here. He would never want us to be friends. I know he is a very influential man and I don't want to provoke any more trouble with him.'

'With my father?' he asks in surprise. His voice breaks. He straightens his shoulders and raises an eyebrow. 'What on earth has this got to do with him?'

I instantly wish I hadn't mentioned it. I wish I'd just taken the card and pretended it was a good idea to keep in touch but, as usual, my honesty trips me up. I can't turn back the conversation now.

'We come from two very different worlds, David, let's not even try to forget that,' I say to him. He shakes his head in denial, but I need to say this. 'Where I'm from in this town and where you're from – well, the two communities just don't mix well. We couldn't possibly have anything in common and—'

'What has my father said to you?' he asks. His pushes one tanned hand through his thick dark hair and his handsome face twists in despair. 'I don't care about any of that. Where is this coming from?'

'I—I looked for you,' I confess in a whisper. 'I'd promised to find you again, so I looked for you and I thought I'd found you. I went to your house.'

He is flummoxed. 'You did? When?' He frowns as he awaits my answer.

'I went to your house when I got back on my feet, so to speak. It was almost a year after the bomb,' I tell him. 'I wanted to keep my promise, but most of all I wanted to thank you in person for helping us that day and to see how you were coping. But your dad told me to never come back again—'

'What the . . .?'

David licks his lips and shakes his head in disbelief. He laughs a little but he is not finding any of this funny. I can tell he is laughing in shock and frustration at the realization that, for all this time, his father has stood in the way of the one thing we both wanted the most. Just to be friends, just to get to know each other properly.

He takes my hand again and presses the card into mine.

'Kate, please believe me,' he whispers firmly. 'I am *nothing* like my father, and I never will be. You can contact me whenever you want. I'd love to see you again.'

I can't help it. I smile at the very idea and allow myself – just for one moment – to imagine a time when we might be able to see each other in a way we want to, and not through the blurred vision of a sectarian divide.

'Oh, Kate,' he says, looking away and rubbing his forehead.

'What?' I ask him, totally puzzled.

He looks down the street and then back at me.

'Nothing,' he says, blowing out a deep breath. 'Look, I'd better get back to Lesley but let's stay in touch this time, OK?'

He grips my hand, lets it go again slowly and I stand there as he walks away down the hill.

'Bye for now, Kate,' he calls back to me. 'Chat very soon, I hope.'

'Goodbye, David. It was nice to see you again,' I whisper, my voice cracking a little as I speak.

He stops and looks back, then he nods as if in full agreement, and turns away from me again. I swallow hard and try to ignore how much my head is spinning right now, then I watch him until he disappears into the crowd and I make my way back to my family.

I found him again and I can't wait to tell Shannon.

I can't wait to tell her I found the ice-cream shop boy.

DAVID

I found her.

I can't stop grinning from ear to ear. My God, her smile floored me in a way that she will never know, which is why I couldn't help but look up to the sky in response.

It floored me even more than what she told me about

my father sending her away did and, as I walk back to the bench where Lesley sits, her head tilted back towards the sun, I realize that when I was at my darkest hours after the bombing – when I heard about Aaron's death and any of the many times down the years where I'd wake in the night with tremors and flashbacks – it had been her smile that had kept me going.

I would close my eyes and I'd picture her smile.

I would remember her that day in the shop, walking past the counter and complimenting me so subtly, and I'd recall later that afternoon when the tears streaked through the ash on her face and she still managed to smile at me then, if only for a second, even though we were both in so much physical pain and frightened beyond our wildest nightmares.

'There you are!' Lesley says, standing up to greet me. She kisses me on the cheek and takes my hand, but I let go, pretending I need to take off my jacket. I feel bad, but I can still feel Kate's hand in mine, and I want to hold on to that feeling for just a little bit longer. 'You feeling any better? You look very different. A lot more settled?'

I didn't get her number, I realize. I gave her mine, but she didn't give me hers in return. Knowing this lights a sense of fear inside me, but it's too late to go back and try to find her again. The event is almost over, and I need to get away from here before the crowd starts moving or we'll be stuck in traffic for ages and my nerves won't handle it.

'Let's go and have a picnic lunch somewhere,' I suggest

to Lesley, feeling a little bit guilty for the thoughts that are running through my head. 'I'd love to switch off from all of this. How does that sound?'

'Wonderful,' she says, linking her arm with mine as we walk towards our hired car. 'I'm so proud of you, David. I'm glad you got through today and that you're feeling better.'

'Me too,' I say, wanting so badly to come clean with her about meeting Kate and how it has shaken me to the core, but knowing that now is not the time to launch back into a past she can't and won't ever understand.

And the other truth is that I can't bear to go home yet, as I don't think this time I'll be able to hold back what I feel like saying to my father. If Lesley thought I was 'angry again' at him earlier, I'm afraid at how this latest revelation will affect me when I see him later.

Our flight leaves tonight back to England and, even though I've always wanted to be as far away from here as possible, there's a tug inside me now that holds me here and I know I'll be counting the minutes, hours and days until I hear from Kate again.

I'm already wondering what she's doing now.

My mother is waiting for us when we get back to the rectory manor later that afternoon and, as always, it breaks my heart to see the light dim from her eyes with every visit.

I remember how she used to laugh so loudly and heartily for such a refined person; her sense of humour was very often the one thing that kept me sane when I was growing up within these walls.

She hands me an Americano and has made some iced coffee for Lesley, knowing it's her favourite. We don't have long before our flight. I feel bad for my mother that I avoid staying for dinner or overnight, but I can't bear to be here in this house for any longer than I have to.

'Where is he?' I ask her, trying to appear calm and cool as I feel my blood bubble beneath my skin. I can't leave here without saying something to him. I need to let him know that I know. I just can't pretend it didn't happen, even if it was so long ago.

'Your father?' she asks, as if I could be talking about anyone else. 'Oh, he's in the garden. He always likes to read out there when the sun is out. How did today go?' she asked, concern in her voice. 'You look tired, David. Are you tired?'

'It's been an emotional time for him,' says Lesley and, although again I know she means well, it irritates me that she can't possibly have any clue of how anyone who witnessed what I did might feel. Plus, I can very much speak for myself.

'I'm glad we went,' is as much as I can muster. 'It was very worthwhile. Now, please excuse me for a second. I need to speak to my father.'

I can hear my mother and Lesley whisper in low, worried tones as I leave them to make my way to the garden. I see him sitting there in the distance with his back to me, on a large custom-made lounger by a dainty white cast-iron table under an oak tree in the shade. A small portable CD player sits by his side and I can hear his choice of music, always Beethoven, grow louder and louder as I make my way towards him.

I practise what I'm going to say in my head, just as I've done the whole while when Lesley and I were sharing our picnic at a nearby forest park, the beautiful scenery and fresh air exactly what I needed to calm me down and let it sink in that I only encountered Kate ten years later than I should have because of him and his blind ignorance.

'You're back,' he says, not taking his eye off the novel he is reading. He doesn't turn the music down either, so I do that for him. A glass of fresh lemonade sits on the round table beside him and the birds sing in the trees above him as soon as the music stops. He lives a life of great luxury here and always has done. He has no idea of struggle or trauma and – for a man in the role he has taken on – he has little empathy. My resentment for him rises like bile in my throat.

'Yes, I'm back, but we are leaving almost straight away,' I say, clutching my mug of coffee. 'Today was worthwhile in many ways, before you ask, not that you were going to. I've no doubt you don't really care.'

'That's good. That's really good to hear,' he says, adjusting his black-rimmed glasses. He turns the page of his novel, licking his finger to do so.

I stare at him until he at least has the grace to look my way. As always, I can see the disappointment in his eyes. The one-time law student, second-chance RAF pilot turned science teacher. I don't live up to his expectations. I know I don't.

I wait for more, but he doesn't speak. I just stand there, and he sits, and we stare, man to man, father to son, eyeballing and waiting, like a game of chess, on who will make the next move.

It's my turn.

'Why didn't you tell me she called here all those years ago?' I ask.

I'm not sure whether it's the tone of my voice or what I have just said, but he puts the book down at last. He doesn't need to ask me who I'm talking about.

'Ah . . . Miss Foley?'

I nod. I had no idea what her surname was, but I believe we are on the same page.

'Kate,' I tell him. 'Why did you send her away?'

He tuts and reaches out his hand to lift the book again, but I slam the mug I'm holding down on the table, fury overtaking me. I want to smash it on the ground right here in front of him.

'You had no right!' I tell him through gritted teeth. 'No right whatsoever to cast your judgement on someone I would have given anything to have seen just one more time! You have no idea how often I've longed to see her again!

How I've wondered where and how to find her! How dare you? You have no idea what we went through together, and luckily for you, you never will!'

He winces as my voice rises and I can feel my chest rising up and down rapidly.

'She doesn't belong here,' he says, looking me firmly in the eye. 'Her type is not—'

'Her *type?* You have no clue about her type at all!' I tell him. 'You're supposed to be a man of the cloth, yet you judged her without knowing one single thing about her!'

He stands up now. He reaches just under my chin and he leans on a stick, but his voice is as big and bellowing as ever.

'I know of her family and that's enough!' he yells at me. 'Her mother served time in prison for hiding firearms in their home! Did you know that?'

I take a step back. My breathing is rapid, and my time is running out, so I daren't mince my words.

'That's nothing to do with Kate and, anyway, I was old enough back then to decide for myself if she was worth the risk,' I tell him in hushed tones.

I had no idea of her mother's background, but I actually don't care right now. Those days are gone, and I won't let history hold me back like it has previous generations.

'You were young enough to be fooled into a world where you don't belong, David, and where you will never, ever fit

101

in,' he says. 'You don't belong with them, especially not with someone related to Annie Foley! Stay away from them!'

I check over his shoulder to make sure my mother or Lesley aren't within hearing distance of our raised voices. I don't care about Kate's family beliefs, I don't care about her upbringing, I don't care if she landed down here from the moon. What I care about right now is that he kept her from me at a time when I needed her, even for just one day, and then I could have decided for myself the way forward, just like I can do now.

'"For in the same way you judge others, you will be judged",' I say to my father, quoting his precious Bible, a verse that was drummed into my head from as far back as I can remember. 'Why do you look at the speck of sawdust in your brother's eye and pay no attention to the plank in your own?'

He looks stunned, like a rabbit caught in headlights, and I know I've got him. I've summed him up in a nutshell. He knows exactly what I'm referring to in his own torrid political history where he has taken a vow of silence for matters he should have spoken up against – confessions he's heard from his own congregation, forgiveness of evil that should have been brought before a court of law. There are rats in the gutter on both our sides of the community, Catholic and Protestant, Republican and Loyalist, and I won't stand here and let him preach that one is more wholesome or righteous than the other. Those days, for me anyhow, are over.

'She is not our kind,' he says, lifting his chin now in defiance. 'I do not want her or her people around my home.'

I am so tempted now to grab him but I hold back as best I can, repeating mantras and techniques used to control the rush of anger I sometimes battle with when I come up against such ignorance and bias.

'I hope to God that no one ever judges me on their knowledge of you, Reverend Campbell, the way you unfairly judged Kate,' I tell him, clenching my fists tightly and knowing I have to leave here straight away. 'I will never forgive you for this. Ever.'

7.

KATE

My best friend Sinead, a fellow nurse from Ballsbridge who works on the children's ward with me, is first at my door the evening after Sam moves out, six days after I met David and on the evening of what would have marked three whole years together.

'Oh, look at you!' Sinead says, shaking her head. 'You're a mess. He's a bastard. Come on. And before I come in, I give you full permission to kick me if I utter those highly irritating words about there being plenty of fish in the sea.'

I open the door to let Sinead in and I can feel my mood lift ever so slightly already, the best it has been since I kicked Sam out for cheating on me. I had actually thought he'd been going to propose yesterday, on the anniversary of the day we met, but I'm too embarrassed now to admit that to anyone, even to Sinead.

What makes it hurt so much more and sting so much deeper is that I know his partner in crime so well. I would even go so far as to say I called her a friend. I confided in her, I trusted her, and I let her into a world I've kept so private since I got here.

I even told her about the bomb and about David, much more than I'd ever told Sam.

She's a married journalist friend called Bridget, with whom we'd spent many afternoons sharing lunch and a chat, and many long evenings that led into nights together over a bottle of wine. She and I would talk about everything from the chances of Obama's election victory, which she'd been lucky enough to be invited to cover live from Washington this coming November, our mutual admiration, awe and respect for his wife Michelle, and our fear of the credit crunch of 2008 that had murdered the Celtic Tiger and brought the country financially to its knees.

'It's like a double betrayal,' I sniffle to Sinead, who arrives with what she calls a 'break-up hamper' full of self-help books she swears by, a host of celebrity magazines to distract me for a while, enough chocolate to give Willy Wonka a run for his money, some M&S Percy Pigs, two bottles of wine, a box of tissues and a home-made joke voodoo doll she'd put together, just in case I ever feel like upping my game and really letting off some steam.

'I know it's like a double whammy, honey. You liked the bitch a lot, just not as much as your boyfriend did,' says Sinead in her strong Dublin accent. She never is one to mince her words. 'But just imagine the torture she's going to go through now, sorting out all her legal affairs with her husband during a recession when most of us can't afford to pay our rent. At least you only had to kick Sam out. She's going to have a rotten divorce ahead of her, so I hope he's worth it.'

'He totally fooled me,' I whisper, doing my best not to succumb to finishing an entire bottle of cold white wine in the space of an hour, but by God it's good medicine right now. 'They both fooled me so well. You know, now that I think of it, I came home last weekend after the memorial service and I thought he was acting differently, but I put it down to my own mixed-up head. I bet he'd had her round here when I was away after all his "Do you want me come with you? I can if you want? Are you sure?" crap that morning. I'm never falling for that shite from any man again. What an utter—'

'You won't fall for it again, no,' says Sinead. 'You'll learn from it. You'll be stronger for it, too, believe it or not, so take it as another lesson in life and allow yourself a time to cry before you brush him off for good and realize he just wasn't right for you or good enough for you either. I wouldn't have said it at the time, but didn't it really annoy you the way he said "wow" so much? Like, wow, what now, Sam? Wow, wee Sam. Big feckin' deal, Sam. Wow, wow, wow!'

'Ah, stop, you're just saying that to make me feel better.'

She laughs and I do too.

'Is it working?'

'A little, I suppose.' I shrug, knowing the emptiness and hurt I've felt inside for twenty-four hours is only being temporarily cured by Sinead's presence and the fact that my brain is a bit numb from alcohol.

I'd always fancied myself as a detective in another world, like an old-school Cagney-and-Lacey type, and if not for the complicated political climate I grew up in, I might have considered it as a career. But it didn't take a detective of any sort to put two and two together yesterday evening when I found a bracelet belonging to Bridget down the side of our bed – down *my* side of our bed, to be precise. I knew instantly it was hers because it had been a gift for her thirtieth birthday from Sam and me only a month ago.

I didn't ask for any big detail on when or how it got there. I approached him with it, he admitted their fling, packed his bags, and even looked a bit relieved in the end.

'What an asshole,' I whisper, staring at the furry rug on my apartment living-room floor. 'What a total knob he is. And to think they were doing it in my own bed, if you don't mind! I wonder did they do the nasty in here in the sitting room too. God, Sinead, I'm going to have to throw everything out and start again, aren't I? Everywhere I look I'm reminded of him and her at it behind my back. That's what gets to me the most, you know? It's not even the sex, it's more the sneakiness and the clever ways they had going on to cover it up while we were all thinking we were best buddies. Oh Sinead, I might be sick.'

Sinead stands up.

'Yes, yes you could indeed be sick, I'm sure, and you could overthink all of it and make yourself *very* sick indeed, or you *could* . . .'

She dramatically pauses for effect.

'You could . . .'

'I could what?' I ask, prompting her to hurry up.

'You could always just get rid of all this stuff and move in with me?' she says, as if someone has just lit a flame beneath her.

I don't answer at first so she continues.

'It makes perfect sense, Kate! I'm skint right now and can barely scrape up my rent since Niamh moved in with whatever he's called from the ENT ward,' she says, 'and you're going to have the burden of this place all to yourself now that rat-face is gone, so you could just start afresh, move in with me and we'll both live happily ever after! Voilà!'

I blink a few times. I know she's tipsy and so am I, but she *is* making perfect sense.

'Like Will and Grace?' I ask, romanticizing it all in my head. 'And you don't snore like a hippo, I take it, like Sam did?'

'Well, I was thinking we might be more like Rachel and Monica from *Friends*, but Will and Grace will do,' she says.

I picture us living in peace and harmony together, coming and going as we please, no painful, lonely nights sitting here, like the ones I'd envisaged, pining over a man who treated me as if I was some besotted fool who would never catch him out.

A smile creeps over my face and I feel so much better already. I hate being on my own, which I'm not entirely proud of, but Sinead's suggestion makes sense in many ways and the deal is done.

'Let's do this,' I tell my friend, feeling a whole lot better than I did just a few hours earlier.

I'll hand in my notice to my landlord and will start the ball rolling tomorrow.

It's on the night I officially move in with Sinead in the rather pretty south Dublin neighbourhood of Ballsbridge a week and a bit later that I take David Campbell's business card from my purse and stare at it, trying to find the courage to go against his father's wishes and send him an email.

For almost three weeks I'd built myself up to it and chickened out every time, though to be fair the shock of my break-up with Sam and moving out of my apartment did distract me quite a bit. Plus, apart from the blips of the past week, I've been travelling along a very positive road in my life. I've worked hard on my mental wellbeing and triumphed by helping others, but I'm afraid that David seems ever so slightly stuck in the past. Will my presence in his life, even with the Irish Sea between us, bring him more stress than comfort?

On top of all that, I've struggled with the huge political differences our backgrounds hold; I've struggled with going against his father's wishes, even though I realize that at – I'm guessing – around 30 years of age, David is capable of making his own decisions in life; and most of all I've struggled with the fear of becoming emotionally attached to him in a way I've probably always been, in case he turns out to be horrible in real life and getting to know him properly might ruin the only positive thing to come out of that day of terror.

This evening, though, after a few celebratory moving-in drinks, I open my laptop and type David Campbell's address into the recipient box. I stare at it for a few moments as I think of what to say.

I shouldn't do this for so many reasons. I know I shouldn't do this, but with Dutch courage, I decide to give it a go.

'*Dear David,*' I begin with.

Well, that's that bit out of the way. I know nothing about him and have no idea where to start.

'*It was really good to see you after all these years,*' I type and, after hesitating for a couple of seconds (I'm not sure if it's the few glasses of bubbles from earlier that get me going or the strange feeling that I know him already, even though I really don't), the words suddenly come easily and I type and type and type until sleep takes over and I can't type any more.

'*I hope you and your fiancée got back to England safely*

after the memorial service,' I write to him. *'It was nice, if surreal, to see you again.'*

Although I'm doing really well, in many ways my mind is stuck in that strange place we found ourselves in that day, and a little part of me will be that frightened 20-year-old for ever. Does that make sense to you? It's like, although life has moved on in so many brilliant ways, a part of me is still there with you in that doorway and it always will be, so I hope it doesn't make things worse for you by hearing from me. In fact, I hope we can both learn to keep going forward, to hold on to the positives and learn from every lesson life throws at us, rather than hide from them.

What happened to us back then is a benchmark for life – I will never be so afraid of anything again, and therefore, if I'm ever scared, I remind myself how I'm strong enough to get through whatever comes my way.

I'm practising what I preach right now as my relationship with my boyfriend Sam is over. I won't bore you with the detail but, rather than dwell on the negatives, I'm looking at it as another learning curve.

I realize we come from very different backgrounds, but I truly hope we see each other away from all of that. I saw humanity and kindness in you that day. I saw you for just being you and I hope it's not presumptuous of me but I'm confident to say that I think you saw me for

*simply the person I am too, and that's the most important
thing of all.*

*So until next time, David, please take care and know
that as always I'm thinking of you and will always wish
the very best for you, and all the happiness in the whole
wide world.*

Your friend, I hope.

Kate x

I press send without even reading it back and then I climb into
bed where I fall asleep more quickly than I've done in a very
long time. I don't have nightmares for the first night in ages. In
my dreams I only see David, and he is no longer the bloodied,
injured ice-cream shop boy I remembered him as for so long.
He is handsome again and he is strong and happy, he is smiling,
and he is getting married next year to his fiancée from Wales.
Knowing all this is enough for me to see that life is moving
on, even if my own has encountered a bump in the road.

A bump in the road never stopped me before, I remind
myself when I wake up, and it surely isn't going to stop me
from living a life that's good from now on.

DAVID

My mind is still on the rugby game I played earlier as Lesley
and I have dinner in our favourite Indian restaurant. It's in

the quaint little English village we've called home since I got my new job in the nearby school two years ago, and as usual the main focus of our conversation is our forthcoming wedding. The subject matter is a tricky one, though, as we contemplate how we are going to push the date back to May next year and move the ceremony across the water to my home town, due to the decision by my mother to have one more blast of chemotherapy to try and overcome the cancer that is tearing through her.

'I've spoken to the florist, to the band and to the hotel of course,' Lesley tells me, her eyes so full of stress and disappointment at how our original plan isn't working any more, 'and they're happy to return our deposits under the circumstances, so I guess that's some of the main things out of the way.'

She pushes her food around her plate, and I can't hide from the fact that she's really stressed and annoyed about it all since I first brought up the issue this morning.

'Look, Les, I know you wanted to get married in Wales, but Mum just isn't fit to travel and there's no way I could go through with it without her,' I explain once more, feeling a trickle of sweat on my brow. The match earlier was tough but dealing with this is almost as ball-breaking. 'She thinks the world of us both, so she'd really want to be there. But we'll make it special and we'll still be married, if only in a different way and a little bit later than we'd planned.'

She pours herself another glass of wine from the bottle

of Marlborough we're sharing and does a thing where she slowly shakes her head from side to side, which tells me she's trying to weigh everything up in her mind and strike some sort of balance with it all. I, in turn, rub my temples at the very sound of florists and musicians and wedding venues. My mother is seriously ill, and my head can't take in much more right now.

'I know it's out of our hands to a degree,' she says, pursing her lips together. 'I just always wanted to get married by the Gower Peninsula like my own parents did, but maybe we can have a party there some time after?'

Despite my inner turmoil, my eyes light up at the glimmer of positivity coming my way from her at last.

'That's an amazing idea!' I tell her, even just to distract her mind a little. 'I'm so sorry about all the disruption and change of plans, Les. But I'll make it up to you in any way I can, I promise.'

She reaches across the table and rests her hand on top of mine, and then her eyes meet mine.

'I know you will,' she says in a whisper. 'And as long as we're married, I don't care deep down if we have to get married in our own back garden. I can't wait to be your wife, David, that's all.'

'I can't wait either,' I try to reassure her. 'It will work out, babe. I love you.'

'Do you?'

Her reaction makes my eyes widen, so I take her hand

and hold it across the table, trying my best to convince her that it's true. I do. I can't imagine my life without Lesley. She has been so solid, so supportive, and although I've often pushed her away as I battle with my demons, I have always loved her deeply.

'Why do you ask that?' I say, my head spinning now as the thought of her insecurity gives me further anxiety.

'You haven't been the same since . . . well, you haven't seemed the same at all since the bomb memorial, David,' she tells me, the look of relief on her face so evident to have spilled it out at last.

'What way?'

I know exactly what way she means. I know exactly how much that day has changed me, and although I have tried so many times to tell her about how meeting Kate again was like opening up an old wound, and how it has made me question every step I've taken in life since the bomb, the timing has never been right as Lesley is always so focused on wedding plans to the exclusion of virtually everything else. The truth is, I haven't wanted to drag her down to my level with old ghosts and painful memories, so I have tried to carry on as normal, but it appears I haven't been as 'normal' as I thought I was.

'You're distant,' she says, looking away with tears in her eyes. 'I feel like I don't know you any more. Something has changed, I can tell.'

I shake my head, wondering if now is a good time to

come clean about how it felt to meet Kate again, but I don't know where to start. I'm not even sure it's relevant, and the last thing I want is to put ideas into Lesley's head that don't belong there.

'It brought back a lot of old memories and pain, that's all,' I say, biting my lip. 'Maybe you and my father were right about me going there. Maybe going back did me more harm than good.'

I'm not sure I believe what I'm saying, but a shrug and a light smile on Lesley's face suggests I've said the right thing for now.

We finish our meal in a slightly awkward silence, which tells me deep down that Lesley is more than disappointed by our change of plans. Her spark has gone, and her enthusiastic planning has come to a standstill.

Now it's my turn to play with the food on my plate. I hate hurting her by changing the wedding plans, but I don't feel as if I have any choice. My mother is so sick, and I just can't celebrate what's meant to be the happiest day of our whole lives in the middle of all that.

We get home and kick off our shoes in the hallway like we always do, then Lesley goes to run herself a bath while I sit down to check my emails, hoping to hear back from a medical friend I'd messaged for advice on how else I could try to help my mother battle this deadly illness.

I rub my temples again in circular movements as I wait

for the laptop to upload. I roll my neck to get rid of some of the tension that lies on my shoulders, a mix of too much activity on the field and what's on my mind lately.

I've prayed so hard every night for my mother's recovery. Even if my father has made sure I have managed to be put off practised religion of any sort, I try to imagine a life without her on the end of the phone to reassure me when things get too much, or to ever going home and not finding her there any more. All I can do is pray that she survives this.

I take a deep breath. I'm thinking ahead of things I can't control, as I often do, and I feel my anxiety levels rise.

I want Lesley to have the day of her dreams, I really do, and I know she had her heart set on getting married by the Gower Peninsula in Wales, but since we got back here to England, my mother's condition has deteriorated again and my mind is all over the place.

I open my emails, ready to face the usual stream from school, but do a double take when I unexpectedly see a name in my inbox.

Kate Foley.

The subject matter says a simple 'Hello from Ireland' but it's enough to make me sit up as I stare and stare at the screen in front of me.

I touch her name, running my fingers along the letters. I don't know her. I know nothing about her, yet I'm so taken aback by her name appearing on my screen and what might lie in her message.

I open it and I read her words over and over again, smiling at her good wishes and relating to her instantly in so many ways, just as I knew I would – from her outlook on how she measures every pain she encounters against the trauma we experienced together, to the way she feels what she has been through has made her a much stronger person. I find myself nodding in agreement when she says that part of her is still that 20-year-old girl, sitting on that doorstep beside me as we waited for help, and I feel sad for her when I read about her break-up.

'Can I get you anything?' Lesley asks me, popping her head around the doorway of the sitting room.

Her voice makes me jump.

'I thought you were in the bath?' I say, closing the laptop with a snap, feeling like a cheating spouse even though I know I'm doing nothing wrong.

'I had a quick shower instead,' she tells me. 'Do you fancy a beer? Or even a glass of wine as a nightcap? Think I'll have a beer then head to bed.'

I stutter and stammer, trying to find a response to her simple question, telling myself that – although I feel bad – I wasn't doing anything wrong but was just reading an email from an old friend.

An old friend my fiancée has never heard me talk about. An old friend I've never mentioned to Lesley through-out our three-year relationship and who I know very little about, yet I seem to think about so much.

'I'll have a beer, please,' I tell her, and then I find the remote control and switch on the TV news to take my mind elsewhere. 'I think I need an early night too. Thanks, Les.'

Lesley brings in two bottles of beer and she snuggles beside me on the sofa, her blonde hair still damp from the shower and the smell of coconut radiating from her skin. I clench my hands in frustration, then kiss her damp hair to try and ground myself again.

If this is the way hearing from Kate Foley is going to affect me, I'm not sure this is a path I should be travelling on after all.

8.

KATE

I sometimes feel as though I've become an expert at pretending to be brave and strong, as if I'm trying my best to be some sort of warrior champion, made of steel, who sword-fights feelings out of my way as if in battle on a daily basis.

Bomb victim? Don't dare label me. *Working-class kid?* Nurse with an honours degree, thank you very much. *Wasn't your ma in prison?* Mind your own business. *What do you mean you haven't seen your father in months?* His choice, not mine. *Your boyfriend was having a fling with your friend and you found out on the day you thought he was going to propose?* I'm so over it. (I'm so not.)

I can handle, or at least pretend to, most of the incidents I encounter on this crazy old path of life, yet sometimes all it takes is the tiniest little problem belonging to someone else to send me into a spin, and I won't stop until I know I can change the world for them, or at least try to.

Take Cassie, for example, an 8-year-old girl who stayed on the ward with us for two days just this week after a minor operation, and who touched my heart and left her tiny fingerprint there when I heard her story. Her mum died when she was just nine months old, her father is a drug addict, and she hadn't seen her two sisters in six months since they were separated in the care system.

The thing she missed most was not her mum, her dad or even her sisters, but her shiny new red bike, which she had to leave behind in the family home. Since her dad had gone to rehab, her foster parents couldn't access the place to get it back for her. I just couldn't get her off my mind, so I made a few calls and, before she went home, a local toy shop sponsored a brand-new, almost identical red bike all for herself that she could ride. I hoped she would be reunited with her sisters and her daddy one day soon again but, until then, at least she had her bike.

'You'll be working for one of those wish foundation charities soon,' Sinead tells me. She loves to hear my stories of goodwill and happier faces. 'Saint Kate, Queen of Deprived and Injured Children.'

'Oh, give over, I'm not that bad,' I tell her. 'I just take stories to heart sometimes and find it difficult to switch off.'

So it's no surprise to me that, when I finally get a reply from David, his despair and angst over his mother's illness affects me in the same way. I find I am spending much of my spare time contemplating what I can do to make the situation just a little easier on him.

Dear Kate, he wrote to me, two days after I sent my own slightly tipsy message to him.

> *It's so lovely to hear from you. I'm so sorry to hear you're going through a break-up – are you OK? Make sure and look after yourself, Kate! It's a tough thing to go through for sure.*
>
> *I have to say you've been on my mind a lot, as has Shannon, since we met again on the day of the memorial service. Ten whole years, imagine? I really hope life has been kind to you after all you've been through. I'd love to hear more about your life and what you've been up to since we met on such a tragic day. Thank you again for all your help. I don't think I'd have got through it without you.*
>
> *Life is a bit of a rollercoaster for me at the moment. Our wedding, which was supposed to happen in March, has now been rearranged for May as my mum is going to have another blast of chemo to try and beat her cancer. She had been in remission a while but now they've found new abnormalities in her lungs and, to be honest, I'm worried sick. Planning a wedding is the last thing on my mind.*
>
> *On a different note, your positive outlook has somehow inspired me to go for something I wouldn't really have*

dreamed of. There's a head of department post coming up at school and, even though it's an absolute long shot as I'm up against two other cracking teachers who have been here for many years, I've taken a punt, 'bought the lotto ticket', so to speak, and thrown my name in the hat.

I really hope we meet again soon, Kate.
Until then, take care,
David x

Sinead watches me pacing the kitchen floor while preparing our dinner – a very easy lemon linguine recipe I inherited from my mother – and reads my mind like only she can.

'What are you plotting now, Florence Nightingale?' she asks as she watches me serve up. 'I just know you're cooking up more than dinner, by the way. You're not listening to one word I said. Who is it? I bet it's the little one, Ellen, on the Disney ward who has chronic diabetes. Have to say, she melts my heart too. Did you see her dad? What a hunk!'

'No, no, it's nothing to do with work for a change,' I tell Sinead as I stir up the linguine. 'Well, not really. I'm on a totally different mission but I don't know where to start. You see, it's a tricky one knowing, or not knowing really, the people involved. I've told you about David, the guy from—'

'Oh yes, you sure have told me about the dreamy David,' she says, her eyes glazing over. 'Have you any photos of him at all? I'd love to see if he's as gorgeous as you described him.'

'Give over and go find yourself a man,' I joke in return, before explaining and updating her on David's email and his despair over his mother's illness when he is so far away from home.

Sinead 'oohs' a lot when she is eating something she enjoys and, given this is one of her favourite meals of mine, at times I wonder if she can hear me at all through her own appreciative noises.

'So, what would really make him feel better,' says Sinead, chomping through her meal, 'is if he knew his mum had someone, not from her medical team and from outside of the family home, who made her feel a bit more human as she goes through her treatment, something more holistic perhaps?'

'That's it,' I say, twisting the pasta onto my fork. 'How about some reflexology or aromatherapy? In fact, anything that involves relaxation and a bit of human touch?'

'Sounds good.'

'I remember when my gran was having her treatment, she looked forward to a light massage with some essential oils just to make her feel human again,' I say, twirling my fork in the air. 'It's worth a shot, yeah. OK, I'll see who I know from back home who does this and suggest it to David. I'm sure I have some contacts, and hopefully it will give him some peace of mind.'

And so I embark on a mission to compile a list of alternative therapists which I send to him, and after his mum receives her first session of reflexology with an old school friend of mine called Bernie a few days later, he calls me for the first time since we spoke in person that day of the ten-year memorial.

'Your suggestion has worked a treat, Kate,' he says, as I sit on a bench in Phoenix Park, watching ducks glide along on the lake. 'I hope you don't mind me calling you to say so, but Mum loved it. Really loved it.'

It's a beautiful, colourful early autumn morning, and I close my eyes and absorb his voice in my ear. His accent sounds like home, like a warm snuggly hug or a blanket of reassurance and familiarity.

'No, of course I don't mind,' I tell him. 'It's nice to hear from you and I'm so glad to hear this about your mum.'

'Yeah, she has really brightened up since the first session, and says she feels so much more relaxed and in touch with her own body, like it belongs to her a little more again.'

'That's amazing,' I reply, sensing his smile from afar. 'I'm so happy for your peace of mind, and hers.'

I'm killing time until I start my afternoon shift at work, sitting here in my blue nurse's uniform while David talks to me from somewhere across the Irish Sea in England.

'Look, I won't hold you back,' he says quickly, 'but honestly, thank you. Your friend Bernie was a real hoot and cheered my mum up no end, so—'

'It's no problem and if there's anything else I can do—'

We talk over each other like nervous teenagers.

'It was really nice to meet you again.'

Then there's a pause. A long pause.

'You too, David,' I tell him. 'I felt some sort of closure by bumping into you, perhaps like we'd fulfilled our promise at last, in some small way, by finding each other.'

Another pause follows, then I hear him take a deep breath before he speaks again.

'I'd like to know you better, Kate. I'd like to at least try to be friends, even from afar.'

I can't help but smile at his suggestion. I close my eyes tight. I grip the pale blue cotton tunic I wear and wish that our backgrounds were much simpler.

'I'd like us to be friends too, David,' I whisper. 'I'd like to get to know you better too.'

We develop an unplanned pattern of almost daily snippets of email conversations, which slowly turn into more spontaneous phone calls in which a natural pattern of conversation flows. At first, this mostly focuses on reflection of the horror we both witnessed together and what we've been up to since. Then the chats progress to covering a mixture of mundane day-to-day achievements, gossip and worries, to discovering little facts about each other that make our friendship grow very quickly, if only from afar.

Sometimes David's messages or calls have me laughing out loud, sometimes his reflections and memories make me want to cry for what we and so many others suffered.

'I had such a horrendous nightmare about the bomb last night,' he told me one day. 'I was looking for you everywhere, but I couldn't find you. It was like I was in a maze full of smoke and there were people screaming your name telling me where to go but I still couldn't get to you.'

In turn, when I am having a tough time, I put it into words to him and he always manages to make me feel better.

'Why don't you treat yourself to something just for you today?' he'll suggest. 'Or go for a walk in your favourite place like you always remind me to.'

I once arrived home from work after a particularly tough day to find a bouquet of flowers waiting for me on the doorstep and a note from him saying, 'You've got this.' It was enough to make me sit down right there and then and thank God for good friends like him.

As the days and weeks go by, his conversations soothe me; he calms me and he makes me feel as though I'm on top of the world. Sometimes, just sometimes, we almost cross the line into a territory neither of us really wants to explore. My heart lifts when I see his number calling and I find myself constantly checking my phone in anticipation. 'You looked amazing when I saw you last,' he says to me one night when I come home from work to his late phone call, moments that I find myself looking forward to every day. 'You haven't changed much, Kate. I would have known you a mile off.'

'You really shouldn't say that,' I tell him, cosying myself in the armchair and knowing I was feeling exactly the same as when I'd had his rugged, handsome, tall, strong physique wrapped around me. His voice makes me automatically close my eyes and imagine his face.

'I know, I'm sorry. I just feel that seeing you again and getting to know you better has changed me. Sorry.'

Lying in bed, I spent the whole night imagining what it would be like to meet him in person again. I know he belongs to another, but in the confines of my mind, somewhere he is holding me again and I'm breathing in his manly scent and feeling the strength and safety of his arms just once more.

And deep down I know that in my mind is the only place that can really happen, because there's simply no way our friendship would be accepted where we come from, yet the more I get to know him, the more I want to know.

I know now that his favourite restaurant at home is the same one as mine, that we both ultimately are food geeks and could spend hours talking about recipes and fine wine to go with different dishes, that we both love psychology and the spiritual mind and an admission to sometimes reading horoscopes for a bit of geeky fun.

Lesley is Aquarius, he tells me – smart and intelligent and a little bit mysterious, which is what he found attracted him to her in the first place when they met during his time in the RAF.

'She sounds like a wonderful person,' I say, feeling just a pinch of envy at how Lesley gets to know him in the real world, whereas my friendship with him is mainly through notes, emails and phone calls. 'She's a very lucky girl.'

I hear him sigh a little before he replies.

'You're right, she is truly wonderful,' he tells me with gratitude in his voice. 'She travels a lot with her job and, to be honest, Kate, we haven't been getting along so well lately. I sometimes wonder if I really deserve her or if I'm good enough at all.'

'You deserve it all, David Campbell,' I say tautly. 'When I say she is wonderful I mean you sound wonderful together. I mean that she is just exactly what you deserve and I'm not at all jealous that you two are living the happy-ever-after dream and I'm still searching for my own Mr Right here in Dublin. I'm totally fine with that.'

He laughs a little, but I still get a sense that something just isn't right.

'And you, Kate, are a Leo, led by the heart and the perfect soulmate match for the fiery, passionate Aries like me,' he laughs, and then he stops before he takes it any further.

We both go quiet.

'We can still be soulmates,' I whisper, pinching my eyes at the unfairness of it all. I wish we had met earlier. I wish he wasn't engaged; I wish we weren't from such opposite backgrounds. 'Soulmates can be friends even if it has to be a secret, you know.'

'It shouldn't have to be a secret,' he says, and I hear a nip in his voice.

'Does Lesley know we talk?'

'No . . .'

'David!' I exclaim, sitting up in my armchair. 'So it is a secret, then!'

'Well, it's not a secret as such . . . have you told your family?' he asks. I have a feeling we might be about to have our first argument. 'Your reasons for keeping it secret aren't too far from mine.'

'I don't live with my fiancé!' I say, my eyes widening. 'And I don't even live with my family back at home any more, so I'm not exactly tiptoeing around this like you are!'

'I don't care what anyone back home thinks. We don't need anyone's permission to be friends.'

I let out a sigh.

'Well, I *do* care what people at home think, David, and I don't want any trouble for either of us,' I tell him. 'The last thing I want is for Lesley to wonder if this is anything more than what it is.'

'Why can't I tell Lesley about you?' he asks a week later. I'm sitting on a bench, phone in my right hand and coffee cup in my left, and I freeze, my left hand stopping in mid-air.

'What?' I reply. 'You still haven't told her about me at all? I thought you said we didn't have to be a secret to anyone.'

'I can't tell her,' he says, whispering now, and I hear the school bell ring in the background which tells me his lunchbreak is over. 'I've tried so many times to put our friendship into words, but every time I do, I just can't find the right way to describe it.'

I pause for thought.

'I know. How about you tell her I'm a woman you met during a horrific bomb explosion ten years ago, after a brief flirtation in the shop you worked in, and who you now talk to almost every single day?'

'Doesn't sound good, does it?' he mutters.

'I guess not,' I agree, putting my coffee cup down on the bench beside me and absent-mindedly drawing imaginary hearts on my leg with my finger as we talk.

'You're not ashamed of being friends with me, because of—'

'Oh, God no!' he says quickly. 'No, no, it's the opposite, actually. It's like – it's like what we have and what we had before is so special and personal to me that I don't want to . . . I know this sounds silly, but I like to think of this as just ours. It's too special to share, not even with Les, because no one else understands. Maybe I know deep down we keep growing closer and I'm—'

'Don't say any more, please.'

'Sorry, OK, I won't,' he tells me. 'Right, I'd better go. I'll chat to you later again, yeah?'

'Of course,' I whisper. 'Bye, David.'

I sit there on the bench for a few moments when he hangs up, holding my phone in my lap. I breathe out, long and slowly, and make my way to work at the hospital, replaying the conversation with David in my mind the whole way.

He said what we had was too special to put into words and he didn't want to share it with anyone, not even his own fiancée. He said we are growing closer and closer. Maybe we should call a halt to it right now, before this goes any further. Maybe we should be honest and true with each other, knowing that – no matter how connected our hearts are on so many levels – in the real world it could never be.

I imagine his father's face that day when I called at the house. I imagine my own family's confusion as to how I would even think we could be friends, and it all frightens me a little inside. I imagine if Lesley heard our conversations or read our messages – how would she feel? And could we honestly say it was always innocent and above board? I don't think we could.

It's going to take me a while to get my head round all of this but equally I'm going to have to do my best not to overthink it.

'Aargh!' I say out loud just before I go in through the hospital gates. Why does life have to be so bloody complicated sometimes?

And why is my unruly heart trying to rule my always very sensible head when it comes to David Campbell?

I already can't wait to hear from him again, which is wrong and I know it.

DAVID

'You've made quite an impression on our young students since you first came through our doors two years ago,' my headmaster Andrew Spence begins. He has called me into his office at home time, gesturing me to take a seat across from him. I do as I'm told, wondering where this conversation might be going as I was really hoping to make a quick exit home and grab a bite to eat before I hit my midweek training session at the rugby club.

'You've a great rapport with the students here, David,' he continues, 'and believe me it hasn't gone unnoticed on a behavioural level, and also on an academic level too.'

I smile at the unexpected compliment from a man who, for some reason, I didn't really think was particularly aware of my existence. St Michael's is a large school, with over 1,200 pupils, and I had been warned that sometimes as a teacher it was very easy to slip into the background and feel as if you were just a number to Mr Andrew Spence. He is known to have a head for practicality and a heart that's sometimes hard to find.

'I think my own life experience helps with that,' I tell him. 'I like to keep in mind that every single one of them has their own story, and never to take it for granted when they turn up and take a seat in my classroom each day, despite what's going on in their own world.'

He smiles as if I've just scored another point, as if what he's called me in here for just made even more sense.

'Are you happy here in your job?' he asks me, and I immediately wonder if there's a right or wrong answer to his question.

'Very much so,' I say. 'I take my work very seriously here, but like to connect as best I can with the young people. They have an important voice and I enjoy hearing what they have to say.'

'It shows,' he says, before a blanket of silence fills the room. Should I speak again? Should I agree or just wait? I've no idea where this is going or what to say.

He opens a grey file in front of him and flicks through the pages as I wait on what might be coming next.

'With all that in mind, I'd like to say congratulations to you, David,' he tells me at last. 'Congratulations on being appointed as our new head of science here at St Michael's. I truly believe you're the ideal candidate for the job and I wish you well in what will be, I've no doubt, a very bright future in teaching our new generation of scientists.'

I feel a bit dizzy as his words sink in and I seriously don't know what to say.

'That's . . . that's a really big surprise but such good news!' I reply to him at last, totally taken aback at his announcement.

I've only been at the school two years and feel in many ways that I'm still settling in, but I know my relationship with my students has been smooth and productive. Nonetheless, this is still a huge but very welcome shock.

'I'll give you a day or two to think about it, of course,' he continues, getting up now to show me to the door. 'Just so you have time to consider all the extra responsibility that comes with the new post, but I've every faith in you and your capability to deliver. I can see our pupils positively glow in your presence, David. You're proving to be very inspirational, and that in a teacher is worth its weight in gold.'

'Thank you, Mr Spence. That means a lot coming from you.'

'Andrew,' he tells me.

There's no way I will ever get used to calling him by his first name, not even if I was to be principal myself one day.

'Thank you, Mr . . . Andrew. Thank you, Andrew,' I mumble, and leave, wondering when will be an appropriate moment to jump up and punch the air.

Flabbergasted and feeling as if I could jump over the moon, I find myself sitting in the car in the school car park, reflecting on all the positives that Mr Spence has just highlighted and also reminiscing on how far I've come in ten years from a confused, anxious 21-year-old whose parents were forcing me into a career in law that didn't appeal at all, to blindly joining the Air Force in a bid to escape my life at home and also to please my father, then finally finding my true vocation by doing my teaching degree at University College London.

Head of science, I repeat to myself, shaking my head in disbelief. I can't honestly believe it. I took a leap of faith, a shot in the dark, and it worked out in my favour.

I think of Aaron and his crazy motto: *Take a chance and buy the lotto ticket, every time.*

I picture my good friend in my head, wishing he was a phone call away to celebrate with. God, I miss him so badly. I know he'd be toasting me tonight and using it as an excuse to go down to our favourite bar at home and drink a few pints of his favourite beer. I can feel his hand on my shoulder.

I got the promotion.

The first person who comes to my mind to talk to is Kate, whose nudge of positivity gave me the urge to go for the job. I have to tell her my good news, so I call her without even thinking of the time. She's probably still on her shift at the hospital but I call anyway and take a chance. She answers in a hurried whisper.

'I've slipped into the loo to answer. Are you OK? What's up, David?'

'I got the promotion!' I tell her. 'The head of department!'

'No way!'

'Yes!' I say, my voice shaking as I speak to someone about it at last. 'You are now talking to the new head of science at St Michael's Comprehensive! Like, what the hell, Kate? What the actual hell?'

I rest my head back on the car seat and try to let this all sink in.

'I'm totally, totally doing a celebratory dance for you in the staff toilets here in Dublin!' Kate says, the sound of joy in her voice so tangible, just as I knew it would be. 'That's awesome, David! I'm so, so proud of you and I'll have a celebratory drink for you tonight. Shit, it's only Tuesday, but I'm sure you'll celebrate loads at the weekend. What did Lesley say? She must be thrilled to bits, and what great timing when you needed some good news!'

I pause and my eyes widen.

'I-I haven't told Lesley yet,' I say, knowing it sounds as strange as it actually is. 'For some reason I wanted to tell you first. I never even—'

'Well, get off the phone quickly and tell her!' Kate says, in her wonderful accent that always makes me feel like home. 'I'm so proud of you, David! I have to get back to work, too. Mwah, big congrats to you! You're an absolute star! Now, go call your fiancée and plan those celebrations!'

I hang up the phone and press the top of it to my forehead. What am I thinking? I should have told Lesley first, shouldn't I? Kate's encouraging words inspired me to take the chance and go for the job, but surely telling Lesley should have come first to my mind.

That used to be the case. There once was a time when she'd be the first person I'd think of when I got news of any sort, so what is happening now?

I search my phone and press Lesley's number, cursing myself for not thinking of her in the first instance to share my good news and, as I wait for her to answer, I feel a little deflated already because I know deep down I'm on the wrong path with her and I need to get off it before it's too late.

I'm all consumed with Kate and it's driving me insane. We need to pull way, way back before it all ends in tears.

FEBRUARY 2009

9.

KATE

I tuck into my boring, effortless dinner of chicken and chips at the kitchen table after my evening shift at the hospital, exhausted but determined to get a hold of my work-life balance again and live in the moment a bit more. I seem to have become more and more internalized, going from working all day or night to waiting on my next call from David.

'It's unhealthy,' I tell myself on repeat, knowing I might be slightly mad by talking to myself out loud. 'You need to live in the real world. *Your* world. Not David's. He is getting married soon and you've become much too attached, for goodness' sake.'

I can't help myself. For the past six months I've spent my days wondering what he is doing and my nights dreaming about him. I know he feels the same way too but, as the date of his wedding comes closer, I curse myself for becoming involved with him to this extent.

I know his daily routine inside out. I know that he plays basketball on Monday evenings, that he goes to the gym Tuesdays and Thursdays, Wednesdays are late at school while Friday he has a few drinks with his friends after work. Weekends are for him and Lesley to catch up, if she isn't away with her own job. I really miss him on those days, yet I know that cracks in his relationship with her are beginning to show.

'You need to be honest with Lesley about your cold feet about the wedding, but most of all you need to be honest with yourself,' I told him one Monday when he rang me and seemed so glad to have the weekend over so we could chat again. 'Are you still arguing a lot?'

He sighed deeply and I could hear the confusion in his voice.

'A lot,' he admits to me. 'It's like we're on two totally different paths, or in two different worlds, and I think she knows it too. She is obsessed by weddings, while I just want to run at the mention of it. And so that's what I do. I go for a run and try to clear my head and pretend it's not happening.'

Our lunchtime phone calls are becoming more regular than we'd ever planned, but recently they are also becoming more and more intense and, if Lesley's obsessed with weddings, I fear that David and I are becoming obsessed too – with each other.

'Stop calling me every day then,' I say, closing my eyes as I await his response.

'OK then, I won't!' he retorts. 'You call me a lot too, Kate, so don't pretend this is all one sided!'

I stand up.

'I never said it was,' I reply. 'I'm just trying to stop you from ruining your relationship with your fiancée without really thinking this through. We're on a very slippery slope here, David, and we both know it. We have to stop.'

He goes silent.

'You're right,' he whispers. 'I need to think this through. I need to—'

'You need to forget about me, and I need to forget about you,' I say, finishing his sentence for him.

'You don't mean that,' he tells me. I feel my lip wobble at the very thought. There's no way I could ever just forget about him.

'Just try not to call so often,' I whisper. 'Let's just scale it way back and see how it goes. I care about you and I really don't want you to get into any trouble at home.'

And so we don't call each other for three whole days and every second of every minute, and every minute of every hour is agonizing as I toss and turn, feeling my skin crawl with anxiety as I long to hear from him. If anything, the silence just makes me want him even more.

So it's a great surprise when my phone rings just as I'm just getting into bed one night.

'Hey, Kate Foley,' he says to me, addressing me by my full title in what has become quite a term of endearment. 'Guess what? Last-minute decision, but I'm coming home tomorrow for Mum's birthday. Flying visit, but I'm landing into Dublin if you fancy a quick bite to eat tomorrow night before I head north? Would be nice to catch up with my good buddy in person again.'

My stomach gives a leap. Me and David at dinner together? I pause. I let this sink in. I close my eyes and I breathe. This could be dangerous, there's no denying it, though I can tell by his jaunty tone that he is trying to set boundaries, just as he should be.

It's been six months since I saw him last in the flesh and, although I feel we know each other very well by now, the thought of meeting up in person gives me butterflies.

There's no mention of Lesley. I take it he is making this last-minute journey alone. I can't pretend I'm not excited about having proper time with him all to myself, and I can hardly wait until tomorrow. We will catch up, just like friends do. We are simply friends.

'Will Lesley be coming with you?' I ask, even though I've already guessed the answer.

'No, no she won't,' he says quickly. 'Not this time. Look, I know what you're thinking and it has crossed my mind too, but don't worry that Lesley won't be joining us. I'm well aware how careful we need to be. We're just friends.'

I pause as a weight of doubt settles in the pit of my stomach.

'I'm not sure, David – look, you know I really want to

see you again but this is crazy. I don't think it's a good idea.'

I can almost sense the disappointment as he tries to answer.

'OK,' he whispers eventually. 'If that's how you feel, I respect that. I totally understand and you're probably right, it is crazy. I just hoped we could catch up, you know as—'

'Friends,' we both say at the same time.

I fidget a little. I push back my hair. I close my eyes.

'I do want to see you.'

I can hear him breathing.

'Yeah, but you're right. It's probably not a good idea in case it would—'

'On the other hand, we are both adults and we know what's at stake if we ruined everything,' I say, sounding like a runaway train as my mind has an argument with itself. 'So, actually yes, I do want to see you, and there's no harm in dinner with a friend, is there?'

'Absolutely no harm in that whatsoever,' he says quickly. 'I totally agree.'

'It's a date then,' I say, squeezing my eyes closed. 'I'll see you tomorrow.'

'No, it's not a date, Kate,' he jokes in return. 'It's just two friends who want to meet up in person instead of talking on the phone or online all the time. I can't wait to see you.'

My stomach flutters at the very idea of being close to him physically again.

'Ditto,' I whisper, before I change my mind again. I know this is risky. I know it's going to be a big test, both of our morals and our self-control. 'I can't wait to see you too.'

DAVID

During the short flight from Gatwick to Dublin, I try to stop myself from going over and over in my head that this could be my mother's last birthday with us. She is still so young at only 57 years old, almost fourteen years younger than my father, and it burns me inside to think that she has given everything to be with him and yet has lived such a sheltered, limited life instead.

'David, you shouldn't taunt him like that!' my mother used to say when I'd tease my father by reminding him of how my mother was once a beauty pageant winner. 'I sometimes wonder if you think of what buttons to press, knowing which will send him absolutely bananas. You're a rascal and it really doesn't help matters around here!'

But I couldn't help trying to expose his true colours at any opportunity.

Yes, as my mother often reminded me, he did give us a very privileged life; to me Reverend Campbell delighted a little too much in having a picture-perfect wife who served him as she should, and longed for a cardboard cut-out son about whom he could boast in the pulpit. Looking back,

I did everything in my power to go against that and show him up. I tried to push the boundaries in school when I could, I was suspended for smoking in the yard and he almost had a heart attack when I dyed my hair purple one summer when I was seventeen and turned up to church, much to the delight of the Sunday School kids I was helping out with but to my father's utter despair. If he said black, I said white, and vice versa.

Kate tells me I need to learn to accept him as he is, acknowledge our differences and make peace with him once and for all in an 'agree to disagree' manner, then focus on my present and look forward to my own future, while Lesley – just like my mother – tries to strike a balance of being gentle and understanding with him and walking a tightrope between us to make each visit or interaction go as smoothly as possible.

I sometimes wish Les was more vocal about her own beliefs, instead of always choosing to sit on the fence, but then I've been wishing for lots of ways I'd like things to be different between us lately. We need this break, even if it's just for a day or two, to let off some steam and release the valve of pressure that has been building up between us.

As the plane touches down, my heart sinks a little as I realize I'm drifting further and further away from the desire to plan any future with Lesley, and I know this has everything to do with Kate. Before she rocked my world I was cruising along on autopilot, but Kate has reignited a fire in me that had been smouldering for far too long.

I know it's so wrong, but as Lesley becomes more and more embroiled in wedding plans, I become more and more agitated and suffocated, which isn't her fault at all. I'm distant, I'm distracted, and I fear that I'm settling into a life with someone who ticks every box in my father's books – the daughter of an army field marshal, a high-flying global marketer, a squeaky clean, beautiful lady who always looks impeccable and is ever so polite. I fell in love with Lesley, yes, and she is a truly kind and wonderful person, but I can't help but feel as if I've had an awakening by meeting Kate again. Or am I making excuses for how I feel? It's like Kate has come along and peeled back the layers I've been hiding under to expose the real me once again.

Because beneath what I've been moulded into, I'm still the guy with the purple hair, the smoker in the back yard, the one who wants to challenge the rules and not stick by them. I want to feel the wind in my sails, to push boundaries and fall in love with life again, just like I used to, and like I do when I'm in the classroom, when I can really let my own sense of self shine through. It's why my students relate to me. I know life can be shit. I know playing by the rules is hard. I want to feel like that all the time, and – well, the truth is, I want to feel like I do when I talk to Kate.

The bomb changed me in many ways, but perhaps mostly in that it made me run away and try to reinvent myself into a different person from the one I was before. I now know that I've been hiding my true self for far too long, and very soon I'm going to have to allow the real me to live again in a way that I want to, and not in a way I'm forcing myself to.

My phone bleeps as soon as I turn it on as the plane waits to taxi across from the runway.

'Look to the left for a hideously bright yellow umbrella when you get to Terminal 1 exit doors.'

I feel my heart lift in my chest and I quicken my step, and sure enough when I walk out into the dark, damp, drizzly Dublin weather, I see her standing beneath what looks like a dazzling yellow sunbeam, waving at me with an enthusiastic welcome which makes me quicken my pace and walk towards her.

'I couldn't have you bussing it into town in that weather!' she says as we huddle beneath the umbrella. 'Plus, it's not every day David Campbell unexpectedly comes to town.'

I brighten up from the inside out when I see her, and her electrifying smile makes me stumble.

'You're an angel!' I say, giving her a quick peck on the cheek to say hello. 'Wow.'

'Well, I wouldn't go that far!' she says to me as we stand there with only the stick of the umbrella between us. 'You don't have much time before you head north, so I thought this would be quicker.'

I feel my pulse quicken and can see my chest move up and down as we stare, grinning in wonder. The silence between us is smouldering, deafening almost. It's like it takes everything in our power to retain some self-control.

'Where have you parked?' I ask her, trying to snap out of my daydream.

'Follow me,' she says, and she leads us across the zebra crossing to the car park, away from the hustle and bustle of families and couples reunited. I carry my case until we get to the shelter of the car park and her nippy little blue Vauxhall Corsa.

'Here, put your case in the back seat,' she tells me. 'The boot won't open, and I've never needed it enough to have it fixed.'

I do as I'm told, and it's only when we get into the car and out of the rain at last that we get to look at each other again.

'Look at you, all smiley!' she tells me as she takes me in. 'Ah, this is such a great surprise!'

Her eyes make me dizzy. This is only our third time meeting properly in the flesh, and as always I'm caught under her spell immediately. I need to hold back. I need to respect both our positions.

'Here, I got you something,' I say, reminded by the word 'surprise'.

I rustle in my jacket pockets to find the small gift I picked up at the airport in London.

'Ah, David, thank you,' she says, tilting her head to the side as she opens the modest gift. I can smell her perfume. It's the same one she was wearing the last time we met six months ago and its scent makes me want to touch her even more.

She looks puzzled as she opens the little bracelet, a silver chain with a ruby stone, and immediately puts it around her wrist, smiling with pleasure. I lean across to help her fasten the clip and our eyes meet.

'It's your birthstone, but of course you already know that,' I say as I clip it together around her wrist. My hand brushes her skin and our eyes meet, and we hold one another's gaze for a few seconds, then she holds her hand up to the light. Just like me, she can't stop grinning.

'A ruby? I'm right, I hope?' I wait.

'Yes, you're right,' she replies. 'David, this is really sweet, but why would you—?'

'It's a thank you after all these years, that's all,' I say quickly, knowing that it looks as though I've totally over-stepped the mark. 'I wanted to get you something to say thank you and for keeping your promise that day of the bomb. I'm glad we've found each other again. It means nothing more than that.'

'You sure?' she asks, her face wrinkling in concern.

'I promise,' I say, hoping to diffuse any suggestion of other motives.

'Thank you,' she says, looking at it again and touching

it with her delicate fingers. 'It's very special. I'll treasure it for ever.'

She reverses the car out of the parking space and I watch her hands on the steering wheel, where rows of other silver bangles jingle as she moves them around and I can't help but wonder how many others she has managed to help with those hands, as she helped me that day.

I turn down the window. The fresh air shakes me up a bit, thank goodness.

'So how's your mum?' she asks, and I'm thankful to her for bringing us back to some everyday conversation. 'She's going to get a great surprise when you get there tonight. Are you sure you're OK to hang out here for the evening? Oh, I bet she'll be over the moon to see you.'

I don't hesitate to answer. 'She's coping so well and with such dignity,' I say, feeling a pang in my heart at the thought that I can't even introduce Kate to my own mother because of my father's bitterness and resentment. 'Bernie – the therapist – is like a lifeline, calling once a week. I'd say she knows more about my mum now than I do myself. It's been great for Mum. I honestly can't thank you enough and, as for hanging out with you this evening, there's no way I could pass through Dublin without saying hello, is there?'

She smiles as she drives and her turquoise eyes, defined like a cat's, light up when I tell her so.

'It's so good to see you,' she says, and I nod in agreement.

I know this is going too fast and too far already. I try to

stay focused, to stay faithful, to stay true to my word and not ruin everything I have. I have made a home with Lesley, we have a future planned, I've a career in England and a comfortable existence that took me years to build up through hard work. But with Kate I have a connection that runs deeper than I've ever known with anyone else, an attraction that could set the world on fire.

But there's a danger in the knowledge that we would never be accepted as a couple with our families. To push this too far could be the ruination of everything, so I must stay in control.

'So, tell me, how was the flight?' she asks, and we laugh at her deliberate attempt to change the subject.

We chat so freely together, just like we did when on our almost daily phone calls, but being here in her presence, in her car, in the city she now calls home, in her daily existence in real life is very different and even a little surreal.

It's like no matter how much we've got to know each other, I sometimes think of Kate as some sort of enigma from another existence – untouchable, otherworldly – so it's strange to be driving along the motorway now in her little car with its worn-out seats and fresh pine smell, talking in real life about her real life and about mine. She is cool and elegant, vibrant and positive, and she radiates even in such a mundane, everyday scenario as driving her car.

Every time I get to know her a little more, I find myself more and more spellbound, which frightens me to say the very least when I think of the backlash we'd have from so many if we were to cross the line tonight. I shouldn't feel this way about her, and I hate that I do, yet I love it even more than I hate it.

'So, what's the address of the restaurant again?' she asks when we stop at traffic lights. 'Did you say Parnell Square or am I totally wrong?'

'Yes, Parnell Square North,' I say, as the lights change to green. She wears a soft leather biker jacket and a long burgundy woollen skirt, which rides up her calf when she accelerates. I try not to gasp when I see a long white line on her tanned leg which makes me wince.

I instantly get a brief flashback again to the screams and the terror from the doorway, but her voice as she speaks soothes me instantly and brings me back to reality just as it has done so many times lately.

'I don't know about you, but I'm starving,' she says, flashing me a trademark Kate smile. 'Is it OK if we drop the car back at mine and get a taxi there?'

'Of course. Great,' I say to her, and as we cruise towards her flat, the wipers screeching as the rain dries up, that's exactly the way I feel.

10.

KATE

'Oh, David, that's hysterical!'
I can barely eat for laughing, and we've been in this constant giddy state ever since we hit the city centre and found the little side-street restaurant that David had pre-booked for our early evening meal together. We are both giggly and excitable, like two teenagers on a first date, trying to ignore the sizzling tension that hovers between us.

David tells me of his days growing up only miles away from me, and we swap stories of teenage life in the same small town.

'Ah, Aaron was something special, all right,' he says, as he recollects times with his dear friend who he's told me so much about by now. 'Do you remember him serving you in the shop? You'd have loved him if you'd got to know him, Kate. I've no doubt about that. He was a natural comedian when we worked together and even more of an eejit in school. We bounced off each other so easily.'

155

'I'll bet I would have, for sure,' I say, seeing as always the pain behind David's gentle eyes. 'He sounds like he was great craic altogether. You miss him.'

'I do. I miss him a lot,' he says, and I long to reach across and comfort him with a friendly hand, but I refrain. We are having such a light-hearted, fun time together so far, and I don't want it to become at all maudlin. Nor do I want to cross the line, as I feel any sort of physical touch might drive us both insane, plus I'll never be the 'other woman' for any man. If we take this too far, we'll break a lot of hearts, and I would never forgive myself for being the reason for another woman's heartache. I've been there myself and it stung so badly.

'I had a friend like that, who got up to all sorts of antics back in the day in school,' I tell him, doing my best to keep us on the straight and narrow. 'There's always a class clown, isn't there? She'd have done anything to give us all a laugh and torture the poor teachers.'

We reminisce about school days and about teenage discos, where I discover David had an almost-encounter with one of the prettiest girls from my youth club, and we marvel at how we spent years and years living so close geographically, yet so far apart in every other sense of the word.

'I went to the local convent school, where the nuns put the fear of God in us should we even look out of the side of our eye at a man!' I tell him, much to his amusement. 'We wore our skirts below our knees – well we did until we hit the school gates at home time – and our punishment was prayer, though I don't ever really recall any bad times there. We had the best of times and I wouldn't change it for the world.'

We marvel at how our lives crisscrossed in the way those of any two people might if they grew up in the same vicinity, yet we both realize that of course it wasn't the norm to be segregated like we were – not only divided into boys' schools and girls' schools, but also of course by religion, so we had no chance of getting to know each other properly, even if we had wanted to. Even our nightlife mainly took place at different ends of town and in different venues.

'You know, the day you came into the shop and caught my eye,' he says to me, holding my gaze as he does every time he speaks, 'I was sure I'd seen you somewhere before. I even said it to Aaron, and I think I've just realized where.'

'Go on?' I reply, totally puzzled. 'This will be interesting!'

'You worked in the bowling alley for a while, didn't you?' he says, his blue eyes wide as the penny drops.

'Yes!' I exclaim. 'Yes, I did!'

'I knew it! Down at the leisure centre? You wore a red tunic as your uniform, like something you'd see in an American diner, and you wore a white hairband? I knew I'd seen you somewhere before! That was you, wasn't it?'

I'm taken aback at his elephant memory for detail, but very impressed at the same time.

'My goodness, I must have been about sixteen at the

time,' I say to him, clasping my napkin in my hands. 'That was my very first job and I loved it! How do you even remember that? Did you go there?'

Unlike other more traditional sports like Gaelic football or rugby, in our part of the world tenpin bowling was one of the few non-segregated activities our community did share, as the leisure centre was deliberately placed in 'neutral' territory for all to enjoy. Under that roof, the deep divides of our town were almost forgotten and, looking back now, I feel sad for all the friendships we missed out on because of the world we grew up in.

'We went there every Friday until we got bored of winning too easily and a notion for playing pool down at the pub took over our interest,' he says, his eyes sparkling at the carefree memory. 'I knew it. I knew I'd seen you somewhere before.'

'Hang on,' I say to him, as my own memory serves me well at last. 'Did you have purple hair back then? Oh my goodness, was that you with the purple hair and biker jacket?'

'Yes,' he exclaims. 'Not my finest look, but yes!'

'Ah, you were an awful rowdy bunch of eejits but we were all mad about you,' I tell him, leaning back in my chair with disbelief. 'You definitely stood out as the, very good-looking I must say, rebel of the pack.'

He shrugs in apology.

'I told you I was a bit of a rascal growing up,' he says,

still savouring each mouthful of his steak as if he can slow down the clock. I'm enjoying his company so much I don't want our evening to end. 'Imagine you caught my eye even way back then. And I caught yours.'

We pause in the moment, an action replay of the innocent teenage years when our paths crossed but we didn't realize it running through my mind.

I blink back any feelings of that sort, forcing myself to imagine his fiancée Lesley sitting in their home in England with no idea of the fun time we are having together, and I shift a little in my seat as the thought of Sam and Bridget getting up to their shenanigans behind my back flood my mind. I don't want Lesley, even though I've never met her, to go through any of the pain and betrayal I experienced with Sam. The very thought of it makes my stomach churn.

'There's no point denying it, I did notice you back then and it wasn't just for your standout purple hair,' I say, 'but we are where we are now in life, David, and isn't it great we found each other and are lucky enough to be here to reminisce?'

I raise my glass, determined to set the boundaries exactly where they should be, as I feel our time together could quickly lead to something a little less controlled, especially if we keep going down a teenage memory lane where I fancied him even then.

'I knew even in those days you were untouchable,' he

tells me, looking up at me as I lean my hands under my chin. 'I knew you were from the other side of the community, the forbidden fruit, if you like.'

'Yes, isn't it mad how we just knew who was who back in those days? My parents would have been petrified if I'd mixed with a Protestant boy,' I say, noticing how he rubs his jawline and his blue eyes flicker as we chat. 'I remember most parents, including mine, didn't allow their kids to cross into certain parts of town because sectarianism was so rife and dangerous. It's mad now when you look back. We were all just kids being controlled by a society we were born into. We didn't have a choice.'

His eyes widen as I speak. If I was untouchable back then, he is more untouchable now, and yet there is a magnetic force across the table, taunting us, teasing us to go as close as we can.

'True. My father didn't allow me to mix in your part of town either,' he says, holding my gaze. 'Catholic girls from the Green Park estate were totally out of bounds. It maddened me how he preached about peace and love in the pulpit yet whispered bigotry in my ear. You stood out back then, Kate Foley. I remember you.'

I swallow.

'And I remember you too, David.'

Our knees brush under the table and I take a sip of water to try and stay focused.

'Here's to those carefree innocent days, and you in your

red tunic and white hairband,' he says, making my stomach flutter.

'And here's to the rascality of you back then, my future ice-cream shop boy with the one-time, very eye-catching purple hair.'

We smile and, as we drink now from our wine glasses, I can't resist just one more longing stare in his direction before I default back into the friend zone. David Campbell is beautiful and strong on the outside, yet I can see that on the inside he is still so vulnerable and fragile. I can also see how his energy rises when we talk or when we are together in person. Being together makes us both feel better, it's obvious by now, but we are also both broken souls who could easily hook onto each other for all the wrong reasons and I'd be devastated if we destroyed what we had by getting carried away in a moment of foolish passion.

'You all finished?' asks the waiter, in a welcome break from the intensity that lingers in the air. 'How was it?'

'Thank you, that was delicious,' I say, trying my best to ignore how David's smile pings on my heartstrings and how, every time our eyes meet, my pulse races. 'Gosh, is that the time already? Where has the evening gone to?'

The last train north leaves in just over an hour and I realize we have time for dessert and not much more, which pains me more than it should.

He asks for a dessert menu and then leans across the table a little towards me in a movement that pulls me in, the ticking of the clock adding to the urgency we both seem to feel. I can't take my eyes off how sexy he looks in the flesh now, ten years on from the cheeky, rebellious young man he was then to the hunky, strong person who makes me ache to touch him.

We sit for a moment in contemplative silence as the veil of tension hangs in the air, no doubt on the very same train of thought as we imagine another us in another world. I want to question him about his marriage, whether he really should be having the thoughts he has when he's about to pledge his love to a woman for the rest of his life. I want him to tell me he's changed his mind, but that's not for me to decide, so I can't and I don't.

'I always like to think we can only deal with where we are right now,' I continue, trying to close the subject and move on for both of our sakes. 'It's healthier to think that way instead of dwell on what could have been, isn't it?'

I can see him swallow as he ponders his answer.

'Yes, that's definitely the best way to look at it,' he says, scanning the dessert menu to avoid my eye. Then he looks at me again. 'Although, I can't help but still feel very angry at my dad for pushing you away back then. We would have been great friends despite our differences, I know we would.'

He lets out a long, frustrated sigh.

'There's no point in holding on to all those negative emotions, David,' I remind him gently. 'We have found each other again now and I'd much rather have you in my life than not. What's meant to be will always find a way and I think we've proved that theory to be correct, yeah?'

He smiles at me and my heart leaps a little.

'You always seem to find the right words, Kate,' he tells me. 'How on earth do you do that?'

I shrug without giving him a proper answer, and do my best to read the blur of sweet options on the menu in front of me.

'Being with you always makes me feel better too,' I say truthfully as I look at the menu without looking at him.

If only he knew how much I'm battling inside with frustration right now at the thought of him leaving here so soon, and of how I hate that I don't know when I'll see him in the flesh again, and how all the pain of Sam and his rejection and betrayal has magically disappeared now that he is beside me.

He heals me a little every single time we talk or meet, and I think I do the same for him.

I can't find any other way to describe it right now but being with him is like filling a void that's been in me for over ten years now.

He heals me.

I don't want him to marry Lesley. Not only that, but the way he looks at me and the way we make each other feel, I really don't think it would be a good idea for any of us.

DAVID

The conversation flows so easily between Kate and me, and time goes too fast for this, our first proper meeting in person after six months of constant contact.

Being with her this evening is even more than I could ever have imagined. She is like a shining light, so full of positivity and joy with her stories of how she goes the extra mile in the work with the children she looks after on a daily basis. The way she can read me and what I'm thinking sometimes takes my breath away, and I know we are treading dangerous waters by meeting up. I know the simmering attraction between us could threaten to bubble over now we are physically together, but I'm determined to stay in control. I want us to be friends, nothing more.

I absorb her as she speaks, while the tick of the clock makes my heart thud with every turn of the second hand, an indicator that my time here with Kate is only borrowed, but every moment is worth it. Her laugh, her eyes, her smile, her teeth, her hair, her words, her voice; the way she looks at me with such intensity, the way she ponders over every-thing she says so that it has perfect meaning, the way she makes me feel exactly how I should.

I really don't want to say goodbye.

She tucks her hair behind her ear, she tilts her head to the side, she is like slow motion to me; she is music to my ears and balm to my soul.

'You've taught me to slow down my mind a lot,' I tell her, 'and give my head some peace.'

She laughs at that.

'It's always good to give your head some peace,' she tells me. 'And your heart . . . don't underestimate yourself either, David. You give a lot out. You're a wonderful listener.'

'Me?'

'For sure,' she says. 'I've spilled out a lot of stuff to you and you've been great with your listening ear and patient ways.'

'Thanks. That's nice to hear,' I reply. No matter how down I feel, Kate always seems to know how to raise me up and here she is doing it now once more.

I know that many would probably say that our bond, our connection, our link to each other is all representation of what happened that day we met in the doorway. It's association, it's a memory of hope, it's a safety net and the knowledge of what could have been, but I think we both know now that it's grown to become so much more. We've joked about our attraction at first sight, and of how it still lingers now, but it's not a laughing matter at all. Our backgrounds are so different, yet we have so, so much in common too.

'So, tell me more about the charity work you did in China?' she asks, tucking her hair behind her ear. 'You mentioned it a few times on the phone. You seem pretty passionate about it?'

I glance away, feeling my cheeks burn.

'You're being modest,' she says. 'You don't have to be so modest. Tell me.'

'I got into it by accident, really,' I say, trying to play it down a little. 'It was through school and Lesley was travelling a lot at the time so I just thought I'd throw my name in the hat when they asked for volunteers to go there to help after the earthquake. I loved the challenge. By doing so I discovered a side of me I didn't even know existed.'

Kate is all ears.

'I hear you,' she says with a smile. 'I grew up watching my mum campaign locally for equality and women's rights and I think it rubbed off on me, so I know what you mean. It's so important to keep pushing the boundaries and challenging ourselves in life. I think so, anyhow.'

'Me too,' I agree. 'I'd love to do more voluntary work eventually.'

'Ha, check us out. We'll be competing for the Nobel Peace Prize soon,' Kate jokes, clasping her hands beneath her chin. 'You're a bit of a force, David. You come across as quiet sometimes but I can see a fiery, competitive streak in you somewhere. It's seeping through. I can see it.'

She laughs and I fear, as I think she does too, that my competitive streak isn't the only thing revealing itself this evening. There's a heavy feeling in the air yet our conversation flows, and I know that the elephant in the room is getting bigger.

I'm attracted to her and I shouldn't be. We are playing with fire and if we keep this up, we're all going to get burnt.

'Oh, this looks delicious,' Kate tells the waiter with a charming smile when our dessert arrives, and when he nods at her in return, I see with my own eyes how she has a magic that very few other people have.

She was right. This is too much.

Kate has the ability to make everyone she meets feel special and I doubt it's only me she can cast her spell on. I imagine there are many people she touches in her job and in her daily life. She is one in a million, and I will always be grateful for this second chance of getting to know her.

We eat our last course with a sense of trepidation and sadness for what was a wonderful, funny, reflective and poignant evening together coming to an end. When it's time to find taxis to take us once more in our very different directions, we both find it so hard to say goodbye.

I stare at the ground, dreading the moment we'll part to go our separate ways.

'I hope you have a wonderful time with your mum,' she says to me when we stand outside under her yellow umbrella as two taxis pull into line in front of us.

I take a deep breath.

'Yes, I'm looking forward to surprising her,' I say to Kate, whose face is full of genuine concern. 'This evening was so perfect in every way. You've made this trip even better than I thought it could be.'

I can feel her breath on my face as we stand so close beneath this shield from the rain.

'I really, really enjoyed seeing you again after all this time,' I whisper.

'So did I,' she says to me, licking her lips and looking up into my eyes as our bodies move closer. We breathe in sync, in and out as the rain lashes down around us. 'So, until next time – you look after yourself, David Campbell. Promise?'

'I will, I promise,' I say to her in return. Our breath mixes now in the cold, damp air. Our faces are so close. 'And you look after yourself too, and as always, if you ever need me, you know where I am.'

'Thank you,' she says with a smile, and I kiss her gently on the cheek, lingering for long enough to close my eyes and wish for all the happiness in the world to come her way. 'Text me when you get home, just so I know you're back safe.'

We embrace into a tight, lengthy hug and I can feel her soft hair on my face. I can smell her perfume and I know that she doesn't want to let go just like I don't. I take her hand just before I leave her, in a tiny gesture that will always be our own. Her hand in mine, mine in hers, in a way that no one else will ever understand.

We look into each other's eyes, our breathing still in the same pattern, and I feel an urge to kiss her properly even more than before. It's like a rush that washes right through me, like a force, and it scares me so much. I can't do this. I promised myself I wouldn't lose control.

But I can't help it. I pull her close, I lean in and our lips touch and for just a few seconds it feels so explosive. Hers are warm on mine, my tongue moves to meet hers and I don't want to stop but she suddenly pulls away.

'God no! Don't do this, David!' she says as tears fill her eyes and her hand goes to her mouth.

'I'm so sorry! I didn't mean to—'

'I want you to kiss me, I really do!' she says. 'I want you to kiss me so badly but I don't want to ruin anything for you. You're getting married soon. You need to think this through.'

We drop hands, our eyes wide at what we so nearly did.

'What if I don't?' I find myself saying. I'm breathless now.

'What?'

'What if I don't get married?' I ask her. 'I don't know . . . I . . .'

We stare at each other for a moment and I gently wipe a tear from her eye with my thumb. Saying it out loud is as stunning to me as it is a relief, and that takes me by surprise. I have that option still. I could call the wedding off, couldn't I? I could sort this whole mess out once and for all and just be honest with everyone, most importantly with Lesley.

I could call it all off.

'Don't say that,' Kate pleads with me, her flooded eyes

looking up in my direction. 'Don't say that if you don't mean it, David. You aren't thinking straight.'

I take a deep breath. I close my eyes. She is shaking. We both are.

'I don't even know what I mean, I'm sorry. I've so much going on in my head. Look, I need to think things over and make some long overdue decisions,' I tell her, stumbling over my words as a million thoughts fly through me. 'Sorry . . . I need to – I'm sorry.'

I stand in the rain, watching as she takes down her giant umbrella and climbs into the back of the waiting car, her eyes on me the whole time.

'Bye David,' she says with a light wave of her hand and the pain of heartache on her face. I'm smiling as I wave her off but inside I'm crumbling. 'Look after yourself. Goodbye.'

And with that we part company, just like we did on that August day ten years ago when the world was falling down around us.

I get into the back seat of my taxi, and as I travel towards the train station through the February wind and rain away from Kate Foley, her life here in Dublin, and the wonderful evening we shared together, I already feel as if I've left a part of me behind with her.

Can I go ahead and marry Lesley after this? I honestly don't think I can.

APRIL 2009

11.

KATE

It's Easter week, one of my favourite times of the year. The feeling of spring is in the air with a great sense of new beginnings, but just as I'm leaving to do some last-minute shopping before I head home to spend the weekend with my family, David's call has stopped me in my tracks.

I feel sick.

I sit down. I stand up again. I don't know what to do as reality hits me like a blow to my stomach. The night we kissed in Dublin plays out in my mind and I can barely remember how to breathe when I think of how I left there thinking everything between us had changed. And everything had changed, but now . . . now it's all finished.

Now, it's all changed again.

'Should I say congratulations?' I manage to say to him, gripping the phone to my ear, but even that word itself makes me fear I might actually be physically sick. I go to my bedroom and curl my knees up in agony at what I'm hearing.

'No, that doesn't sound right coming from you,' he tells me. 'I'm sorry.'

'You don't have to be sorry,' I say, feeling my pain turn to anger. 'It's just the last thing I expected. God, David!'

'It's a surprise for me too!' he says, but his words are like mumbo jumbo as I try to control my reaction. 'It's a really big surprise for both Lesley and me. My God, I don't know what to think, Kate. I don't know what to do!'

This is more than a big surprise. It's a shock to my system. It could easily bring me to my knees, but I'm doing my best to sound as if I'm delighted for him. I am not delighted. I am heartbroken even though I know I have no right to be so.

'Just goes to show,' he says in a hurried whisper. 'As I was busy trying to make life-changing decisions, the universe decided to make them for me. God, I'm all over the place, Kate. We've just had the big discussion about calling things off and now this. I had absolutely no intention of this happening at all.'

I know exactly what he means. Since our last meeting in February, David has been in deep discussions about his future with Lesley, while I tiptoed around the subject trying not to lean him in any direction or influence his decision in any way, but now, all that pondering is over. Even after the 'big discussion' took place, it means nothing now. It sounds as though he is going to go ahead and marry Lesley after all.

'How do you feel?' I ask him. 'Is this what you want,

David? Ignore me. I don't even know what I'm saying. It's not even my business, is it?'

I can hear David pacing the corridor of the hospital where he is calling me from, and I can also sense the nerves in his voice when he speaks.

'I just felt like I had to tell you first,' he says, his voice shaking so badly. 'Are you working? I'm sorry if I've rung you mid-shift but I needed to hear your voice. This is such a mess.'

'David, try and breathe, for goodness' sake. It's all going to be OK,' I tell him as my insides burn just a little more. I'm just about keeping it under control. 'Having a baby is the most wonderful blessing in the whole world and there's no one I can imagine who would be as good a daddy as you will be. This is obviously meant to be. Just look at it that way. It's all we can do. This is how it's meant to be.'

I know my voice is flat, but I'm doing my best to act grown-up through this and accept that this is way out of my control.

Lesley is having a baby. She has been feeling sick for a few weeks and was having pains in her side for the past few days (which I've almost lived through myself, David has called me so many times for advice). When they finally went to the doctor's this morning they suggested an ectopic pregnancy at first but when they scanned her after admitting her to hospital, they have discovered that it is not in fact an ectopic, but a fully formed, ten-week-old foetus who is perfectly placed in her perfect womb and will be due to pop out some time in early autumn.

Oh God.

'It's just – well, with the wedding next month and all my nagging doubts, it's the last thing I was expecting,' he tells me. 'My head is mangled, Kate. I don't know what to think.'

I want to scream. I want to tell him exactly how this news is making my stomach curdle. I want to tell him never to contact me again, but I also want to kick myself because of course I should have known something like this could happen. They're engaged to be married for goodness' sake and I knew that from the start.

'Kate, I'm sorry. I'm so sorry,' he says. 'You know this wasn't planned at all. I don't know what to do!'

'You'll stay with your fiancée, that's what you'll do, David,' I say feeling sorry for myself and trying to steady my shaking voice. 'In fact just do whatever you want to do. Forget about me and do what's best for you and Lesley and your new—' I can't finish my sentence.

'You don't mean that,' he whispers. 'I can't just forget about you.'

I shake my head as tears stream down my face.

'Well what do you want me to say?' I ask him. 'Congratulations? Is that what you want? OK, congratulations, David. There you go. Congratulations!'

'That's not what I want and you know it!' he says firmly.

'Jesus, Kate, I've just told Lesley I didn't want to get married and now this. What a mess! I'm sorry.'

I take a deep breath and do my best to compose myself.

'And I'm sorry too,' I whisper.

In fact I've a feeling I'm going to be even sorrier when I realize how foolish I've been.

Since our meeting here in Dublin two months ago, David and I have become closer and closer and there's not a day that goes by when we don't speak to each other for at least half an hour at a time. We recalled our wonderful evening together in detail, we talked about how meeting each other again has changed us both and how much we each feel we continue to grow by having each other in our lives. We talked of how we kissed for seconds before we said goodbye – a heart-stopping moment we've eventually brushed under the carpet, afraid to ever mention it again until David knew what he wanted to do regarding his marriage to Lesley.

I lingered over that moment for nights on end, imagining in my mind what it would have felt like had we kissed for a little longer. I could taste his lips on mine, I could feel his warmth and passion in my dreams, and then I'd force myself to snap out of it and to realize that, although it almost did happen, I did the right thing by pulling away.

But I continue to let it play out in my mind when I want to, and I have to admit I enjoy where it takes me.

My near-miss with David led me to tell my mother about our growing friendship on my last visit home and, while she thought it to be a truly beautiful thing that we'd found each other after all this time, she did do a double take when I told her exactly who the ice-cream shop boy was in real life.

'He's a very handsome man I'm sure,' my mum said as she recalled seeing David years ago when he was just a teenager. 'He looked very like his mother back then, not like the grumpy old reverend who always looks like he is chewing a wasp.'

But my sister wasn't letting me off the hook so easily.

'Friendship?' asked Mo as she dried the dishes by the sink. 'Is that what they call it these days?'

'Yes, men and women can be good friends without having to take it any further.'

But Mo just laughed.

'Ah, you're setting yourself up for an almighty fall, sister,' she said, delighted to be up on a pedestal of righteousness for a change. 'It's not often I'm the one to give you advice, but I can see it a mile off when you're best buddies with a soon-to-be-married man. There's a steam train coming your way. It's called reality.'

'He's so gorgeous,' said Shannon, flicking her hair back, her teenage eyes going all dreamy as if she was talking about her favourite boy-band member. 'At least, what I can remember of him, he was.'

'You couldn't possibly remember a lot about him, Shannon,' I said, trying to dilute their admiration over his good looks and trying to ignore the sting of what Mo just said. 'And thanks for your concern, Mo, but there's no steam train coming my way. He's a very, very good friend – in fact I'd now call him one of my best friends – so you can all calm down a bit.'

'Just be careful,' my mother said with concern, and I knew she wasn't referencing his forthcoming marriage. 'There are people around here who wouldn't exactly approve of David's background and your friendship or whatever it is with him.'

I don't need to ask who the people around here are. Sean McGee and his cronies might think they rule the world, but their patch is very, very small and they like to guard it tightly when it comes to the political divide especially.

'Didn't he go off to join the Navy or something?' Mum asked me. 'My God, Kate, are you—?'

'The RAF,' I corrected her, knowing she is exactly right in her warning, 'but he's a teacher now and he wants nothing to do with military life, just like I'm nothing to do with my background. Neither of us chose to be born into the family situations we were brought into.'

I didn't mean to jab at my mother or sister, but their own choices of men, especially Shannon's father, the notorious Sean McGee, left a lot to be desired.

'Be careful, darling,' my mother said, giving me a stern warning again. 'As well as those in our own neighbourhood breathing down your neck, the old reverend has been up to some antics too. He's had his hands dirty in the past by protecting a lot of his own, believe it or not, and his circle of friends would never be mixing with ours. They're arch enemies.'

'Really?' I asked, interested more than ever now.

'I'm saying no more.'

'And you talk to him every day?' asked Mo, taking off her glasses to dry off the steam from the sink beside her. 'Never mind your very different backgrounds for a second, you talk to him every day and his fiancée knows this and is fine with it? Huh, maybe she's blinder than I am, and that's saying something.'

She fixed her glasses, laughing at her own joke.

'Lesley has absolutely nothing to worry about,' I insisted, as my stomach gave a twist knowing deep down that was a lie. 'And neither do any of the watchdogs around these parts, or the old reverend, so let's just leave it at that. I should never have mentioned his name.'

'I think you'd be best to leave it at that with David Campbell,' said my mother. 'I'm sure he's a lovely person, but I don't think he's for you, Kate.'

I left my family home after that conversation and ran back to the safety of my own nest in Dublin where I could talk to David every day if I wanted, where I didn't have to worry about others' opinions, and where no one, not even Lesley, could come between our close bond. Until now of course.

Until this baby news that has made us both come back to earth with an almighty thud.

Will this huge and important change in his life change our friendship? Once the baby comes along he will be so busy, and rightly so, and I doubt our daily updates and deep and meaningful conversations will be at the forefront of his mind. Not to mention our close-to-the-edge conversations and that kiss . . .

'I just didn't see this coming at all,' says David, who is now on a one-way-track rant that I'm only just zoning in and out of at this stage. 'I was so focused on other stuff like work and all my responsibilities, not to mention Mum and her sickness. Lesley says she really wants us to get married now and keep the baby. Kate, I've really fucked it up but I need to stand by Lesley and I know we kissed and I can't help the way I feel about you but—'

'I really need to get ready for work, David,' I interrupt him.

I can't listen to any more. My shift starts at four p.m. and it's already past lunchtime, so I need to make some proper food and get ready, but the very thought of food makes my stomach churn. It's like I'm a third party looking in on this little family-to-be. When it comes to the crunch, my sister is actually right: all I'm doing is setting myself up for a fall. I need to step back. I need to walk away and let them get on with their lives before my involvement is damaging to either of us.

I clutch my own empty womb, feeling its pain as it yelps out in agony for the sadness I feel. I need to end this conversation because I need to sort out my own feelings about this and, right now, I feel like I could cry.

DAVID

I try to control my clashing emotions as I sit here in an unfamiliar hospital corridor, and do my best to ignore the urge to run away and jump on a plane to take me away from here.

I hate myself for feeling this way. Why do I feel like I can't breathe? Why are the walls of this place closing in on me? Like everything is so out of my control and everything is falling down around me.

I lean my head back on the cold wall behind me and I force my mind back to when I first met Lesley at the recruitment afternoon for the RAF three years ago to help me realize just how 'lucky' I am right now. She stood out in the crowd so much with her neat blonde hair tied back, her bright red lipstick. I followed her around the room with my eyes, knowing that when it was my turn to discuss career options with someone for the team, I'd be sent over to her. I'm instinctive like that and always have been. If I'm thinking of someone out of the blue, chances are I'll hear from them on the same day, or if I've someone on my mind, I could easily bump into them moments later.

It was like that with Kate that day in the shop. I knew I'd seen her somewhere before but I also knew that – given the chance – we'd get to know each other and become great friends, or even more. I felt the connection with her, and as I sit here digesting this unexpected news, I try to cast my mind back to the day when I felt a similar connection to Lesley to help me process the fact that she and I are going to have a baby.

She had an open, welcoming and friendly smile that day, and I saw her eyes light up when I came her way. We flirted instantly as she handed me leaflets and explained in detail all the options that lay in front of me.

'I think you'd make a really fine pilot,' she said, and the way she held my gaze at that moment led me to signing up right then and there on the spot.

My father was over the moon when we got together. Lesley's own parents were both in the forces and her dad was field marshal in the Royal Irish Regiment, which almost gave the old Reverend Campbell a multiple orgasm. I can only imagine how utterly thrilled he is going to be when he hears his own grandchild will be part of such a prestigious lineage. Hell, he might even hug me again like he did after he had dinner in Cardiff with John and Josephine Taylor, her parents, when Les and I first introduced them all a few years ago.

Lesley is going to wake up soon and she'll have a range of emotions to go through now too as we readjust our lives to what this year will bring – in the best possible way, I hope.

I hope.

'Kate,' I whisper to the person who, deep down, I really

want to be with. 'I should probably get back to Lesley so I'm there for her when she's ready to go home.'

I wait for Kate's response, but she's gone quiet.

'Are you still there?' I ask.

'Yes, I'm here,' she says, her voice cracking a little. She doesn't say any more than that which is really not like her.

'Kate?'

She takes a moment before she answers.

'It's fine, David,' she sniffles then there is more silence. 'Yes, you go and see to Lesley. She has had a rollercoaster of a day. You both have and it's a lot to absorb, I'm sure. It will all work out for the best.'

So this is it, then. This is the hammer blow I've been waiting on, the sign I've needed, the wake-up call, the wise-up moment of realization that I've been playing with fire and just how much I could have let Lesley down. But Kate? I'm letting her down too and it's not fair on her either.

'Look, this isn't going to change our friendship, Kate,' I tell her, standing up now. 'We'll still be as close as ever. In fact, maybe you could be godmother to the baby. Would you like to—'

Oh my God, what am I even saying?

'Stop, David, please!' Kate tells me in a tone I've never heard her use before. 'This baby has nothing to do with me so don't say that. It's your baby, yours and Lesley's. I don't want to be godmother!'

184

She waits. I can hear her breathing and I'll swear she is crying. I don't know what to say.

'You can't even introduce me to your parents, and Lesley knows very little about me, for God's sake,' she says with a touch of laughter through her tears. 'I don't want to be godmother. Thanks, but no thanks.'

'Kate, I'm sorry, that was so stupid of me to suggest that,' I plead with her. 'I'm not even thinking straight, sorry. I'm just trying to say that we'll still be close after this. We still have something amazing between us.'

'Between us?' she says. 'What exactly is the something amazing that's between us, David?'

'What?'

'Look, I'm sorry, but it's about time I tried to protect my own feelings instead of always looking out for yours,' she tells me. 'Yes, do go to Lesley and stay by her side where you should be. I'm happy for you, deep down I really am, but I need to look after myself too.'

'Kate, but—'

'I have to get ready for work.'

'OK, we'll talk tomorrow at lunchtime as usual?'

She doesn't answer.

'Kate?'

'I can't, David,' she whispers. 'I'll check in with you in a while, all right? I think we need some time out from this, whatever it even is. I don't know any more.'

She hangs up and I fall back down onto the two-seater

sofa behind me, throw the phone down and lean my head in my hands.

I can sit here and pretend to wonder, but I know exactly what Kate means when she asks what exactly is between us.

I've asked the same question to myself so many times. We are more than friends and there's no point denying it. I want to call her back and say how sorry I am for leading her along on this road to nowhere with me. I guess I've been on auto-pilot, plodding along as time ticks by to my wedding day, taking too long to find the courage to tell Lesley I don't want to do it and trying to make sure my mother is feeling as good as she can and trying to hold on to Kate like she's some sort of security blanket when I'm having moments of darkness; yet, she is expected to just sit on the sideline and cheer me on from afar as I now move on in my life with Lesley.

She doesn't deserve to be treated like this. She deserves the very best of me and I can't give her that. I certainly can't give her any more than that *no*w. What the hell have I been doing, playing with her emotions like this?

'There you are!' says a nurse, who was with us earlier. I look up at her. 'Ah, it's been a really big day for you, Daddy-to-be! Your wife is ready now. She's asking for you.'

I jump up.

'She's not my wife. We're not married,' I tell the lady, who looks at me as if I'm a prize moron for feeling the need to correct her. 'Sorry. Sorry, yes, it's been an emotional day for sure. I'll go and see Lesley now.'

MAY 2009

12.

KATE

'Why are you not at work?'

I wake up to see Sinead at the bottom of my bed, two cups of coffee in her hand and what looks like a flap-jack wrapped in plastic between her teeth. She sets the coffee down on my bedside locker, opens the flapjack and offers me half but I shake my head. The very notion of food right now is enough to me make me nauseous, plus I've barely woken up yet after a disastrous sleep full of dreams where I was lost and couldn't find what I was looking for.

'I'd booked the day off in advance to be here with you, lady,' Sinead tells me. 'There's no way I was letting you stew here on your own today, crying into your pillow. Come on. Get up and we'll do something nice. It's a gorgeous day outside. Shit, you probably don't really care if it is, do you? In fact, the sun shining probably makes it even more unfair.'

It's David and Lesley's wedding day – a day that I've been dreading for so long – and even though David and I deliberately haven't been talking as much as we used to over the past couple of weeks, the countdown to the big day has slowly chipped away at me as I come to terms with the fact that I was much more dependent on his calls and his friendship than I ever should have been.

'Thank you. You're a sweetheart,' I tell Sinead, as I try and peel myself off the bed. 'In hindsight I really should have made sure I was on the rota today for work instead, but I'd booked it off ages ago on the slim chance that I might have been invited to the wedding. How naive can I possibly be?'

Sinead shoots me a look with a raised eyebrow.

'And you're telling me you'd have gone if they'd invited you?' she asks, munching a mouthful of her convenience breakfast. 'You mean you could have actually stomached watching him kiss her and say, "I do"? Sorry, I didn't mean to put that image in your head, but you know what I mean.'

My stomach churns at the thought.

'No,' I tell her simply, 'There's no way I would have gone, but a few months ago I seemed to think I could have.'

No matter how much I try to erase it from my head, the image of David in his sharp navy suit today, watching his bride walk up the aisle towards him, has kept me up most of the night, and to be honest it's making me really nauseous.

'We need to let go,' I told him on a recent phone call. The wedding was approaching faster and faster once Easter had passed and May came around. With the baby coming along now, everything had changed, and I needed to give us both some space. 'You're having a baby with your future wife. I can't pretend to just fit in around all that.'

He protested and insisted we could keep our friendship going, just like I expected him to, but deep down I think he knew that we were growing way too close for comfort. My sister Mo was right. I was setting myself up for an almighty crash by growing so intensely close to someone who was never going to be mine in the way I'd secretly wished for.

He was like my crutch and I was his, so it was no wonder that when Lesley had a miscarriage just ten days ago, he called me during the night sobbing his heart out, and I coached him through it until I couldn't take any more.

'We can't keep talking like this, David. It's unfair on us both and it's unfair on Lesley. You need to focus on your future with her. She needs you now more than ever.'

And so slowly over the past few weeks, apart from the night of the miscarriage when I couldn't turn him away, I gradually learned that – no matter how much it pained me – it was for the best to deliberately 'miss' David's calls. It was best to leave long gaps between his texts, to stagger the times I'd email him something I'd found online that I thought he'd find funny or of interest and, in an attempt to shield myself from the inevitable crash, I very, very slowly tried to wean myself off him, if only on the surface, as this dreaded day came around.

'I don't think that you and David Campbell will ever be able to stop orbiting each other,' Sinead tells me as I nibble on a piece of toast downstairs when I finally do get up. We both sit in our cosy pyjamas, the sound of a lawnmower outside making it sound like a normal Saturday morning in May, even though it's anything but normal to me as my heart is being torn to pieces inside. 'You have a deep, unbreakable bond that no one else can touch, but if being in his life is going to cause you both this heartache, I think you're right to step away totally, Kate.'

'I know,' I say, putting the toast down, its blandness doing nothing for me. The wedding is this afternoon, it's just past nine in the morning and I've tried my best to message him good luck but I can't just yet. 'I'm trying to totally step away, I really am. I wish we could just be friends without it feeling so intense and so across the line. I wish I could just be happy for him getting married without it being a threat to our friendship, but I can't.'

'Are you in love with him, Kate?' Sinead asks me, staring at me now so there's no escape and no way to avoid her very direct question. 'You can tell me the truth. There's no need to deny it either to your own self or to me.'

I shrug and stare at the mantelpiece.

'I . . . I know that I can talk to him more than I could any other man I've ever met.'

'OK.'

'He makes me feel like no one else has ever done, and

I know we have some sort of magic between us,' I say, unable to hide a smile as I recall some of our tender conversations. 'We have a bond from ten years ago, yes, but it's more than that, Sinead. The last time we met in person, we had the most wonderful time together. He tried to kiss me before he left and I really wanted him to but we stopped before we took it too far.'

'OK,' says Sinead again, her eyes wide like saucers.

'And I wanted him to kiss me so badly, I really did,' I confess. 'There's a hunger between us that's insatiable. I've never felt anything like this before.'

'So, you're in love with him then,' she whispers, nodding her head as it all sinks in. 'Oh, Kate.'

I feel my eyes burn and my lip trembles.

'What on earth do I do now, eh?' I ask my flatmate and great friend as the inevitable tears flow down my cheeks. 'What do I do to let him go? I can't just sit here for ever wallowing over a man who is getting married today to someone else. I have to know what to do.'

'Ah, you poor thing,' she says, joining me on the sofa. 'We'll figure it out, don't worry. I'll help you in any way I can, I promise; anything you want me to do, I'll do it if it makes you feel better. I'm just trying to figure out what that could be.'

We sit there for a few moments as I let it all sink in. Images of David – so handsome, tall and smart in his morning suit, soon to be smiling at the lovely Lesley in her iconic white dress, their smiling families looking on – flood my head again. I hear him clear his throat as he makes his after-dinner speech, shy and blushing as he takes the mic in front of the gathered crowd of guests from both sides of their family. His voice will break a little and she'll put her hand on his to reassure him he's doing a great job.

I hear them laughing as they gaze into each other's eyes, I see him whisper in her ear as they share their first dance to a song that means nothing to others but the world to them. I see his father look at Lesley in a way that he would never look at me, and it tears me apart for how unfair life can be.

But, aside from all that, I also know it will be a day tinged in sadness too as they grieve the loss of their baby. I try and change the focus of my mind to sympathy and joy for them instead of sympathy for myself, but it's hard to shift gears in my mind when in my heart I'm so deeply devastated.

'So, how about we get dressed up and go for a nice lunch, somewhere out of the city where we can sit outside and have a nice old drink and feel the sea air on our faces?' Sinead suggests, trying to brighten me up. 'It's the best I can come up with for now, but it might help you get through the day and stop thinking about fairy-tale weddings and torturing yourself?'

'Yeah,' I reply, trying to build myself up to getting changed out of my fleecy pyjamas. The idea of putting on make-up and fixing my hair seems like an arduous chore, but I also know that if I lie around here thinking and overthinking it will drive me insane.

'Did you message him good luck for today?' Sinead asks me, nodding at my phone.

I glance at my mobile as if it's a disease, shake my head and look away.

'I can't even look at my phone,' I tell her. 'I know I should send him some sort of a message, I really do, but I think it would be best for me to stay out of it totally. Plus, in a selfish way, I think I need to focus on me.'

'Fair enough, whatever makes it easier,' says Sinead. 'OK, you go make a start to get ready and I'll tidy up here a bit. Once you have today behind you, you'll start to feel better. You'll see.'

I only wish I shared Sinead's confidence in my ability to put David into my past with Sam and all the others I thought I'd loved before. Maybe this will ease off eventually, but I know in my heart this is different to what I felt like with anyone before, even with Sam who I one day thought I was going to marry. Thank God for unanswered prayers – and who knows, maybe this is another one of those things that just wasn't meant to be?

David slipped into my life for a fleeting moment, but he left a wound in my heart so deep that it's going to take a long, long time to heal. I honestly thought we were soulmates as far as friendships go, but my stupid heart got involved and ruined it all. I dig deep inside and close my eyes before I get up from the sofa, doing my best to send good vibes from me to him for his day.

I force myself to lift my phone.

'What are you doing?' asks Sinead, as if I'm about to jump off a cliff.

'I'm being the bigger person,' I tell her as I type a message into my phone, my hands shaking as I type and I press send before either of us can change my mind. 'I'm wishing my good friend all the happiness in the world for his wedding day. There you go. Done. I feel better already.'

Sinead puts her hand on her hip.

'Well done, Kate,' she says, nodding her head like a proud mother. 'That's step one out of the way. Now, up to the shower you go. We're going to have a lovely day and each day that comes after this, you'll be one bit closer to your new future.'

And so I do as I'm told. I go to the shower and stand under it for far longer than I intended to, but all the time I stand there, I force myself to smile for David and Lesley on their big day.

Inside, though, I'm falling to pieces, and I know I'm broken in a way that will never be fixed. I just have to find a way of never letting it show.

DAVID

I'm sitting in the garden, in my father's chair, under the tree where the birds sing a pleasant morning melody that couldn't be further from my mood right now. My stomach is in bits, my head is banging after I tried to numb my feelings with too much whisky last night. I feel as if my blood is curdling as it runs through my veins, as despair grips me and leaves my head in a very dark place.

I picture Lesley and her family getting ready for today in a nearby hotel, and every time I think of her, buck's fizz in hand, having her blonde hair styled just like she'd planned it, her white dress hanging on the door as her sister and her mother fuss over her, and the dainty shoes she bought from America waiting to be worn for the first and only time, I feel as though I'm going to be sick.

It's 9.30 a.m.

I check my phone and my heart jumps when I see there's a message from Kate at last. As well as imagining with dread what Lesley is doing now, I'm also pining to know how Kate is feeling. I haven't spoken with her in almost ten days since I spilled my guts out to her about the miscarriage and, although there has been so much going on, as Lesley and I packed up on autopilot and we made our way across the Irish Sea on the ferry for the wedding two days ago, every second without having Kate in my life to talk to has felt like someone boring holes in my heart.

'*Thinking of you. Have a wonderful day x*'

Oh God. My head throbs like a beating drum and I pray for some direction. I beg for some spiritual guidance, for some advice to come from somewhere, anywhere, to please help me. I've never felt so alone in my life.

I can hear footsteps behind me and, from the way they are light as they patter across the gravel, I know it's my mother.

I knew she'd find me here eventually. I try and focus on my breathing, wondering where to start to try and explain to her, if I can find the words, how I'm feeling on what is meant to be the happiest day of my life.

'I thought you'd be in the shower by now,' she says, putting a mug of cappuccino on the table beside me, her jolly smile tinged with just a hint of uncertainty. 'You didn't eat your breakfast, David. It's probably nerves, mind you. I remember on my wedding morning I couldn't eat a bite, but you'll be glad you did later if you can manage something. Even a piece of toast?'

'I don't want anything to eat, but thanks, Mum.'

'I could do you some porridge? Or even some fruit?'

'Honestly, I can't even think of food,' I say to her, staring ahead. I swallow hard, wondering if I can spit out what it is I want to say.

'David, what's wrong, love?'

Mum pulls a chair beside me and takes my hand.

'I'm so sorry, Mum.'

'Sorry? What for?' she whispers so gently. 'Has something happened?"

'I can't do this,' I whisper, waiting for her face to crumple but instead she just smiles and squeezes my hand.

'Oh, darling, it's normal to have cold feet on your wedding day: you do understand that?' she says. 'But Lesley adores you and I know you love her too.'

I shake my head from side to side. Where do I start? My parents know nothing about the surprise pregnancy last month and the subsequent miscarriage just ten days ago. They know nothing about how I've been so distracted by the insane pressures of work that meant the days just ticked by and this date came around so quickly, or how I've been so consumed with Mum's illness and making sure she was going to get better that I didn't stop properly to think about what it was I was actually going ahead with.

As my parents prepared the house so it was freshly decorated, as they ordered in a catered breakfast for this morning and fresh flowers to fill the hallway, as they chose their outfits so carefully, as they sent through a list of friends they'd like to see invited to our reception, as they talked to Lesley's parents and let the excitement of today take over, they had no idea that all that time all I wanted was Kate.

The only person I wanted to be with was Kate.

Kate Foley, the girl from the doorway who held my hand and fixed my arm, the one who makes my world spin in the best possible way; the one who lights me up inside. I can see it in every move she makes and I can feel it in every word I say in return. She brings me to life like oxygen with her words and advice and her soothing tones. She makes me feel, when I wake up clouded by darkness, that I could jump the moon if I wanted to. She is like no one I've ever met before.

'I hate the thought of letting Lesley down,' I tell my mother. 'She has gone through her own private hell all week in a time when she should have been looking forward to the best day of her life and now I'm going to destroy her even more.'

'I don't understand,' says my mother. 'Have you really changed your mind?'

I breathe out slowly and nod my head.

'I'm so sorry,' I repeat. 'I'm so sorry.'

She squeezes my hand again which makes me feel just a tiny bit better.

Looking at her frail face, dry and worn out by months of chemotherapy, her blonde bobbed wig so perfectly placed for what was to be a very proud day for her, I feel so angry at myself for the devastation I'm about to cause. Despite her own physical pain and all the internal worry she has had lately for her own wellbeing, she can still set that to the side here and pledge her support, even though I'm about to shatter so many worlds.

'I've left this too late, Mum, but I was hoping somewhere along the way I'd change my mind and see some sense,' I continue. 'I should have acted quicker, I should have read the signs earlier and more honestly. I hate myself for doing this to Lesley. I hate myself for inflicting so much pain on her. I hate that I feel the way I do.'

Mum's eyes fill up and she shakes her head slowly.

'David, darling, are you really telling me—?' she asks, as sadness and shock creep over her kind, delicate face. 'Are you really telling me . . . you're not going ahead with the wedding today?'

I nod, unable to watch as tears fill her broken face.

'That's what I'm trying to say, yes,' I tell her. I bite my lip and look away.

She is stunned and I'm brought back to so many moments here in our home when bad news was broken – the aftermath of the bomb when our whole community was stunned, losing Aaron so tragically and suddenly that cold winter morning, all of the standout moments in life that have defined us. And now I've landed this on my mother.

She shakes her head as she stares at the grass beneath her.

'Lesley is a wonderful young lady, David, and we are all very fond of her,' she whispers gently. 'This will devastate her and her whole family.'

I put my head in my hands.

'I know it will,' I say, looking up to the heavens. I close my eyes. 'I never wanted this to happen. I can't believe it's happening.'

201

'Are you sure?'

This time I don't cower out of my decision. As much as the pain of what I am going to do engulfs both of us here right now, I know it's the right thing. I need to face up to it head on.

'I'm sure, Mum,' I tell the woman who brought me into this world. I hate disappointing her, but right now I know there is simply no turning back. 'I'm sorry, but I'm sure. I can't risk living a lie for the rest of my life, and I know it would hurt Lesley more in the long run if she thought I was going ahead with this against my gut feeling.'

We sit there together, with only the sound of morning bird song breaking our silence. I already feel a slight weight off my own shoulders having spoken out my truth, but I dread the day ahead as I face the music and break Lesley's heart.

'Well, it looks like you've made your decision,' my mother says eventually, her voice a little stronger now, 'and even though this is the last thing I'd want either of you to have to go through, you must be true to yourself and to Lesley. She deserves the truth. I'm so sorry for you both. I won't lie, this is very sad to hear, but I respect your decision.'

She puts her frail arms around my neck and softly kisses me on the forehead as a swarm of butterflies attack my insides. I have a fleeting urge to backtrack, to chicken out of pulling out of today, but something Kate said to me in her very first email comes back to me and gives me the push I need to get through this.

What happened to us back then is a benchmark for life – I will never be so afraid of anything again, and therefore, if I'm ever scared, I remind myself how I'm strong enough to get through whatever comes my way.

I close my eyes, hearing those words over and over again, and when I open them my mum is still there, waiting for me with her arm stretched out. I take her hand in mine. She is so small now, so weak and so fragile on the outside, yet a powerhouse from within as always. If she has never loved me more, I can say that I feel exactly the same for her.

This is going to be horrendous, but I've made my decision once and for all.

'You're a disgrace to me, and a disgrace to this family name,' says my father as he looks out of the front window of the drawing room, staring out to the lawn. 'What are you thinking, David? Are you even thinking at all? Does it thrill you to hurt people like this?'

He pinches his eyes and thumps the table beside him.

'I'm not intentionally out to hurt anyone out, Dad,' I tell him, jutting out my chin. 'This is one part of my life that you won't be able to control or ever make me feel like I'm doing the wrong thing, because believe me I already know how painful this is going to be for Lesley. I feel bad enough, and I'm going to have to deal with it, so I really don't need your "letting down the family name" speech, thank you!'

'But Lesley is perfect for you!' he spits, taking his tie off and throwing it on the floor. 'She's the daughter of a field marshal for goodness' sake, David! She couldn't be any more perfect for you if we'd hand-picked her ourselves, but now we'll be the talk of this town for all the wrong reasons!'

I shake my head as I try to find the words. I'm stunned in a way I never thought I'd be, my head spinning.

'Yes, Dad, that's exactly it, you see,' I say in bewilderment, almost laughing in frustration now. 'Lesley is an amazing person, yes, I already know that, but you can't tell me who's perfect for *me* – no one has that power over any other human being. It's absolutely tearing me apart inside what I'm about to do to Lesley, but all you can think of is what other people will say, as bloody usual.'

'She doesn't deserve this and neither do I or your mother.'

'But it's not about you, Dad!' I plead with him. 'And while I'm sorry you're disappointed in me, I'm much more concerned that I'm about to break a beautiful woman's heart on what should have been the biggest day of her life. I only wish you could see it that way, instead of thinking of yourself and your fine reputation as always.'

'You can leave now,' he tells me, still staring at the floor as he points towards the doorway. 'I will speak to Lesley's parents in my own time and apologize to them for this sorry mess you've left us all in.'

My stomach flips as I picture the scenes ahead when I see Lesley. Once more I consider taking the easier short-term option by pretending this conversation never happened and meeting her at the church this afternoon as planned.

'I'll come with you, David,' I hear my mother say to me. She stands in the hallway with her light pink summer coat in her hand. Her eyes are red-rimmed from crying and I feel my heart crush in my chest.

'No, Mum. Thanks for the offer, but please stay here and rest. This is one mess I'm going to have to deal with myself, and the quicker I do it, the better for all of us involved.'

13.

Sinead and I spend the early afternoon walking along the beach at Sandymount in Dublin, and I do my best to distract myself from what time of day it is. I've deliberately left my phone at home to allow my mind to switch off and default, back to a time when I didn't know David Campbell in real life, back to a time when my world was just me and Sam in our apartment and I thought I had the world at my feet.

'Funny how you think you've everything under control in life and then boom, it all falls down around you,' I say to Sinead as we sip coffee in the Sandymount Hotel, where Sinead is insisting I at least try to eat some lunch. My untouched sandwich stares at me from the table, but I can't think of digesting anything yet. Every time I experience any kind of upset, it goes straight to my stomach. My mother says I inherited it from her while Mo wishes she had the same trait, joking that she turns to food for comfort and piles on the pounds, whereas I turn away from it and lose weight I can't afford to lose in the first place.

'Look Kate, I know this is going to sound a bit like tough love, but you found David right on the cusp of your break-up with Sam, so maybe you gave your friendship with him too much energy on top of what you already were going through,' she tells me. 'I'm no relationship expert, but perhaps this is a good time to focus on yourself and start planning out your own future. You've so much to live for.'

I know what she says is probably true. I need to shake myself off and accept that Sam and David were both life lessons – Sam has taught me that people you love can cheat on you and friends can lie, but that's their problem and their loss, while David taught me that falling in love with someone at the wrong time can hurt so deeply, but that life isn't always fair and you just have to roll with the punches, treat your wounds and reboot.

'I'd love to do something really spontaneous,' I mutter, staring at the table in front of me. 'Like, something totally mad, something from the bucket list, you know what I mean, Sinead? Something we always say we'll do before we die but we never actually do it. Like, a parachute jump—'

'Hang on, don't most people just change their hairstyle or join a gym?'

'Or going on a jungle trek? Actually, I've always wanted to go to Africa,' I say, as my mind runs away with itself.

'You know, like on a proper safari adventure! Would you come with me?'

Sinead sits back in her seat and holds her arms out straight with a shrug.

'Well, I was thinking more of spending a week in the sun by a pool somewhere like Ibiza this year, but why the hell not?' she says, looking at me as though she thinks I'm just a little bit bonkers but she likes it. 'Imagine the two of us in camouflage!'

'Will we book it now? Come on! Let's go find a travel agent, call work and book in some annual leave and we'll start making plans!'

I lift the sandwich and take a bite, as Sinead claps like a seal in front of me.

'You see!' she says in triumph. 'Mind over matter and it's all your own idea! It will give us both something to look forward to! Right, eat up and let's go and book our jungle holiday, Kate. I knew we could make today a good day if we tried!'

Half an hour later, we are armed with brochures, we have a deposit paid and our holiday leave booked off for the last two weeks in July. We giggle in disbelief as we make our way back home, already planning our next shopping trip and all we'll need to pack for the adventure.

'I can't believe we just booked that on a total whim,' I say as I pull into my parking space outside our apartment. I'm still talking nineteen to the dozen, recalling the advice of the travel agent on all the lotions and potions we'll need, the jabs we'll have to get as soon as possible, and all the things we have to look forward to like the Virunga Amani tour to see gorillas and Kahuzi-Biéga National Park which we were told is astonishing, when Sinead goes exceptionally quiet. I pull the handbrake, take off my seatbelt and follow her eyeline towards our home, where I see exactly what, or should I say who, it is that has stopped her in her tracks.

'David?' I say, scrambling out of the car and running towards the steps where he sits with his head in his hands. 'David, oh my God, what's happened? Why are you here?'

He swallows hard, looks up at me and shakes his head. 'I couldn't do it and I didn't know where else to go.'

My heart is in my mouth and all the joy of booking my spur-of-the-moment holiday fades away as I try and work out if this is some sort of dream.

So he didn't marry her? He came here when he was meant to be celebrating his big day after months and months of planning? He didn't marry her, and he drove all the way here to be with me? I feel like I'm in some sort of cyclone of emotions – I'm totally overwhelmed with euphoria one second, which plummets to guilt and grief in the next. I blink back shock as I realize that this is indeed very, very real.

I gulp back tears and I can tell from the red rims around David's blue eyes that he hasn't slept a lot lately. He looks so exhausted. Sinead slips past, apologizing, and says she'll give us some space, her face pale with shock just like I'm sure my own is right now.

'I'm so glad you thought to come here,' I whisper, not even knowing what it is I'm meant to say. I touch his face. I look into his tired eyes. 'I'll always be here for you, David.'

This changes everything. All the pain I've felt in the build-up to today is whitewashed now with a huge relief, but at the same time my stomach is sick with a mixture of fear and excitement. Does this mean we might have a chance of being together some day? Could we really risk the wrath of his family and mine to try and make that happen? I put my arm around him and lean my head on his shoulder as we sit there for a moment in silence. As we do so, I can't help but think of Lesley and how someone is probably doing the same right now with her. Oh, the poor girl. I feel queasy again when I think of what she must be going through.

'Come on, let's get you inside and you can tell me all about it,' I say to David, urging him up from the step. 'I'm nearly sure I've some brandy in the cupboard. I'll get you a glass of that for a start. It's good for shock. Maybe I'll have one too.'

I'm rambling as I link my arm through his and lead him into my home for the first time, my head still racing with the possibility that maybe, just maybe, David's decision today might have been something to do with me, but I'm not ready to ask him that yet.

'One step at a time,' he says as we make our way inside.

I couldn't have put it any better myself. My heart is bursting with anticipation of what could happen now, but my head is telling me not to get carried away or out of control.

There is much more to David and me ever being together, even with Lesley out of the picture.

There always has been.

DAVID

The brandy burns my throat like liquid fire, easing calm through my veins as I sit here at Kate's table in her tiny Dublin kitchen. I've no idea how I made the two-hour journey south in my car without ending up in a ditch or taking a wrong turn, but I got here, numb and grey with shock, grief and sorrow at what I have just done.

'I feel so bad but also so relieved,' I tell Kate, who is sitting beside me, holding another glass of brandy. I can imagine her shock levels are pretty high right now too, having found me waiting for her, when in her head she would have assumed I was going through with my wedding day. I look at the time. We would be dining by now and, in a parallel world, I'd be preparing to make my speech. The thought of it chokes me.

'You've really floored me but I'm so glad you knew you could come here.'

I shake my head.

'I'm so sorry for all the hurt I caused, Kate, but I just had to see you,' I tell her. 'I couldn't go home to my parents, I was too embarrassed to go to any of my friends who were all looking forward to a good day out, so after I'd done what I had to and contacted our guests to say the wedding was off, I was politely asked to leave by Lesley's dad. I say politely. He's an ex-field marshal in the Army so you can imagine how he defines "politely".'

I laugh at this, but Kate looks serious still.

'Poor Lesley,' she whispers as she looks at me with such concern. 'How was she? I can only imagine.'

I take a moment as the reality of today hits me once more. How did it all come to this? So much has happened. I know it is all of my own making, but it's still hard to take it all in.

'We sat together in the hotel room that should have been our honeymoon suite,' I begin, feeling my voice tremble as I relive the moment I broke the news to Lesley. 'It was so hard to find the right words, but she knew when she saw me at the hotel that there was something terribly wrong. She cried and I cried and then she got angry. Very angry. It was awful for her, Kate. So awful.'

Kate looks on, crestfallen.

'She asked was there someone else.'

'Oh no.'

A heavy silence hangs in the air between us. I feel my eyes sting and a wave of nausea settles in my stomach.

'And what . . . what did you tell her?' Kate asks me.

I shake my head and stare at the floor as she waits on my answer.

'She asked if it was you,' I reply, then I rub my throbbing forehead, 'but I couldn't hurt her any more so I said no. I told her there was no one else, but I don't even know, do I, Kate? I don't know what's going on. It's such a mess.'

Kate reaches across and lightly rests her hand on my arm.

'I feel heart-sore for you both,' she whispers. 'But David, this will work itself out. You're not the only person ever to change your mind about getting married, even if you did leave it till the very last minute. As much as Lesley is hurting right now, which I'm sure is excruciating, she will know in time you were right to be honest. Why the hell didn't you talk to me sooner?'

I look up at her.

'I suppose I thought that by talking to you, I'd confuse myself even more,' I try to explain to Kate. 'But I actually did try to call you this morning, not to mention at least ten times before I left my parents' house earlier today and twice when I stopped on the motorway to get a bottle of water. Lesley is in pieces, she really is, and I feel rotten with guilt right now. But I'm not a bad person, am I, Kate?' I try to grasp for some comfort.

Kate tilts her head to the side, pushes her dark hair out of her eyes and bites her lip.

'You're not a bad person, David,' she says, reaching out and resting her hand on my lower arm. 'You are compassionate, caring, sympathetic, and also incredibly honest in everything you do. This too will pass. You've done the right thing, even if it doesn't feel like that right now.'

Her smile lights me up inside and she reassures me just like I'd hoped she would.

'I can't get it out of my mind – the look on her face,' I say to Kate, as the image of Lesley, heartbroken and tearful, flares in my mind. 'I just can't understand why it's taken me so long, why I left it so late to tell her . . . I've no doubt she is devastated. She said she wants me to move out of our house immediately of course, which I expected. She said after today she never wants to see me again, not that I'd blame her for one second. My dad said the same.'

I take another sip of the brandy, glad of its neutralizing effects on the swirl of emotions that engulf me right now. The relief of seeing Kate and her healing, unconditional welcome, the guilt of running away to her when deep down I know it's my feelings for her that made me push through with my decision, and the horror of causing someone like Lesley so much heartache when today was meant to ease the pain of losing the baby just as she was getting her head around the fact that she was unexpectedly pregnant. Not to mention how I'm going to face up to all my friends and relatives who had no doubt spent a fortune in preparation. I don't know how I'm ever going to forgive myself.

'Lesley is well within her rights to be mightily pissed off right now, but your dad should be supporting you through this, not throwing you out on the street when you need him,' Kate says. 'And your friends and relatives will forgive you, don't worry about that.'

'You've met my father,' I whisper. 'So you'll know that his reaction was as if I'd murdered someone. The shame I've brought on him. How is he going to explain this to his congregation? How is he going to face Lesley's parents? It's all about him and his reputation and his big fat ego. He doesn't seem to care about Lesley's pain, only his own embarrassment.'

Kate looks as if she might burst with frustration.

'Well, none of us has a clean slate to work from, and I very much doubt that he does either,' she says, wringing her hands as she speaks. 'It's called being human! You know, some people say that life is hard, but it's not life that's hard, it's being a human that's hard. We all have our ups and downs in life. There's not one of us walking this earth who can say we have never messed up, or stepped out of line, or hurt someone by our actions no matter what our best intentions were. None of today makes you a bad person, David, and it's unfair of your father to turn his back on you, but at the end of the day it says more about him than it does about you.'

I manage to smile a little at Kate's rant. She looks so passionate as her eyes dart around the room when she talks and I can just imagine her as a campaigner of sorts one day, fighting from her very core for what she believes in.

'What's so funny?' she asks me, looking totally surprised and even a little bit offended by my expression.

'You are funny,' I try to explain to her. 'You're so loyal and fierce and I love . . .'

I stop at that.

I almost said something else, but today isn't the time to go that far. If I feel bad now about Lesley, I'd feel a million times worse tomorrow if I declared my love for Kate while Lesley is wiping away tears and packing up her wedding day to make an early return back home.

'I can't help it. I'm just very passionate when it comes to you, David,' Kate tells me, which takes me by surprise. It's not the response I was expecting at all from her. 'This probably sounds weird, but I feel pain when you feel it. If you're hurting, I'm hurting too, and I hate that your father is treating you this way. When you're upset I get upset. I feel what you feel.'

Wow. No one has ever said anything like that to me before.

'Do you really mean that?' I ask her, finding her hand across the table. 'About me? About us?'

She gets up from the table to compose herself and, when she walks past my way, I stop her and pull her close, wrapping my arms around her waist. I lean my face on her belly and close my eyes.

'I can't help what I feel, David,' she tells me, and I hold her tighter. Then I stand up and cup her face in my hands.

'And I can't help how I feel,' I say as I drink in her soul.

Then, I lean in and kiss her lips so tenderly that the room spins around us. She brings out a hunger in me and a passion that runs deeper than I've ever known and yet I'm also terrified of this. I'm so afraid of getting it wrong. I'm vulnerable to this and so is Kate, and I want to make sure this is absolutely perfect because if we get it wrong, we are so raw and so attached that I know it will damage us both so deeply, like no other wound we've ever suffered, not even those from a bomb.

We kiss and tug and hold each other so tightly here in her kitchen, breathing faster and faster and out of control. She puts her hand under my T-shirt, sending sparks of electricity through me at our first intimate skin-on-skin contact, and I do the same to her, feeling the velvet-soft skin of her back on my hand.

Her slender waist pushes into mine, our bodies throbbing and thirsty for more, until Kate pulls away just like she did before.

My heart skips a beat with fear of what might be going through her mind right now.

'I can't – I just don't think we should do this today, David,' she says, her beautiful face crumpled up in despair as she shakes her head, breathless and flushed. 'Out of respect to Lesley and also to ourselves, let's wait a while. If you hurt me or if I hurt you, David, even if we don't mean to, I know it will destroy what we have for ever.'

I nod, totally understanding what she means and glad that she is stronger than I am, able to resist the one thing we've wanted for so long.

'You're right,' I tell her, feeling my heart rate slow down. 'You're so right.'

'Can I just hold you?' she asks. 'I'd love to just hold you for now.'

She reaches out her arms for me and we stand there, locked in a comforting embrace. For this moment I know that it's all I needed and was worth every devastating step of today and every single mile of the journey that brought me here to find her.

14.

KATE

'Ah, that is so cute! Look at the gorillas! I can't believe you got so close, Kate!'

Shannon is in my mother's kitchen, eagerly looking through the photos from my Republic of Congo trip. My father is sitting across the table from me, staring at me with pride. It's been almost a year since I was in the same room as him, but I've come to accept that's just the way it is, as he battles his internal demons that stop him from doing the things he'd sometimes like to do – like seeing his own daughter.

Now, though, he is showing great interest in the extra-ordinary experience that Sinead and I have just undergone over the past two weeks: in the wildlife I've encountered, the amazing rainforests we walked through, in the intensity of the jungle. Deep down, though, I know that all he really wants to know is how my job is going, if I've found the love of my life yet and if I'm going to 'settle down' and give him a grandchild one day soon.

He flicks a cigarette into a home-made ashtray and I can smell beer on his breath from where I sit but, as always, beneath his devilment and periods of absence that sometimes last for years, I always find his charm so endearing and his humour tickling and contagious, even if he sometimes annoys the hell out of me with his flippant ways.

'You're the image of your mother when she was your age, Kate. God help you,' he says as he sniffs, a habit that again I associate only with him. 'I'm joking, you know that, pet. Your mum was a cracker and still is.'

'She'll crack you if she finds you smoking in her kitchen,' says Shannon, always one step ahead of all of us. 'Try and compliment your way out of that one, you old charmer.'

Shannon may not be related to my dad through blood, but they have always had a great bond and banter that entertains me every time we're all together, which isn't as often as I wish it could be.

'Jesus, Peter, put the fag out,' says Mo when she breezes through with a stack of washing in a basket. 'Mum will freak out if she doesn't smell washing powder and fresh linen when she comes back here. You're pushing it and you know you are!'

Dad does what he is told and sheepishly goes out to the garden to finish his cigarette, while Shannon and Maureen open windows and do their best with air fresheners to disguise his bad habit which makes me sneeze uncontrollably.

I've had a really bad headache since I landed into Belfast Airport, having taken the opportunity to pop home for the evening while Sinead made her way back to Dublin for a shift in the hospital, but I haven't been feeling myself at all.

'So how's lover boy been coping with you away trekking in the jungle?' Mo asks me as she loads the washing machine.

I stutter, trying to find my response. After my mum's subtle but stern warning about our very different backgrounds, I try not to talk about David to my family, though I did let it slip before I left for Africa that he'd called his wedding off, and Mo put two and two together and suggested it might have been something to do with me.

'*What?*' asks Shannon, while I eyeball her directly, pleading for her to be quiet. 'Kate, are you and the ice-cream shop boy an item?'

'No!' I say, giving her a look to quickly zip it.

I can see my dad make his way back inside and I feel hotter and hotter by the second. I'm hoping my hot and cold flushes are not health related and are just from the intensity of keeping mine and David's new, if still pending, relationship status a secret from the vultures in my neighbourhood. I can't afford to be sick. David and I have waited for these summer months and we've so much planned for once he finishes school this week.

'So, darling daughter, can I take you for a drink before you go back to Dublin?' my dad asks when he comes back

223

inside, the waft of tobacco following him again being enough to send our Maureen into another spin of air freshener. 'How about you and I go for a pint? Maureen and Shannon can come too if they want to join us? It's a beautiful day for a beer garden.'

I feel so shivery now and my head is fuzzy. I quickly check my phone and see a flurry of messages from David, as I expected I would by now, but all I want to do is lie down in bed and sleep off my exhaustion. Our tropical holiday was extremely enjoyable, but also very full on, as Sinead and I stuck to a very action-packed itinerary in Africa.

My dad waits for my answer.

'I'm sorry, Dad, I'm absolutely knackered,' I try to explain to him gently. 'I'm going to have to go and lie down a while, but thanks for calling by to see us. Do you mind? We'll do it next time, I promise.'

He pats his pockets, searching for his keys, and he gives me one of his twinkling smiles from beneath his scruffy beard.

'Are you happy, my girl?' he asks me at the front door before he leaves, a question he has asked me so many times from the day I was born and I already know what his next response will be.

'I will be after I catch up on some sleep,' I tell him, longing to lie down. 'But yes, Dad. I'm really happy with my lot. I've a good life. I'm in a really nice place in here.'

I point to my head and to my heart in a gesture that we always share.

'Then I'm happy too,' he says to me, thumping his chest, and he gives me a hug before he leaves. My father's hugs, though he is always a little bit rough around the edges in his appearance and outlook, with his unruly greying beard and unkempt ways, are always so genuine and heartfelt to me, and I nuzzle into him feeling like I'm just a child again. He hasn't always been present or consistent in my life, but I've learned so much from him and I've also learned to forgive him for his weaknesses. As a fully grown adult myself now, I can accept him as a person in his own right with flaws and not just as my father.

And the truth is, out of all my family – Mum, Maureen and young Shannon – my dad is the one who can always read me the best. When I tell him I'm happy, he knows that I'm telling the truth.

'You've love in your eyes, girl,' he says with a smile as he leaves the front door of our terraced home for his flat across town. 'He's a lucky beggar, whoever he is. He'd better treat you like a queen.'

'He does, Daddy,' I tell him, lighting up when I think of David and how I've planned to spend a glorious weekend with him when his school term ends next week, then a dread fills my stomach as I fear for how I might never be able to introduce the two main men in my life for fear that – if they ever crossed paths in person – there might be fireworks, at least on my dad's part. He would be shocked to the core if he heard I'd fallen in love with someone from David's part of town, not to mention the son of the renowned bigot Bob Campbell, who my mum claims isn't as pure as he might lead everyone to believe. This is not just about religion or politics, it's about a deep opposition that has haunted our small town since for ever and, unfortunately for David and me, we are from different ends of the spectrum.

'Do I know him?' he asks, his sparkling eyes lighting up. My stomach flips.

'Er, I'm not sure,' I say, my pounding head getting worse by the second at the idea of telling the truth. 'I'll fill you in some day when I'm feeling a bit better.'

He leaves and I fall into bed in Maureen's room. When David calls me, I can barely find the energy to hold the phone to my ear.

At the sound of his voice, I drift away to a place where I'm with him in real life properly, without this pretence and denial to our families, without this distance, in a world where his parents accept me and mine accept him and welcome our growing love with delight.

'I'm glad to be back, David, but the truth is I'm exhausted,' I confess to him. 'I wish I could magic myself back quickly to my own bed in Dublin, and to the weekend when we'll be together properly at last.'

'It's been a long two months,' he says in agreement, 'but

I've my new little place well lived in by now here in Bromley and, with school ending next week, we've a whole summer to spend together in Dublin if that's still what you want?'

'It's still what I want for sure,' I tell him, allowing for just this moment to forget about the tension this whole reality might bring to us. 'I can't wait.'

In the eight or so weeks since David called off his wedding and left to go and pick up the pieces of his life in England, to find a new place to live and finish his school term, we've been talking like lovers even though we've really only spent one night together, but what a night it was. Lying in David's strong, sexy arms was like floating on a cloud, feeling his skin on mine was like my whole world was safe and complete, and when he kissed me properly for the first time I knew we were meant to be.

It was electrifying, it was soft, sensual and time-stopping, and I knew right then I wanted to be with him, even if we had to fight the world to make it happen.

'I want that more than anything,' I tell him, wanting so badly to fast forward to the day when I would be able to feel him in my arms again. 'Hurry up and get here. I want us to be in the same place at the same time once and for all.'

DAVID

'Are you going to see your *girlfriend*?' Stacy, one of my A-level students asks me as we finish up on our last day of term. 'Brianna is so jealous. She really fancies you, sir.'

'They all fancy you,' says Edward, one of my top pupils who is normally also the quietest. 'They think you're hot. Even the other teachers do. We think Miss Harper is in love with you too.'

'Now, now, that's enough!' I tell my three eager students, who are swarming around me like bees round a honeypot as I do my best to disguise my delight that today has finally come. 'You've all a whole summer ahead to get all that built-up adrenaline out of your system. I'll see you in September, OK?'

But there is no hiding it from anyone as I stroll out of school, saying goodbye to my team in the science department and to my groups of eager students, that I am like the cat that has got the cream.

I'm mad to see Kate and I can't disguise how I'm now counting down the hours to my flight the next morning.

We are a perfect fit, if there's such a thing. Well, we are perfectly imperfect, as we both know the challenges that lie ahead when we break the news to our families that we are more than good friends, but I'm actually looking forward to the day I tell the world of my love for her. I want to tell everyone soon, but Kate keeps urging me to wait until the time is right for proper introductions. For me, it can't come soon enough. And neither can tomorrow until I'm on that plane to see her.

'You didn't tell me you played tennis?' I say to Kate when she presents me with a tennis racket on the second day of our long-anticipated weekend together. We've spent most of our time since I got here chilling out, in bed, eating takeaway food and hiding away from the outside world, but now it's time to get up and get out of the apartment for a while and Kate's idea of fun for today is – it seems – to play tennis.

She wears a tiny skirt that shows off her tanned legs from her recent holiday, and the sliver of the white scar that travels up the back of her calf and up the side of her thigh only makes her more breathtaking to me.

'There's a lot about me you still don't know, David Campbell,' she says, thrusting the racket into my hand. I put my hand on her waist and she runs her finger down my chest. 'Are you any good?'

She bites her lip and does a thing where she looks up at me from beneath her eyelashes, and tilts her head to the side.

'I'm pretty good, yeah,' I tell her. 'You?'

She shrugs. 'I'm good.'

We stare for a moment, teasing and taunting in a game that has already begun.

'OK, let's do this,' I tell her, leaving her thirsty for more. 'I'll give you a good run, that's for sure.'

'I bet you will,' she says, and leads me out of the apartment and into her car, where we drive the five kilometres to a local tennis club, her tiny white skirt bouncing as she skips along in front of me, showing me the way.

Moments later we're on the court and, after a few practice rallies, the competition heats up between us as our shots become harder, faster and trickier, and we sprint and chase until we are both breathless. Kate stands opposite me, our stances mirror-like with feet apart, hips bent forward as we wait for the ball to come our way.

'Harder!' she calls to me from the far side of the court. 'Don't be afraid of giving me your best shot, David! I can take it, you know!'

I shake my head.

'It's not the first time you've said that to me!' I say as I stretch and serve with a bit more force this time. The shorts I brought with me for the weekend ride up my leg and I catch her staring in that direction several times.

In turn, the sight of her in her purple vest against the white of her skirt leaves my head spinning as much as the ball does as it hurtles towards me. I see a fiercely competitive glint in her eyes as we bat back and forth, game after game.

'Faster this time!' I shout to her as she bounces the ball, her eyes glancing my way with a light smile but a gritty expression that shows she means business. 'Get on top, Kate! I thought you were going to whip my ass!'

'Oh, I can do that for sure!' she calls in return.

I twirl the racket in my hands and sway from side to side, bent over as I await her next move, doing my best to focus on the game and not the anticipation it's bringing our way.

The net and distance that divides us creates a barrier that only makes me want her more, yet represents so much that still sits between us. I know all about her mother's past now, about how she was arrested and convicted for hiding arms intended for paramilitary use all those years ago, but those days are gone now, thank God. I know about her dad and how he drifts in and out of her life, yet she idolizes him and she lights up when she talks about him. Her family have been forced apart but are a tight unit, whereas mine are forced together but fragmented and weak in comparison, and while we've no doubt a battle ahead when we come out in public with our flourishing romance, I know every risk we take will be worth it.

'Well done, Lieutenant!' she says when I ram the ball a little too hard in her direction to take the final game, set and match. 'To be honest this whole idea was just an excuse to get you hot and sweaty in a pair of shorts.'

We walk towards the net and shake hands, her eyes smouldering when she addresses me by a title I haven't heard in a very long time. She pulls my arm over and tenderly kisses it where my own scars of that awful day riddle my skin.

'Lieutenant?' I repeat, and she gives me a sultry salute in return. 'And what would your daddy say if he knew you were getting hot and sweaty with someone like me?'

I pull her gently towards me, our hands gripped together across the net; she is so close I feel her breath on my face. Her cheeks are pink and damp, I can feel a river of sweat on my back and the adrenaline of the physical activity on the court only heightens the desire we both feel when we're together.

'My daddy doesn't need to know what we get up to,' she whispers. 'No one does. Now, let's go home. I think we both need a long shower. Together.'

'I think that's a really good idea and very badly needed for sure,' I respond, as our lips almost touch. There are people waiting to get onto our court and we have to step back from each other to contain ourselves. 'Let's go home and shower.'

But I seriously doubt we'll make it past the bedroom.

15.

KATE

The summer rattles by in a flurry of day trips away with David, hotel stays on my days and nights off from work. As August rolls in, I'm excited to get to see some of the places David calls home when we make the trip to England together so he can take part in a charity rugby game in Bromley.

'Good luck,' I mouth to him from the stands when he steals a look my way as he runs onto the pitch. I bite my nails in anticipation as I watch him warm up on the sideline, his strong thighs on show; the way his blue and white jersey clings to his skin makes my own skin tingle.

He commands a presence on the pitch just as I feel he does in his everyday life. The more we spend time together, the more attracted I am to him, not only to his physical being but to his integrity, his beautiful mind and his critical thinking.

I love how he reads to me when he comes across something interesting, how he plays me his favourite James Taylor songs and then listens to my own chosen artists with the same interest, and how he tells me the most random pieces of information he hears on the news. We make plans for the future, we talk about where we might one day live, we describe our dream home and we even decorate our very own virtual bedroom that we'll have when we get together properly at last.

'You should be a storyteller,' I tease him when he reads me out some trivia from the newspaper one afternoon. 'Your voice is like Liam Neeson's. Now, there's a compliment and a half.'

'You're very, very funny,' he replies, too bashful to agree.

We can argue too, and he doesn't let me get away with anything, which both challenges me and pushes me, but the huge elephant in the room is my insistence on keeping our relationship a secret from our families.

'We can't go on hiding for ever, Kate,' he told me as we lay in bed one morning in Dublin before our trip across the Irish Sea for this match. 'It will suffocate us eventually, all this sneaking around in a city so far from home. It's like we're pretending when we both know this is very, very real.'

I tried desperately to change the subject, the bile in my throat rising every time I thought of us travelling north to face the music with our families.

I imagined the pressures of my community, bringing David into our small-minded housing estate, where middle-class locals are the enemy to the low-life thugs who set up my mother, and then the look of disdain on

David's father's face if I should ever dare to darken their door again.

'It's still early days,' I told him. 'I'll go get some breakfast. What would you like?'

'What I'd like is for you to address this once and for all and stop skirting the issue!' he said, not mincing his words, his voice rising on his way to the shower. He stood at the door of my en suite, naked and confident, his face determined.

'I'm afraid to address it still, David,' I confessed to him. 'My family background is so different to yours, more different than you will ever understand. I grew up in a concrete jungle with soldiers on my front doorstep, in an overcrowded housing estate which was in a constant state of oppression, whereas you were practically born with a silver spoon in your mouth by comparison. Even now, my family live in the shadow of a very different world to yours and the life you've known. They still battle to keep their heads above water from the bad boys like Sean McGee who make the rules. Surely you understand this?'

'I think I've been very understanding for months now!' he retorted. 'This is childish, Kate. I'm not afraid of anyone in your community and I'm surprised that someone like you would let this ridiculous underworld that tries to control a tiny part of your world rule *us*. You're acting like there's never been someone like me in your family's world.'

'There hasn't,' I said, my eyes widening with honesty. 'As crazy as that might sound, it's true.'

'Wow.'

'Can we talk about this later?' I pleaded as tears sprung to my eyes. 'Please don't push me, David. I'm doing my best to deal with this before we can go totally public.'

'I'm not hiding this for much longer,' he said, and at that he stood under the shower, singing at the top of his voice, like a person who had said his piece but who didn't want to let it linger.

Now, as I stand in a cold shelter in an unknown English rugby ground, I feel a sense of freedom that I didn't even feel when we were in our cocoon in Dublin. Here, where David lives and works, we are just an ordinary couple; we can tell everyone and we don't have to worry about who might be watching or who knows who from our own part of the country. I've had dinner with his friends, we've posed for photographs that I know will never be seen at home, we kissed in public without worrying who was watching and he introduced me proudly as his girlfriend.

I look for him on the field and feel my heart soar when I spot him. For a fleeting moment in time, part of me wishes we could stay here for ever and forget the world we've left behind, but it's not as simple as that. And I know it never will be.

So instead I choose to drift and dream a little as I stand here alone, my eyes locked on the man I love more than I've ever loved anyone before. I watch as he steps backwards on the grass, as he claps his hands in preparation for the big match, as he bends forward and shouts instructions to his teammates. I watch as he pushes his hand through his hair, as he eyes up the ball in the distance, and when the whistle blows and the game begins, I feel my heart skip with anticipation as I cheer him on.

He is my man. He is my everything, and one day soon I'll find the courage not to hide us away and live the life we deserve.

The after-party celebrations take place in the rugby club's sports hall where I'm introduced to more of David's fellow teachers and some people from the chosen hospice in aid of which the game was played. As I stand there with a glass of wine in my hand, watching as David goes to accept the winner's shield, I catch the eye of one of his colleagues who makes her way across to me.

'You must be Kate?' she says to me, her hand outstretched in greeting. 'We've heard so much about you from David. It's so lovely to meet you in person!'

My eyes go wide as I wait for her to introduce herself.

'Meg Harper! Sorry, excuse my manners,' she says. 'I work with David and he talks about you a lot. I have to admit, you are the envy of a lot of ladies around these parts. He's a bit of a dreamboat!'

'I have to agree,' I say and we clink our glasses. 'It's lovely to meet you too, Meg.'

I watch as she giggles and twirls her hair, looking towards the makeshift stage where David poses for photos from eager fans and she outwardly sighs in approval. It's like a breath of fresh air to see David in this new environment, in a place where it's all about him. He seems so relaxed and different, away from the tense surroundings in which we've spent our last month together. Dublin may be a big city and is miles from the segregation we grew up with, and deep down I know that no one knows or cares who or what we are there, but here we can just be ourselves and I can see David truly shine, which makes me appreciate him even more.

'He does so much charity work for our school, and now he's doing this for the hospice,' Meg drools. 'Honestly, we are all in awe of his generosity, and his organization skills are impeccable. He's such an asset. Don't be stealing him away from us now!'

She lightly taps my arm, and I don't need to hear any more of how much he is thought of here as I can feel it in the air.

I can feel it in my bones too, because he only has to glance my way and I feel goose bumps. I'm a very lucky lady, and suddenly it hits me that I need to come clean at home or I fear I might risk losing him one day when the pressure gets too much. I can't ever take him for granted. I need to sort out our real life world, and fast.

'Hey handsome,' I say, when he eventually makes his way past his admirers to find me with his colleague. He wears a black T-shirt and jeans now after showering off the muddy rugby game and he smells like a dream. 'Were your ears burning? We were just agreeing how fantastic you are.'

He tips his head and leans in to kiss me on the cheek.

'Don't be giving me a big head,' he jokes, and I swear Meg beside me looks like she might need a fan to cool her down. 'Did you enjoy the game?'

'I enjoyed watching you, yes,' I say, also enjoying the tease as poor Meg looks on. 'I didn't really see much more than that, to be honest.'

He blushes now a little and shoots me a look not to take it any further.

'You're such a sweet couple,' Meg swoons, when David casually drapes his arm around my waist as he surveys the room and I stand beside him glowing with pride.

'Thank you,' I reply, looking up at his chiselled dark good looks and I make a wish that it could be like this all the time.

It should be, shouldn't it? It really should be like this all the time. I lean my head on his arm and hope that it will be very soon.

DAVID

'You're a life-saver, thank you!' I say to Kate the next morning when she brings me a pint of cold water and paracetamol to bed. 'How could you possibly have known?'

She slides beneath the covers beside me, and the feeling of her skin on mine soothes my busting head already, but I need to hydrate quickly so I sit up and down the water with vigour.

'I think watching you down those ghastly bright blue shots like you were a teenager last night gave me the foresight to look after you this morning,' she says, kissing my shoulder. 'It was a wonderful evening and I was so proud of you. Thanks for making me feel such a big part of it.'

I get a brief flashback of the drinks she is talking about and how we danced so closely under the flashing disco lights into the wee hours in the little sports hall, her arms entwined around my neck and mine round her waist. Part of me cringes when I realize how many of my colleagues were probably making notes when we became a bit too amorous. We couldn't help it. The adrenaline from the rugby game, the drinks and the music and having Kate so relaxed by my side made everything so perfect.

'It wouldn't have been the same without you,' I say, feeling the need to lie down again quickly. 'I can't believe how much the game managed to raise for charity.'

'It was awesome, well done to all of you,' Kate replies, running her fingers lightly along my arm. 'The whole thing inspired me, to be honest, and it was so lovely to hear everyone singing your praises. They think the world of you round here.'

It's nice to hear that from Kate. I smile in appreciation as she continues.

'It also made me realize just how lucky we are on so many levels for everything we survived, David,' she tells me softly. 'But sometimes I feel like I should be doing more, you know, just in gratitude for having this wonderful second chance at life.'

I tuck her hair behind her ear, listening with intent to what she has to say. I know exactly what she means. Surviving an atrocity like we did makes you rethink everything in life and, once my initial anger after the bomb subsided, I've had many moments of gratitude where I feel very lucky to be alive, which is why doing charity work when I can feels so fulfilling.

'What do you have in mind?' I ask her with a smile. 'A skydive? A bungee jump? A sponsored walk?'

She pauses and looks at me intently then lightly slaps my shoulder.

'Ha-ha, no I'm thinking of something much more structured and long term,' she tells me seriously now.

'I know you are, I'm teasing.'

'I'm a trained trauma nurse. Every day in work I see little children fight the biggest battles of their lives,' she says, looking at the ceiling, 'and I know that while we see how they heal on the outside, they have to heal so much on the inside too, so I'd love to help fund a way for them to do that, you know?'

I nod in agreement. I know the physical scars we both still bear are incomparable to the trauma in the minds of so many others who experienced the bomb that day.

'I love the idea of planning something permanent, you know, to give something back in a way,' I say to her. 'Maybe we could do something together?'

She looks lost in thought and I can feel her energy rise as her plans start to shape up in her mind.

'Sorry, what did you say?' she asks when she catches me trying to read her mind.

'Nothing, I'm just thinking along with you,' I tell her, letting her go back to her own train of thought. 'I know you'd lead a great campaign for trauma victims. You'd be perfect at it.'

Her eyes widen.

'Silent Steps!' she says. 'How does that sound? You know, to represent the quiet little steps we take towards our future that say big things.'

'Yes, Silent Steps,' I whisper, and she looks at me in return as though she's just won the lottery. 'For sure.'

'That's it!' she says, sitting up on the bed now. 'That's perfect! I can keep it general like that and fundraise under that umbrella name for all victims of trauma, of all ages and from all walks of life. I could talk to them about my own experiences and how I've learned to deal with both the physical and mental scars since the bomb. I really want to do this, David. I have a big story to tell and I know I can help others!'

'You sure do,' I say in bewilderment, as I wait for her to acknowledge that I too have a story, quite a similar one, and have loads of experience by now in fundraising, but she is already miles ahead of me. I wait for her to suggest we could work on it together around our day jobs. It could be a project for us both to get our teeth into and I know it could be life changing for so many who could benefit.

But she doesn't, and once again I'm reminded that we are miles away from ever doing anything properly together in public as far as Kate can see. I feel my stomach twitch and I swallow hard as she goes off on an excited ramble about her plans.

'I could work with schools and hospitals, plus there are so many community groups my mum has been helping out with, so they would be a perfect audience too for what I'd have to say,' she tells me. 'What do you think, David? Do you think it sounds good?'

'I think you'd be amazing,' I tell her, biting my tongue.

'What's wrong?' she asks.

'Nothing is wrong, Kate,' I say, getting up from the bed. I need more water. 'I think it's a fantastic idea. You'll be wonderful.'

I feel her eyes on me as I leave the room, and when I get to the top of the stairs I stop and take a deep breath, feeling a fizz of frustration run through my veins.

It's not the charity work – or that she wants to do it alone

– that bothers me at all deep down. In fact, I'm delighted to see her so passionate. For her to go off and do her own thing in any field if it makes her happy, but I'm not sure how much longer I can tolerate being totally invisible in Kate's real world or her long-term plans. This has hit a nerve; it's a reminder that that's exactly what I am for now: a secret.

It's surely a road to nowhere for our so-called relationship, but for now I'll be excited for her. As hurtful as it might be sometimes, I'll do my best to swallow my pride and support her every step of the way.

'Where are you going?' I hear her call after me just before I slam the door behind me, leaving it too late to give her an answer. I need some fresh air. I need to go for a long walk, and most of all I need to take some time out from being a secret.

JANUARY 2010

16.

KATE

You could hear a pin drop in the audience in the Dublin community hall where I'm launching my brand-new venture. I've notes in front of me, but I haven't really needed them, as – after lots of planning – I knew exactly what I wanted to say. I am coming to the end of my debut speech.

'I honestly thought at one point the doctors were trying to kill me, even though they were doing everything in their power to save my life,' I explain to the gathered crowd of potential volunteers and local media. 'That's how frightened I was back then. I was so, so scared that I thought the people who were trying to save me, who were trying to build me back together, were trying to kill me.

'Like so many others I'll never forget the horror of that day,' I tell them. 'I've looked death straight in the eyes and I've constantly asked myself since – why on earth am I still here?'

I pause.

I've practised every word of this speech so many times. I look at the audience, making eye contact with several of them.

'And I am grateful every single day for this second chance,' I continue, 'so from now on I aim to try and help others through this brand-new umbrella charity organization I've set up called Silent Steps. Please join me in my local campaign to help others overcome trauma, so their new world can be a better place and so their futures can be as positive and fruitful as possible.'

The audience applaud me with great vigour and I fill up with adrenaline at what I've just achieved. My heart is thumping, I thought at one stage I wouldn't be able to find my breath, but I just focused on David who sits in the audience willing me on, and now I have managed to get through my speech just as I'd planned.

David had been with me when I first thought of Silent Steps; it has been his drive and ambition that has inspired me to keep pushing it forward, and yet he is willing to sit back and let me take centre stage.

'You totally rocked it, babe!' he whispers into my ear when I find him in the audience. 'You're amazing! Once you're finished up here let's go celebrate! Dinner and drinks are on me!'

'And dancing,' I tell him, still totally buzzing inside as a few journalists approach me to ask a few questions. 'Don't forget how you promised me dancing.'

David playfully rolls his eyes. He looks so damn sexy in his white shirt and faded denims and I can't wait to get my hands on him properly.

'I'll think about it,' he teases. 'Although, I'll be saving my best moves for the bedroom later.'

A journalist approaches us, meaning David is saved by the bell when it comes to his commitment for now to go dancing, which is now a bit of a running joke between us. He always gives in, and we've spent so many nights on the dance floors of bars and clubs in both Dublin and London as our relationship has gone from strength to strength and become hotter and hotter as we continue our long-distance romance.

'Kate, my name's Jen from the local *Herald*,' the lady explains. 'Can I just ask you to come this way for a quick photo? Maybe we could get a shot of you over here by your banners and merchandise?'

'Of course, that would be fantastic!' I say, delighted to have such a positive response to my campaign launch. I stand up to make my way to where a photographer awaits.

'Is this your partner?' Jen asks me, referring to David. 'It would be great to get you both together. It would be nice to have a glimpse into your everyday life behind the bigger campaign.'

David looks at me and I bite my lip.

'Er,' I mumble.

'No, no, I'll step back for this one,' he says, and I can feel his hurt radiate right through my bones. 'This is Kate's moment. It's her time to shine. I'll sit this one out, but thanks for asking.'

I walk across the community hall with my heart feeling heavy. Standing for the photo, I urge myself to smile but tears prick my eyes. I want to have David in the photo so badly. I want him by my side today in a way he should be, so proud and so very much part of this campaign's growth to date.

But he can't. And that's all down to me.

'I'm so sorry.'

I hear my heels click on the pavement as we make our way outside.

'It's fine. Don't mention it again,' he says, quickening his pace as we leave the community hall for the shelter of one of our favourite Dublin pubs.

'But—'

'Honestly, just leave it, Kate,' he says tartly. 'This is an evening of celebration. We can talk about it some other time. Not tonight.'

I drop the subject and we eventually spend the evening laughing, eating and drinking around Dublin, and when my guilt subsides about the photo incident and I accept that David really does want to park it until another time, we once more become so carefree and light on our feet in reflection of how far we have come over twelve months and I'm reminded of how deeply we have fallen in love.

David has been my backbone, cheering me on every step of the way as my dream of launching my own charity came to life. We have never felt more together. He believes in me, and I in turn believe in him, even when he decided to register again with the RAF as a part-time reservist. He also wants to give something back, by carrying out humanitarian aid missions to war-torn countries; even though it means more time apart, it makes me admire him even more.

We have both experienced life so close to the edge, and we are both determined now to do more than ever to help others.

Between our relentless work schedules as I juggle my time around my nursing commitments and charity planning, visiting him in England when I can and welcoming him to Dublin on his time off from school or RAF commitments, we do the usual things any other couples do. We go dancing, we go to the cinema, we go ice skating and mountain climbing, we go running together and we go swimming in lakes. All this feeds our thirst for adventure, and gives a two-finger signal to all the elements that have threatened our very existence, including the demons that still live in David's head and that creep up on him from time to time.

I know there's still some darkness in there about to explode and I know that a lot of it has got to do with my silence over who we really are and what we mean to each other in public.

It's not David's fault, it's totally mine, and I can feel it threatening to boil over more and more as we become closer and closer.

The morning after my debut public speech, David brings me coffee as I lie in bed in an afterglow. We have just one more day together before he jets off from Dublin on an aid mission to bring supplies to the victims of the devastating earthquake in Haiti. We snuggle between the covers and talk, as we often do, about our future.

'Are you happy, Kate?' he asks me, and I know exactly what he is getting at. We still haven't gone public as a couple at home among our own people, sticking to my terms of coming and going from Dublin and London.

When my cousin got married in November, I went there alone. When David's aunt passed away in mid-December, I didn't accompany him to the funeral. I pretended to my mum and sister that I was working so David and I could spend our first Christmas Day together and, when our families ask questions about our love life, we brush any suggestions off. I play it down as well when Mo gets too inquisitive, denying we even keep in touch any more, never mind share a bed and a deep love together.

I prefer it this way to ease any outside influences or pressures, but I know we can't go on like this for ever.

'I'm happy for now, yes,' I tell him as I stare at the ceiling in my bedroom, but in truth I'm really beginning to wish things were different.

I'm fed up with sharing an apartment in Dublin with anyone other than David. I'm fed up with tearful airport scenes and Skype calls, when all I need is a hug from only him, and most of all I'm fed up with myself for not being braver like he is when it comes to telling the world how much we love each other.

The bomb changed my whole outlook on life; it lit a fire in my belly to do even more to test the strength of the person I can become, by making my mark on this world in every way I can. So why can't I be honest about the person who means more to me than anyone else ever will?

Where I'm the public speaker, David is the engine room. Where I'm the hands-on carer, David is the wind in my sails when I wobble, and when I'm the opinionated know-it-all, he's the brooding, thoughtful and quiet deep thinker whose words and knowledge could sum me up in seconds. He is inner and I am outer, he is the one with whom my soul connects, yet he is the one I'm letting down the most.

'I'm not happy, Kate,' he tells me as we both lie side by side, which takes my breath away. 'I don't want this to be a secret any more and I know you don't either. I don't think this is healthy at all. I couldn't even stand beside you in a photo yesterday for something we both believe in. It's crazy. It's so wonderful on the surface, but beneath it all I feel we're struggling already and it's going to smother us one day.'

I lean on my elbow to face him and I can see his mouth twitch as a million thoughts go through his head.

'We're hardly a *total* secret, David!' I say with a lilt in my voice, trying to play it all down, even though deep down I feel exactly the same. 'All my friends here in Dublin know about us and they adore you, especially Sinead who thinks you're almost as wonderful as I do.'

'That's not what I mean and you know it.'

'I've met loads of your teaching colleagues in England,' I say, again trying to play it all down. 'It's not like we're sneaking around like two love-struck teenagers from across the barricades when we're here on a normal day, is it? Yesterday was a one-off. I know you were upset and that it isn't exactly the norm, but we have good reason, at least for now.'

'Good reason?' he says looking my way. 'What is this good reason, Kate? The big bad boys up in the north are going to be upset because a wee Catholic girl from the housing estate is going out with a Protestant whose da is a bit of a Bible-bashing mouthpiece? I'm thirty-three years old, not some teenager growing up in the 1980s! This is a joke and you are making it so!'

'I'm sorry,' I whisper, as guilt ripples through me. I know he's right. I know we can't go on like this for much longer.

We lie there for a moment in silence, his rapid breathing catching my attention. I understand his anger and I feel it too, but I just can't imagine the day when this will all be acceptable. Could we really walk around our home town with our heads held high – the daughter of a Republican prisoner and the son of a church minister who has his own staunch beliefs on the opposing side?

I could, I tell myself. I could if it meant the alternative was losing David.

'Look, when you put it like that, it does sound a bit ridiculous,' I agree with a sigh. 'I'm sorry for letting this drag on for so long. I really am and I don't want it to smother us, ever.'

I take a moment to admire him as he lies there, even though I can feel a storm brewing inside of him. I know all the signs when his anger and frustration start to build up. He goes quiet, then he disappears for a while, and before I know it he's spilling out a rage that bubbles from deep within.

His dark hair is still damp from the shower; his heavy eyelashes that frame his blue eyes flicker on his face as he blinks back his frustration. His tanned, muscular arms lie above the snow-white duvet and his golden skin glistens in the morning sun.

He is my whole world, and I want more for us as much as he does, but I'm just so afraid of it all going wrong.

'I need you to know, once and for all, I'm not afraid of any of that shit, Kate.'

'I know you aren't but—'

'But nothing!' he interrupts me. 'We are bigger than that. We live in different times than your parents and mine did, thank God. I want us both to go together to see them and face the music. Let's get this all out in the open once and for all and suck up the consequences, whatever they may be.'

I close my eyes, trying to picture the scene. I imagine the Sean McGees of my world and how they would torment me if they found out. He may be a waste of space in my eyes, but he has an influence and an ignorance that wouldn't stop him from hurting me, David or – worse – one of my own family, just to stake his claim on what he believes to be right or wrong.

'David, my mother served time in prison for doing something which is the direct opposite of what people like your father believe in,' I say, feeling tears of frustration prick my eyes. 'We couldn't be more different if we tried on that level. We have to take it slowly.'

'I don't care any more!' he pleads. 'I want you to meet my mother and I want to meet yours. I'd love to meet Shannon again. Can't you understand that? This is not normal! It's so far from normal and it's going to eat us up inside, no matter how much we just choose to float along and wait for a magic wand to make it all better!'

I get out of the bed and go to the window, wrapping a towel around me on the way. I stand there, looking out on the tree-lined streets I've called home since I moved out of my place with Sam. It feels like a lifetime ago. It feels like a different me.

We both have come so far, and we deserve so much more than what I've allowed for us. It's been totally my decision to put a cap on how public we are, and I hate myself for being such a coward.

'You are absolutely right,' I tell him, deciding once and for all to rise above my fears.

'What?'

'I'm saying you're right. When you come back from Haiti, we'll travel home together and we'll visit your parents and mine in a united front,' I say, trying not to imagine it in reality as it makes me so nervous. 'The one thing I believe in more than anything is me and you.'

I turn to him and all I want to do is lie beside him and wish this all away.

'Are you sure?' he asks me.

'Yes, I'm sure,' I say, slipping back beneath the covers, beside the warmth of his manliness that makes me feel so safe and secure always. 'Let's tell our families when we get home and we'll plan our future properly at last.'

DAVID

'How about, the first one to get a proper job that's worth-while on either side of the pond makes the move?' Kate says just before I leave as she steps our plans up a gear at last. 'I'll start looking up nursing jobs in the wider London area and I'll have a look at science teaching posts for you here in Dublin as an alternative. I'm excited.'

I put my arms around her small waist and pull her close to me, hoping that a day will come when this won't be part of our normal routine. My decision to sign up as a reserve for a year was only to gain some wider aid experience, as our bigger plan is to grow Kate's charitable efforts to a much larger degree in future, a project we can easily work on together and build, with her nursing experience and my practical nature.

'That sounds like a deal,' I whisper.

'I'm going to miss you,' she says to me. 'So, so much.'

'Ditto,' I tell her.

My mission tomorrow to the earthquake-shattered island of Haiti is my first aid expedition with the RAF reserves out of the country since Kate and I got together, and to say I'm nervous is an understatement.

Haitian airspace is becoming dangerously congested with the vast number of aircraft trying to get to Port-au-Prince to provide assistance. There's talk of looting, of machete-wielding gangs and attacks on aid vehicles, as devastated locals panic to get supplies to their communities fast, but I'm hoping to put it all down to experience.

'This will be all worth it, I promise,' I tell her, kissing her forehead. 'When I get back, I'll come over here for the weekend again and we'll head north, clear the air, and start our proper plans to settle down together.'

Her bright eyes light up my soul.

'I've even planned baby names,' she says with a cheeky smirk.

'I bet you have,' I say, knowing she is pretending to joke but really isn't. Nothing in Kate's world goes unplanned as far as she can manage it. 'We're going to make this work, Kate. I don't care if hell or high water, bombs, illnesses or bigoted parents come between us. When I get home, this is the start of us for real.'

She leans her head onto my chest and rests it there as I stroke her hair. I can tell she is worried about this trip. The truth is I am too, as it will plunge me into horrific scenes similar to those I've experienced first-hand and worked hard to overcome, but I've committed to this now and I can't back out.

The news has been terrifying as the world's media conveys what's been happening in Haiti, and the scenes are all too familiar. There are thousands of people sitting in the streets over there with nowhere to go. Rescuers are trying to dig victims out in the dark using flashlights. Bodies covered with white dust are piled on the back of pick-up trucks as vehicles ferry the injured to hospital. It echoes desperately the carnage Kate and I witnessed together and, although I won't admit it to her, I'm dreading reliving such an atrocity.

And so we won't discuss that in detail. We'll just get this over and done with and then we'll start as we mean to go on.

'Did you say a red front door or a green front door in our dream home?' she asks me playfully as I walk down the steps of her apartment to the taxi waiting to take me to the airport once more.

'Red!' I call back to her.

'Green!' she says in typical protest.

I glance back as she waves at me in her dressing gown, a picture of beauty that I carry with me everywhere.

'I love you, Kate!'

'I love you more, David!' she says to me, and I leave for the unknown territory I've pledged to, but also knowing one thing for sure.

The whole world stops, yet passion and ideas come to life when I'm with Kate Foley, and I can't wait to get back to stop the clocks and make more magic with her again.

17.

KATE

I watch the world news on television when I come back from work after a particularly trying shift. Sitting there, my mouth is open in awe and I'm frozen to my armchair as the scenes of destruction in Haiti are played out in front of me on screen.

I can taste the smoke in my mouth, I can smell the blood, and I can feel the fear for real as battered and bloodstained bodies are piled high in the streets. Rescuers have been forced to dig through the rubble with their bare hands to free trapped survivors.

My heart thumps for David, so far away amidst a natural disaster that measured 7.2 on the Richter scale, leaving up to half a million people dead, with aid workers missing and frantic family members screaming out for loved ones who are long disappeared.

'Oh, David, you shouldn't be there!' I gasp, fearing for the post-traumatic stress and flashbacks he will suffer when he sees this for real. It's all too familiar from before but it's on an even bigger scale. Schools have collapsed, hotels have collapsed, neighbourhoods have disappeared and gravely injured Haitians call out for help, their bodies covered in dust and blood, survivors holding hands and singing hymns as they wait for help to come.

I feel bile rise in the back of my throat and I check my phone to see when I'd last heard from him. It's been almost twenty-four hours since he landed in Haiti, and on his first phone call he sounded traumatized just as he was bound to be with such harrowing scenes.

'I spoke to a little boy,' he told me, 'I think his name was Reuben, who was looking for his father in the rubble but his father was dead.'

'That's so awful,' I said to him. 'Please stay safe.'

He took his time to speak again.

'We're arranging to get him to Fort Lauderdale, working with the US forces to reunite him with some family there, but his eyes will haunt me for ever,' he told me. 'I tried to distract him by telling him stories about airplanes and machinery as he seemed so interested and gave him a chocolate bar and my badge. It's heartbreaking, Kate, but I'm glad I came here.'

He sounded exhausted but strong and determined.

'I'm so proud of you,' I told him. 'But please come home safe.'

'Don't worry, I will,' he replied, but that was almost a day ago.

As the news unfolds it's frightening me more and more, giving me the most horrendous gut feeling as stories emerge of UN aid workers, Red Cross volunteers and many other helpers being caught up in the destruction as buildings continue to collapse and after-shocks ripple through the country. The scale of the devastation is unimaginable.

I'm still waiting for news from David when Sinead arrives in from work, rummaging through cupboards for a late-night snack as she normally does.

'Any word yet from him?' she asks me, and I shake my head.

'Ah Kate, try not to panic. It's pretty normal, right?' she says, sitting on the arm of the chair beside me. 'I mean, he's in a very different world at the minute, so making phone calls or sending texts isn't going to be something he can do very often. David's a bit of an action-man hero, isn't he? He'll be fine and he'll be back soon.'

'I know that, but I've just got an eerie feeling, Sinead, and I'm not going to settle until I hear from him.'

I toss and turn and barely sleep a wink when I'm eventually forced to bed by Sinead, and when I do wake up the next morning I get an international call to say that my instinct was right.

My blood runs cold. I've always had this underlying fear that as soon as David and I are happy and settled together, something awful is going to happen to destroy it all.

'Is this Kate Foley?' a strange voice on the phone asks me.

'Yes,' I say, sitting up on the bed and gripping the covers until my knuckles turn white. 'What's happened? Oh God, what's happened to him?'

'It's David, yes,' the man says. 'Try not to panic. He's going to be fine, but he's been injured and has a badly broken leg. We were caught up in a looting gang desperate for medication, but David is being stabilized before we can fly him home. We'll get him home to you very, very soon.'

I've no idea who I'm speaking to. I can hardly hear him with all the thoughts and fears going through my head.

I knew it. I just knew it. When he hurts, I hurt. I just knew it.

'Oh David, oh God you scared me so much!' I scream into nowhere, and Sinead comes running to my side.

I can't breathe.

'He's coming home,' she whispers. 'Come on, that's my girl. You're going to be strong for him like you always are. Big deep breaths. He's coming home.'

After a cup of hot sweet tea, a shower and a fresh change of clothes, I call my boss to explain what has happened and request some annual leave, then I fly to London as soon as I can get organized and go straight to David's apartment. I plan to be there when he arrives back on home turf.

I know his physical injuries aren't extreme, but I fear for what this will do to awake the sleeping demons in his own mind from the bomb, and when he is dropped off the following morning, hobbling on crutches and with a bandage on his arm, the same arm I bandaged up with my coloured neck scarf in a bloodied doorway when we were so much younger, I burst into tears.

'We can't go on like this, David,' I tell him, shaking my head as I wait with my arms open to greet him. 'No more of this. Please, no more.'

He wraps his arms around me, letting the crutch go as he does, and I can smell fire and danger on his skin. I cup his beautiful face and look into his glistening eyes.

'I will never leave you again,' he promises, and I know I'll look after him with all my heart. 'It was a crazy idea to begin with, but I thought I was doing the right thing. We've suffered enough trauma, Kate. It's over.'

I take him inside and spend the next few days tending to him, washing him and cooking for him. We watch trashy TV and listen to our favourite songs as he heals on the outside, but I know that on the inside he has seen far too much in his lifetime.

'Should we try and come over to see you?' his mother asks him when he talks to her on the phone. She too has been frantic with worry, and a little bit angry at him too for reopening old wounds, quite literally, by putting himself forward for such a mission in the first place, plus on top of her ongoing health struggles it was a stress she didn't need.

'No, no, please don't worry, Mum,' he tells her. 'I'm being very well looked after by Kate and we both plan to come home and see you all as soon as I'm back on my feet.'

'Kate?' his mother asks him, a rise of delight in her voice.

'Yes, Kate Foley, my girlfriend,' he says, giving me a cheeky look of defiance as he sits with his broken leg resting on the sofa. 'But let me tell Dad in person all about her when we get home. I'll look forward to introducing you all in person.'

I spend the next few days tucked up with David in his apartment in Bromley, and I spend my days job-seeking for the future, as well as making sure David has all he needs. I shop for food, I drive him to the nearby parks where we feed the ducks in the winter sun and, when it snows heavily at the weekend, he watches me build a snowman at the front of his apartment block, taking photos as he does and laughing as I pretend to pelt him with snowballs at the window.

I bathe him and wash his hair by candlelight and to the soothing sounds of his favourite James Taylor songs; he reads me poetry in bed and my heart feels so full that I know I never want to be apart from him again.

'I'm looking forward to getting back to the classroom in a few weeks,' he tells me as I'm drifting off to sleep one night, so desperately grateful to have his teaching job to look forward to after his period of leave is up. 'It's science and cheeky teenagers for me from now on, Kate. No more heroic missions or action-man adventures. I know for sure where my heart lies and it's firmly here with you, not trekking across the world on a plane. I'm so sorry for putting you through all that worry.'

'I'm so glad to hear you say that,' I reply, lost in a floating haze with his arms wrapped around my waist as we spoon in the luxury of his king-size bed, just the two of us as the rest of the world does its own thing. 'It's me and you from now on, David, and that's all we need. Let's never forget it again.'

I decide there and then that I can't go back to Dublin while David is living and working here in England, in a place where we can totally be ourselves with no hiding, no worrying about what others might think and no pressure to fear how we might upset others.

One of us has to make a move and that someone is going to be me. I'm serving my notice, both at work in Dublin and with my apartment, and then I'm coming back here to stay with David once and for all.

DAVID

'What is it with my limbs that I seem to attract such drama?' I joke as we leave the fracture clinic on an afternoon in early April when I have my cast removed from my now fully healed leg. 'I mean, as if this poor arm hasn't suffered enough, I get to thrash it again, but now you and I are both even in the broken leg stakes.'

Kate links her arm through mine as we walk towards the car park. She's settling in really well over here and we're about to embark on a whole new chapter of our lives once more, but this time, we're together at last.

'I don't know what it is with either of us, but what I do know is that if I'm going to work here in this hospital from next week on, I certainly do not want to be passing you in the corridors ever,' Kate jokes with me.

We stand outside the hospital and look up at the children's wing in the distance, where she will soon start as a nurse after sailing through a job interview and clinching a post in a new and exciting role.

'I'm still going to keep up some charity work and public speaking, so I'll be keeping my ear to the ground for that,' she tells me as we make our way to the car. 'I'm thinking my next element of Silent Steps will be focused on an awareness of childhood trauma, you know, in line with what Shannon experienced at such a young age. She's turned out such a dream, but I know for so many others such scenes can haunt them for ever.'

I know exactly what she means and, as I drive us out of the car park and towards the city, where we plan to have a picnic lunch in the grounds of Kensington Palace, I fear that someday Kate will realize just how much I'm battling with my own trauma inside, when she lies asleep and I lie there beside her at night with scenes of blood and carnage keeping me awake and messing with my head.

I can't tell her just how bad it gets sometimes: the night-mares, the night sweats; the times I have to slip out of the apartment in the still of night and just breathe as the darkness threatens to choke me. The fear that someone is after me for my life, the sense of hopelessness at my inner ability to take any more, and the worry that this is going to get a real grip of me one day soon.

'Today is a good day,' Kate says with a smile, oblivious to my thoughts, and she puts her hand on my leg as I drive with the windows down and the fresh air on our faces. I look across at her, sitting in the passenger seat with her eyes closed and the wind in her hair, and I remind myself just how lucky I am. As long as I can still see that, I know we are going to be just fine.

I can't wait until I see her face in just a few days on Friday, when I plan to make it so much more than just a good day.

It's the day we both go home to Ireland to see our parents, but it's also a day for a whole lot more and I can't wait to surprise her.

We arrive in Belfast early on Friday morning and set off for the coast, to a sandy hideaway I've chosen as the perfect location for what I'm planning, under the guise of an excuse to see some of our own Irish countryside and coast before we face the wrath at home, where we plan to officially break the news to our parents that we are indeed a couple.

Kate's face is full of wonder as we park up the car in view

of the famous Carrick-a-Rede rope bridge in the distance, and the magnificent sights of the Causeway Coast with its breathtaking scenery reminding us that we are very much back home.

'I've no idea why you've brought me here, but I'm enjoying this sea air and all this beauty,' she says as she takes it in. 'I'd already forgotten how spectacular it is here at home. Doesn't it just fill up your soul to stand here and breathe it in?'

She turns to me to catch me staring and pushes her dark hair away from her face.

'You're beautiful,' I tell her. 'You really are so beautiful and I'm so lucky.'

She puts her hand on her slender hip and tilts her head to the side.

'What are you up to now, David Campbell?' she asks me with suspicion in her magnificent eyes. 'You're up to something, I can tell. This isn't just a detour for the sake of a detour, is it?'

I take a deep breath and put my hand into the inside pocket of my jacket as her eyes widen in front of me.

'I don't want to introduce you to my family as my girlfriend, Kate,' I say to her, emotion catching my throat so that my voice breaks a little. 'You are so much more than that and I want the world to know it.'

I take her hand and kiss it gently then, in a very carefully practised move, I flip open the box in my hand and show her the Celtic band I've had especially designed for her, with a diamond in the centre that represents all the love I have for her.

'Kate Foley, will you marry me?' I ask her, and she puts her hands to her face in delight. 'I want to spend the rest of my life with you, for ever and ever.'

She nods as tears burst from her eyes and she wraps her arms around my neck and kisses my face all over, and then we lock into each other's arms, the ring still in the box in my hand behind her back. She hasn't even looked at it yet, but that's what I love about her most.

We both have realized that nothing is bigger or more important than us just being together – especially the opinions of others any more. I kiss her fully on the lips and breathe in this wonderful moment.

'Is that a yes then?' I ask her, when we finally feel our pulses slowing down again.

'That's a million yeses, David Campbell!' she says, then she gives me the most striking stare right into my eyes that makes my breath catch in the back of my throat. 'My God, I love you so much. I love you, so, so much.'

'Let's go and tell our family our news,' I say, and I put the ring on her finger, then we walk back to the car hand in hand, feeling a new sense of confidence in our stride.

18.

KATE

David and I arrive at his parents' house on this cool April afternoon where the wind has blown cherry-blossom petals over the driveway like confetti ready to greet us. I can't help but glance at the sparkling diamond on my left hand as David drives the car beside me, and my heart swells with pride as we take this next step in our lives, one we have put off for far too long.

'They're here!'

Martha Campbell waves at us with frail excitement from the front door of the Old Rectory Manor and, just as I did the first time I came here on my own so many years ago, I can't help but gasp at such grandeur. I shudder to think how my own home, which we'll visit next, will look so humble and modest in comparison.

'Here goes,' I say to him. 'I'm nervous.'

'Don't be,' he says, kissing my hand. 'My mum is going to love you.'

We step out of the car and the light breeze blows my yellow dress into the wind as the trees rustle around us, and Mrs Campbell comes our way.

'You're so, so very welcome!' she calls as she slowly walks to greet us. She is waxy in her complexion, but her ferocity and determination to beat cancer again, now for the third time, gives me such a sense of wonder. I can tell immediately she's a very strong lady who has seen it all.

'Mum, I'm so, so delighted to finally introduce you to my beautiful fiancée, Kate,' David says, and I blink back tears at hearing him say those words for the very first time.

'Your fiancée?' she says, clasping her hands to her chest in delight. 'Oh, that's the best news and such a great surprise! When did this happen?'

'Just about an hour ago, so you're the very first person to know, Mrs Campbell,' I explain as I hold out my hand for her to see the exceptional ring David has had made for me. 'He just surprised me today on the way here when we stopped off by the Causeway, so excuse me if I'm still in shock.'

Martha Campbell shakes her head and grins as her fine blonde hair wisps out from under a coloured headscarf in the light spring breeze. She was a beauty in her day, I can tell, and she radiates glamour, warmth and sophistication, like an older Grace Kelly in her royal blue woollen dress. I can see immediately why David has so much love for her.

'I just know you two are going to adore each other,' he says with ease.

'It's so nice to meet you, Mrs Campbell,' I say to her, my flurry of nerves calming with the warmth in her eyes. 'How are you feeling?'

'Ah, I've good days and bad days, Kate, but every soldier has to fight her own battle,' she says, guiding us in through the front door of her beautiful home. 'Your father is in the drawing room, David. Go ahead on in. This is just wonderful news altogether!'

If being with Martha Campbell is like standing beneath a gentle ray of sunshine, all I can say about being in the same room as David's father is that it's like being locked up in a refrigerated room.

I could almost bet that if I blew out some breath I could see it linger in the cold air that surrounds him.

'Everything has already been decided. It was known long ago what each person would be. So there's no use arguing with God about your destiny,' he quotes to us as we sit around the dining-room table having afternoon tea. 'Ecclesiastes 6:1.'

He has become more shrunken in his old age, like an old Churchill dog squashed into his black shirt and trousers. I wonder how someone with Martha's inner and outward beauty could ever have ended up with someone as bitter and twisted as he is. David told me how he inherited money which changed him almost overnight, giving him a sense of great power and confidence towards anyone who dared go against his staunch beliefs.

'I'll cut to the chase and tell you both this,' he says, before spluttering and coughing into a handkerchief. 'I'd already heard rumours about your fledgling romance, but I decided to let fate and the hand of God take care of things, which he will of course. Whatever is meant to be is all up to him; it's not for me to interfere.'

I glance at David as I nibble on a very delicate salmon and cucumber sandwich, afraid of putting my elbows in the wrong place or saying something out of line, and terrified even more that David's frustration with his dad could blow up at any moment.

'If that makes it easier for you to swallow, then so be it,' David says, sitting back in his chair and stretching his arms up high above him. He is relatively calm so far, making him very much at home in the most exquisite surroundings, which feel like the very opposite of any sense of home I've ever known. 'Looks like news spreads as fast as it always did around here. It's good we give the locals something to gossip about.'

Reverend Campbell clasps his hands and leans his elbows on the table.

'It's not the gossips or whispers, but the sound of the underground you should be more concerned about,' old Bob says, looking directly my way. 'I did warn you many years ago, Kate. There was good reason behind my wishes and what I instructed on you that day. Did you forget what I said, or are you just ignoring it in the hope it will all go away?'

My heart jumps at the direct question and David pushes back his heavy, velvet-seated mahogany chair. I wince as it scrapes along the highly polished floor.

'You will never instruct her again!' he says, standing up. 'And don't ever speak to her in such a tone, ever!'

'Kate, why don't I show you the garden?' says Martha, ever so calmly, which indicates she has witnessed scenes like this before. 'It's so peaceful out there. Let's go for a walk.'

I stand up, not knowing what to do.

'No, Mum, I want you to hear this too,' says David, standing tall and proud beside me. He puts his arm around me and juts out his chin. 'This is it, all right? I want no more bullshit, no more threats, no more warnings. This is it. Either you accept us for who we are as a couple who will be married one day soon, or you don't. It's your call, Dad. It's black or white. I don't ever want to come here again to hear your snide quotes from the Bible or your idle warnings as you twiddle your thumbs and look down on me and Kate. You either take us as we are, or you don't. There can be no in-between.'

'Well, if it's black or white you want, then it's your choice! You can have your parents in your life, or your new fiancée!' says Reverend Campbell, trying to grasp back control of the argument, and I hear his wife gasp from across the table. 'There is no in-between, David, you're right. And it's your choice! It's us or it's her.'

He doesn't even have it in him to say my name. I want to scream at him, but I won't give him the pleasure of seeing how much he is hurting us both.

'You don't speak for me!' says Martha, her beautiful face full of scorn. 'David and Kate, he doesn't mean it and, if he does, he doesn't speak for me!'

'I do mean it this time and I speak on behalf of my family which is within my rights!' says the reverend, his voice rising. 'It's your family, David, or it's her!'

He sharply points at me this time and I jolt backwards. David clenches his fists and I hold onto his arm for fear that he might launch himself at the old man.

'How *dare* you make me choose?' he says in a tone of anger I've never heard before. 'You despicable man! I choose Kate over you and I always will! Always!'

'I expected as much,' says his father, and Martha leaves the room ahead of us in tears. 'You've always been a stubborn fool, David! You can go now. I won't be seeing either of you again.'

David pulls me close and kisses my forehead, then leads me out of the parlour, just like I was led out before, but this time, just as before, I stop to get the final word.

'He's more of a man than you ever will be,' I say to his father, unable to bite my tongue before we leave this palatial, miserable house of horrors. 'You should be ashamed of yourself, Bob Campbell. You don't even know your own wonderful son and it's your loss entirely.'

We walk away and I do my best not to let David see me cry, or indeed say I told you so. This is exactly what I feared would happen when we tried to come out in the open. It's not exactly a good start, but instead of putting me off what we set out to do today, it lights a fire inside of me. I'm ready to take on the world to fight for what we believe in – our right to be together.

DAVID

'That rotten excuse for a man wouldn't know the meaning of love if it hit him between the eyes!' I say as I thump the steering wheel in the car. 'You know what, I'm fucking glad to have this clean break from him once and for all. He can rot in hell for all I care! I hate him, Kate! I hate my own father!'

'David, don't say that,' Kate pleads, and I pull back, not wanting to upset her any more than she must already be, but my blood is pumping and I need to let off steam. 'I feel so bad for your mother, though,' she says. 'I mean, we didn't exactly expect a red-carpet welcome from your dad, but she'd put in so much effort.'

I start up the engine in the car and rip through his precious gravel on the way out of the driveway, determined never to darken his door again; he has told me not to do so enough times in my life. I will make plans with my mother soon, different plans. I never want to see his face or hear his voice like a worm in my ear for the rest of my life. He may have been a good man at one stage of his life, but his power behind the pulpit has turned him in recent years into a hypocrite, a bigot and a bully.

We grab a coffee in a filling station and drive to a nearby beauty spot to sit by the lake so I can compose myself before we go to see Kate's family.

'This was meant to be a day of celebration but of course he has ruined it,' I say, staring out onto the black water where swans float around, looking so peaceful and serene while their feet do all the paddling out of sight. I feel that way sometimes.

'He has ruined it because you are giving him that power,' Kate tells me. 'Don't let him have that hold on you, David. We both knew today was likely to be difficult so let's try and accept him for who and what he is to you, and move on. You have to let that grip he has on you go, once and for all. Please let today be that day.'

As always, Kate's words make perfect sense, but years of having had my whole personality chipped away by the man who brought me into this world sometimes gets under my skin, no matter how much I try to rise above him.

'Thanks for what you said to him, by the way,' I say, flashing Kate a smile. 'I felt like giving you a high-five but refrained.'

She bursts out laughing and leans across in the car to kiss me tenderly.

'I meant every word,' she tells me. 'You're the best.'

'OK, I'm ready for round two now. Are you?' I ask her, my eyes brightening at the ridiculous lengths we have to go to. 'We will laugh about this one day, I know we will. Your family's reaction can't be any more dramatic than old Bob's, can it?'

'Who knows?' says Kate, squeezing my hand with a nervous smile. 'Let's just get it all over and done with, yeah?'

We cruise out of the forest park and back out onto the main road into town, where Kate directs me past the memorial at the bomb site, out of the town centre and just a few streets away on the other side, where I steer into a sprawling grey housing estate with rows and rows of terraced pebble-dash houses, streets lined with cars battling for minimal parking space outside. A few kids bounce a ball along the pavement and another rides a bike with both hands up in the air, a sight that makes me have to swerve as he comes speeding towards us.

'Welcome to Hollywood,' Kate jokes. 'I'm a bit nervous now.'

'Don't be,' I tell her, feeling protective and strong now after my own showdown. It's my turn to be there for her.

We find a parking space by a row of dilapidated, graffiti-clad garages, and Kate leads me across the way to a smart mid-terrace house with window baskets full of spring flowers. A red-and-blue-framed swing sits in the front garden.

'That swing is almost as old as I am,' she says, and I put my arm around her just before we go through the black iron garden gate. 'It mightn't be the most glamorous set-up, but I have only fond memories of swinging here in this tiny garden.'

'I love you, Kate,' I say, kissing her forehead. 'Let's do this.'

A long-limbed, wavy-haired teenage girl wearing a tracksuit with a crop top that shows off a pierced belly button greets us at the door just as we make it up the path. I stop on the doorstep, frozen in time.

'The ice-cream shop boy!' she exclaims.

It's Shannon, and before I get a chance to catch my breath at the fact she recognizes me, she bounds towards me and wraps her arms around my waist as Kate looks on with pride.

'Thank you for helping me to feel safe that day,' she says, looking up at me with huge tear-filled eyes. 'I was so scared and alone and I've wanted to say that to you for ever.'

She stands up straight and wipes her eyes as black mascara leaves snail trails down her face. I hold my arm out for Kate to join us.

'And I've been looking forward to meeting you again so much too,' I say to her as flashbacks play in my mind of the little girl crying in the middle of the war-torn street, so frightened and helpless. 'Kate has told me all about you and I can't wait to get to know you better at last.'

281

We stand there in the doorway, the three of us reunited for the first time, and I'm filled with a strength I'd forgotten I had within me since I left my father's house earlier this afternoon.

'You must be the famous David Campbell,' says Kate's mum, Annie, whom I recognize from photos when she comes to the door. 'Please don't look so nervous. We don't bite. Not on the first visit anyhow. Come in, you're very welcome.'

She dries her hands on a tea-towel and Kate smiles with relief as we go inside. The hallway is narrow, with family photos lining either side; there is a small sitting room to the left then a flight of stairs, and at the back of the house is a kitchen that runs along the width of the house, looking out onto a small garden and another row of houses that run parallel.

'David, this is my sister Maureen,' Kate says, her voice confident and sure, while Maureen looks on at me more sceptically.

'You didn't tell me he was a pure ride,' says Maureen. 'You're very welcome, David, even if your dad and our mum are old arch-enemies.'

'Maureen!' Annie pipes up as she fusses around the kitchen. 'I don't think my politics is of concern here, even if I can't say I could have ever predicted I'd see Reverend Campbell's son in our kitchen, but Kate seems happy and that's all I'll ever want for her.'

I feel my face flush but, before any sense of embarrassment overcomes me, Kate holds out her left hand.

'Yes, well politics and history are going to have to be put to the side, because David and I have some big news.'

Kate links my arm with her right hand as the three women – Annie, Maureen and Shannon – look at each other open-mouthed.

'No way!' says Shannon, as Kate proudly holds out her left hand to show off her engagement ring, but Maureen and Annie look lost for words.

'Does . . . does your father know?' asks Annie, then she seems to remember the sense of occasion. 'I mean, wow, that's lovely news. Congratulations.'

She swallows after she speaks, as if she is masking her true feelings, but manages to paint on a smile to cover her shock.

'No, I haven't told Dad yet,' says Kate, her voice a little nipped now. 'It was a surprise for me but I'm sure Dad will be happy if I'm happy, like you just said.'

'Oh, come here!' says Annie, holding out her arms as she walks towards us, her eyes glistening with tears now as she embraces us with a light hug. 'I am happy for you both. I really am. It's just very unexpected but a lovely surprise all in all.' We stand in an awkward embrace until Kate's sister interrupts.

'Kate, you should have warned us! We'd have had some bubbles on ice!' says Maureen, in full excitement mode now that her mother has given her stilted approval. 'Don't move! I'll run to the shop. It's not every day your sister gets engaged and I bought new flute glasses the other day! I must be psychic!'

Maureen leaves immediately, while Shannon keeps staring at me as if she doesn't quite believe it's real.

'You and the ice-cream shop boy are engaged!' she says dreamily. 'That's like the coolest thing ever.'

'At least someone thinks so!' Kate says, looking at me as she rolls her eyes and shakes her head.

'No, no, don't say that. I'm genuinely very pleased for you both,' says Annie, who seems a bit more relaxed now. 'Sit down and I'll put the kettle on for a cup of tea while we wait for Maureen to come back with something a bit more appropriate. The ring is beautiful, by the way. Very Kate.'

She looks in approval in my direction.

'He had it designed especially,' says Kate, and I see the little girl in her for the first time ever. This home has known its own traumas, from what Kate told me about her child-hood, but it's a homestead of very strong women and a place where Kate still feels very safe and secure; it's a far cry from the heartless mansion I grew up in, despite the efforts of my mother to make it more homely.

We sit down on a little two-seater sofa in the kitchen as Kate's mum makes some tea. I notice how her hands shake as she does so. She flicks back her hair a lot and I can tell that – although she is putting on a very brave front for me and Kate – it's like she is constantly looking over her shoulder for something to go wrong, despite her own happiness for her daughter. I shift in my seat, trying to ignore the signs, and I'm glad when Maureen comes bounding back in armed with a bottle of Cava which she pops with great delight. She hands us all a glass just as her mother is stewing the tea.

'This is more like it! Now . . . to our Kate and David!' she says, her eyes filling up behind her dark-rimmed glasses. She looks nothing like Kate with her fuzzy curls and thick glasses, and I know they don't have the same father, but she has the same warmth and honesty and I like her instantly.

'To Kate and David!' says Shannon, still gawping at me as if I'm someone off the telly and not her aunt's fiancé.

'Thanks Mum, thanks Mo, thanks our darling Shannon,' Kate says as her eyes sparkle with delight. 'We are so happy and I'm glad you are too, even if it took a wee while to sink in!'

We clink glasses and take a sip of bubbles, but just as I'm swallowing my drink I feel the mood change at the slam of the front door. Everyone jumps a little and then freezes, and I suddenly feel unwelcome.

'Daddy,' says Shannon. 'What are you doing here?'

Then, just like mice scurrying from a cat, all four women hurry away from our circular party and I'm left standing alone in the middle of the kitchen holding a champagne glass.

I quickly follow their eyes towards the doorway of the kitchen to see a thickset man a few years older than me, I'm guessing, and I automatically clench my fists at the sight of him, feeling my skin prickle in defence.

'Sean!' says Maureen, looking very sheepish now. I blink back my bewilderment at how one person can enter a room and change its mood entirely. 'What are you doing here?'

He flicks his head back in my direction, in a move I assume is asking who I might be.

'David Campbell,' I say, to save anyone else the trouble of introducing us, pushing my shoulders back as I say it. He doesn't intimidate me in the slightest.

'David Campbell?' he nods. 'Yes, I've heard about this little love affair but thought it couldn't possibly be true. I knocked the door but you were all too busy partying to hear me. What's the occasion?'

No one answers, but Annie quickly lifts a dishcloth and wipes around worktops that are already gleaming.

'We weren't expecting you at all, Sean,' she says.

'You didn't say you were calling.'

Kate stands up from where she had quietly sat down at the table and stands by my side.

'The occasion is that David and I just got engaged,' she says, holding out her left hand like a weapon towards him. 'That's why we are celebrating. We're engaged to be married.'

Sean McGee scratches his shaved head and folds his burly arms like a bouncer at a nightclub door. His legs are parted and he glares my way, an eyebrow raised as he shakes his head.

'You're taking the piss!' he says with a hearty, snarling laugh. 'Come on, you can do better than that, Kate. You're the brains and beauty of this lot. You're the real pick of the bunch yet you go to the bottom of the barrel to hook up with a—'

'Get out!' shouts Annie, her voice shaking as she stares at the kitchen floor.

Kate and Maureen glance towards their mother in disbelief at her spontaneous outburst.

'You weren't invited in here in the first place to give your snide remarks, so I'd like you to leave right now, Sean!' she says. 'Take your bullying tactics and your arrogant ways away from my front door, please, once and for all. You've caused enough heartache in this family and you won't cause any more, do you hear me?'

'Kate, are you really going down this road?' Sean McGee snarls. 'You're going to marry the son of a Bible-thumping bigot? Talk about letting the side down! I always thought you—'

'You know nothing about me and it's none of your business,' Kate says firmly. I want to speak up but so far she's in control. 'You may be able to roam around here like some underworld mafia chief, but you don't scare me, Sean. Now, get out and do us all a favour. Stay away.'

'You desperate bitch!' Sean hisses and I lunge for him,

but Kate gets there first and she whacks him a slap across the face. He spits on the kitchen floor and tilts his chin out towards her.

'Get out right now,' Kate tells him.

I step forward but Kate grabs my arm.

'Don't bother, David, he isn't worth it! He isn't *worth* it!'

Maureen stares at the floor, fixing her glasses and tucking her hair behind her ear, while Shannon sits with her head in her hands, staring at the table.

'Prick!' he spits out in my direction, and stomps away, then slams the front door shut as Shannon sniffles behind me.

'I'm sorry,' she says to us when I turn back to face them all.

'Maybe we should go,' I suggest, but I'm met with a flurry of whispers and a sense of business as usual. I get the impression these outbursts are what this family are used to.

'No, no, let me get some tea,' Kate's mother fusses. 'Look, this isn't ideal so let's not pretend it is, but there's no way in the world we're ever going to let the thugs of this community dictate to us what we can and can't do with our lives. People like Sean think they can tell us all how to live our lives around here, but we need to let him know that those days are gone.'

She wrings out a dishcloth again and Kate sits down, signalling at me to do the same.

'I agree, Mum. Cheers everyone!' Kate says, grabbing my hand. 'I'm not afraid of him, David. He thinks he can control everyone around here with his threats and his bullshit, but he won't threaten us, no way.'

'That's my girl,' says Annie Foley. 'You make your own decisions in life and don't let anyone ever tell you different, even if they go against the grain. I'm proud of you. In fact, I'm very proud of you both.'

I sense Maureen and Shannon shuffle in their seats. I can see how Kate takes after her mum with her defiance and no bullshit tolerance, but Sean McGee looked at me as though he wasn't finished with ruling the roost around here, and with my father not yet on board I'm not sure if we're much further on at all beneath the surface. When Kate clasps my hand beneath the table for reassurance, I fear she might feel the same too.

CHRISTMAS 2011

19.

KATE

'Penny for your thoughts?'

David lies in bed beside me as the light snow falls outside. My arms are draped around his waist but he may as well be a million miles away. His face is in a deep trance, but he snaps out of it as soon as I call him out.

'Just money stuff, but all good,' he says, turning to face me now. 'I'm calculating in my head.'

'Oh?'

We've been saving hard and talking a lot recently about finally setting a date for our wedding. We plan to have it somewhere in Europe, like Positano in Italy, or a beachside ceremony in Mykonos, Greece, so I'm guessing he's thinking about something along those lines, especially as lately we've upped our game and gone through brochures and spoken with wedding planners. We just need to pin a decision down and take the plunge.

'I'm wondering if we should look for a new place to buy

locally instead of renting here, you know, somewhere more affordable where we have more space,' he suggests. 'What do you think?'

His suggestion really surprises me.

'To buy? Gosh, I like it here in this apartment, but yeah, I know what you're saying,' I reply, with so many thoughts going through my head. 'Do you think we can afford to make a move like that along with paying for a wedding, though?'

'I do,' he says, then laughs at his own joke. 'Yes, I do.'

The winter wind batters the windowpane outside our suburban apartment where we've lived for almost two years now, a little hideaway from the lives we left behind in Ireland, yet near enough for family to come and visit, and thankfully they do as often as they can.

Maureen and I spent an amazing weekend with Shannon and Mum sightseeing along the Thames, taking in a West End show and screaming in horror at the Tower of London dungeon tours back in the autumn, and Shannon has pledged to come back again as soon as she can for a long weekend to see more musicals and see more of a city she has fallen in love with.

'I think it's actually David she's in love with,' Mum joked with me when Shannon's back was turned as we rode into the sky on the London Eye. 'She's quite besotted and sees him as her all-time hero, so you need to watch your back, Kate. You've got competition.'

Shannon's admiration for David has fast become a bit of a private joke between me, Mum and Mo, but I could see exactly what they meant when Shannon was here. She, like a lot of David's students in his school, looks up to him with adoring, idolizing eyes. As much as I find it funny I can understand why they are all taken by him. David is firm but gentle in his ways with young people, wise but willing to learn, open but decisive, strong but vulnerable, and outside of his work his love for me is like a never-ending fuel that gives me hope and faith for the long future we are planning together.

Even my father, who will arrive into London today to spend Christmas with us, has overcome his own barriers and accepted David for the wonderful person he is, now that he has realized that as a couple we mean business.

'How about we start house-hunting in the New Year, then?' David suggests after breakfast, shortly before I leave to collect my dad from the airport. 'On your salary and mine we can afford something bigger, even if it means a bit of a commute, and we'll still have enough to set aside for our wedding. What do you think, babe?'

I kiss him on the cheek on my way past, with a piece of toast in one hand and a coffee in the other.

'Let me work it all out with you after we get Christmas behind us,' I say, checking the time. I need to leave in half an hour. 'We've a lot to look forward to, David. I'm excited.'

He pulls me close to his bare chest where he sits at the

table, rests his hand on my belly and gives me a cheeky look.

'And as for a junior Kate and David, do you think we have time for a very quick practice run before you leave for the airport? You look very, very cute in that nightshirt.'

I roll my eyes at his reference to my faded, thigh-skimming nightshirt that has definitely seen better days.

'You're so naughty sometimes but I love it,' I tell him and, after some passionate lovemaking in the kitchen and a very quick shower, I'm off to pick up my dad and feeling quite on top of the world with my lot.

'You like it here, love?' Dad says to me as I confidently cruise along the roads back from Gatwick Airport towards Bromley. 'I wish I'd travelled more in life, I really do. It opens both the heart and mind in ways that nothing else can.'

'I'm enjoying it here for sure. It's rural and quiet but close enough to the bright lights of London too.'

'I also wish I'd gone to school a bit more often and got myself an education, instead of slogging away as a gopher, labouring on building sites for a pittance, but you live and learn, eh?' he continues.

It's more a statement than a question, so I don't have to agree or disagree.

'Life takes us in all sorts of directions, Dad,' I tell him softly. 'David and I have to work very hard to make it work but I love my job at the hospital here and we've a great circle of friends.'

'That's good to hear . . . you're really going to marry him, so?' he asks, and I glance at him with a smile.

'Yes, I am going to marry him and I'm a very, very lucky lady to have him.'

Dad lets out a sigh which makes me laugh and then he giggles too. Our opposing backgrounds are a bitter pill for him to swallow, but David and I have made it very clear that nothing like that will ever be an issue, having firmly closed down that discussion on our now infamous visit home to announce our engagement.

'And he's fine with your mum's history with his dad, all that trouble and time in prison?' he asks. 'I'm not suggesting he shouldn't be, I'm just trying to understand how it has worked out now that I'm over my own worries about it all.'

I focus on the road ahead while I answer his question. Dad has taken his time to come round to my relationship with David, having given me a recap of the many occasions on which my mother and the reverend clashed on everything from abortion to homosexuality to civil rights for Catholics like us, and how the religious divide in our country instilled a hatred among so many.

'David and I don't see religion, Dad, I've told you this many times,' I explain. 'Our parents' history will not come between us. We won't let it.'

I glance at my dad who looks genuinely impressed.

'And he's not afraid?' he asks, just as I expected him to. A pause hangs in the air. 'It's not really common to see anyone of his sort around Green Park estate.'

He laughs nervously at the very idea.

'We have no interest in hanging around Green Park, or anywhere near it, Dad,' I say to him. 'I'm not saying we won't come and visit, but our life is here now and we're getting on really well.'

Saying that out loud makes me feel as though I'm betraying where I come from, but I also know I need to keep moving on if David and I want to be together. There's a whole big world out there, and if we do decide to go back and settle nearer home, there are many, many beautiful and much more desirable places to live in Ireland than the infamous Green Park estate.

'I'm happy for you, I really am,' Dad says, pointing out names on signposts he recognizes as we drive into Bromley. 'Gosh, it's just like living in a wee village here. Really lovely, and not what I expected at all.'

I feel a pang of sorrow for him when he says that, realizing how he – like my mum and so many others of his generation – was a victim of the times he was born in. My dad is a gentle soul, and his own worst enemy with the antics he was involved in, not to mention how his character changes when he decides to really hit the bottle, but if he had been born into a different era, when bombs, bullets and barricades weren't a way of life back in our beautiful country, he could have made so much more of himself. Watching him admiring scenery and pointing out a red London bus shows an innocent and childlike side of him that I've never seen before. It's so endearing but also just a little bit sad.

He's looking fresh and new for his visit, if a little thinner than before, with his clean-shaven face and neatly cut hair, with just enough left to sweep back into a smooth quiff at the front. He always had a very distinctive look, and I'm delighted not to smell the usual whiff of alcohol from his breath.

'We are hoping to buy a house in the New Year, somewhere in the same area but a bit bigger,' I tell him as he drinks in every word I say and every sight he sees. 'You should come over more often. I think you'd really enjoy the culture and the way of life here.'

My father, for all his lack of education and travel, instilled in me my love of poetry from a very young age, and he used to quote Irish writers like Seamus Heaney and Benedict Kiely to me as he walked me to school back in the day. I just know he would have loved to have seen more of the world through his own eyes than life allowed him to.

'I will come back, you know,' he says, nodding his head. 'Thanks, love. I think I've had my eyes opened already.'

'So, who would you normally spend Christmas Day with, Peter?' David asks my dad as we tuck in to a magnificent dinner with all the trimmings two days later on Christmas

Day. It does my heart good to see my father enjoy his turkey and ham, and when he laughs or tells a very humble story of his own festive memories, I want to wrap him up and keep him here for ever.

'Ah, I'm a bit of a drifter, David,' he says as I pour him a top-up of white wine. 'I always have been, I suppose. Some years I go to Annie and the girls for Christmas if they'll have me, but mostly I could end up anywhere. I've a few friends who live alone like I do, so I'm never stuck, but this is a real treat. Actually, now that you ask, I don't know when I last spent Christmas with my beautiful daughter in such welcoming surroundings. Thank you both for having me.'

I calculate in my head that it could be at least five years since my dad and I shared a proper meal together, which makes today all the more special.

'Well, you're very welcome to come here for Christmas anytime from here on in,' says David. 'Hopefully next year we'll be in a new home, and maybe my own mother will be still here and fit enough to join us too.'

'And your father?' Dad asks, glancing my way to make sure he hasn't suggested anything wrong. 'I know he wouldn't exactly be rushing to share a table with the likes of me, but maybe someday he'll—'

'I'm afraid we've accepted that isn't ever going to happen,' David says, his knife and fork clashing with his plate just a little louder than it probably should. 'But I do see my mother when I can. Families, eh?'

I shudder for David when I hear him speak of his father and the wounds that continue to fester between them. It's a stark reminder to me that, while we are living a beautiful life here in England, we are still a long way off fixing everything back home, but for now it's the best it can be.

We close the subject at that and, after a dessert of home-made pavlova, we relax in front of the TV until we all fall asleep, our bellies bursting and my heart full up too with having my dad here.

With a new year, a new home, and hopefully some firm marriage plans in place to look forward to, I'm not sure I've felt as content in my whole life.

DAVID

With Kate at work in the children's hospital on Boxing Day, it's my turn to take the reins and show Peter O'Neill around the area we've decided to settle in here, which is a perfect opportunity to clear up any fears or past encounters once and for all, man to man and eye to eye.

I take him to one of my favourite haunts for a pint, and it's not long before the small talk is out of the way and the elephant in the room takes over, leaving us to address the bigger picture that surrounds my love for Peter's daughter.

'Look, David . . . there's an element where we live that

will never want to accept you and Kate, but I'm praying you both are stronger than that,' Peter tells me. 'I know you are.'

'Small minded people are nothing to me,' I say with a nonchalant shrug. 'What matters is Kate and I, the rest is just white noise.'

'I totally agree,' says Peter, 'and it's an outdated mentality in a very small minority that is slowly fading away in most parts of society, but there are still pockets of thugs in our neighbourhood who are just waiting on the opportunity to pounce in the belief that stuff like this is under their control. They don't like newcomers on their territory, especially from families like yours who they would see as the enemy and vice versa. It's the same on both sides. There are some very small minds who are stuck in a past they can't move on from.'

It's nothing I haven't heard before, but it's good to hear from Peter that he can now see past the blinkers he once would have worn.

'I've heard of Sean McGee and his tribe from Kate, and he's a fierce fella it seems, but he doesn't scare me,' I say, knowing that a lot of my bravado is born out of the physical distance between us.

'Yes, I hear you stood your ground when you met him in Annie's last year,' says Peter with a deliberate nod of his head. 'And that Annie chased him on his way too. You know, Annie and I might not be together any more, but she'll always be the true love of my life and that will never go away. We're still in love behind it all, and I'd rather have her in my life than ever be without her.'

I picture Peter and Annie together, two very strong and striking people, and I feel sorry for the love they lost, whatever their story may be.

'I'm sad to hear it didn't work out for you both,' I tell him.

'Ah, it's a long story, David,' he says. 'But Sean McGee knows his targets, and Annie has been a pawn for his gang for long enough, so I was delighted to hear she stood up to him at last. Surprisingly, he's left her alone since, but of course he's always going to want to call there to see Shannon. That's the trouble. They're linked to him for ever.'

I shake my head at the pity of it all. Shannon is a delight, a wonderfully bright girl who has a strong head on her shoulders and doesn't deserve to be dragged down by a father who chooses to live in the gutter.

'To be honest, David, between you and me,' he whispers, 'there's great darkness in a very small corner of our community that will always be there as long as Sean and his types are around. It's gone way beyond politics at this stage. It used to be about paramilitaries and their hunger for war, but now it's about drugs, it's about power and street crime, but most of all it's about control. I can feel their eyes on me everywhere I go. I made mistakes in my past by getting caught up in their world and it seems they want me to pay for those mistakes for ever. They don't like you and Kate being together and they're already calling me out as a traitor for "allowing" this to happen.'

'How do you mean they want to make you pay?' I ask him. 'Do you owe this gang money, Peter?'

He rubs his weary eyes.

'They want to make me pay in more ways than one,' he whispers. 'Put it like this, I won't be broadcasting that I've come here for Christmas. Sean McGee thinks I owe him some sort of loyalty and, no matter how much I beg him to loosen his grip, it's like he has a noose around my neck. One day I fear he'll tug that noose too tightly.'

The lines on Peter O'Neill's face are drenched in the history of a world that neither Kate nor I choose to recall any more, but I also know that what Peter is telling me is pretty serious on so many levels.

'Are you afraid, Peter?' I ask him, hoping the answer will be no. I'd hate for Kate to have to worry about her dad when she is so settled now, enjoying her life and happiness at last.

'Afraid?' he asks me, his frightened eyes already answering my question.

'If you're in any sort of trouble, please don't keep it to yourself,' I say to him. 'I'm not claiming it's better here than it is where you live, but if you ever want to get away from it all, even for a break, there's always a bed for you here. No one would need to know.'

Peter looks away, then stands up from his bar stool and pats his pockets where he finds a pack of cigarettes and a lighter. He puts a cigarette in his mouth and talks to me as it hangs there. His eyes are yellowing, he is thin in stature, and I feel sorry for him now in a way I never dreamed I would.

'Of course I'm afraid, but I'm used to it by now,' he says, and then he has a change of heart. 'For God's sake don't tell Kate I said that! I mean it, don't breathe that to her or she'll be on the next plane home and I don't want her anywhere involved. You'll promise me that now, David?'

His eyes plead with me so there's no way I can say anything different. I know he's right. If Kate thought her father was living in any sort of fear, she'd believe she could fix it right away and could end up in a lot of trouble herself, plus it would confirm all her biggest fears about us and the risks she has always believed we've been taking.

'I promise,' I say to him. 'I won't say a word, but if it's about debt or if I can—'

'Just leave it. I've said too much as it is. You're a good lad, David,' he interrupts me, putting his hand on my shoulder, and I can see for real now that his eyes are indeed clouded with fear. 'You're a good, good lad. You mustn't tell Kate, for God's sake.'

We stand there in silence as the noise of the pub fades into the background around us, and then Peter takes the cigarette from his mouth, takes a breath and speaks again.

'You know, the world is full of stupid, ignorant and judgemental people, and I'm only sorry that I was once one of them,' he says to me, 'but when you get to my stage in life, David, you realize what's most important.'

'I hear you.'

'Everyone has a story, everyone has a background, a reason to believe in what they believe,' he says, 'and everyone has a right to stand up for those beliefs. However, with respect to all that, I've learned not to judge a book by its cover. In my old age I've learned that a person's true self is much more than their politics or religion. It might just take them a while to realize that.'

I slide off my stool and stand up tall beside him, and then I shake his hand.

'Kate loves you very much, Peter, don't ever forget that, and I know you've been good to Maureen and Shannon as far as life has allowed you to, even though they aren't your own flesh and blood.'

'I have, in my own way.'

'Kate once told me not to be so hard on myself,' I tell him, 'and although it has taken a while and a bit of hard work, I'm learning to do just that. Nobody's perfect.'

He blinks back tears and then squeezes his inner eyes with his right hand.

'Do you fancy one more for the road?' I ask him.

I nod to the barman for service without having to wait for him to answer. He walks away slowly towards the smoking area at the rear of the pub but then, as if he's just remembered something, he makes his way back to me again.

'In case I forget to say it to you,' he says, his yellowing eyes looking into mine. 'Try and make it up with your da, for goodness' sake, David.'

I pay the barman and then look back at him.

'Ah, Peter, I don't know,' I tell him, shaking my head. 'I think that bridge has been well and truly burned by now.'

'Never.'

'I'm afraid so,' I tell him. 'He and I will never see eye to eye, so it's probably for the best we stay apart. It's more peaceful that way for all involved.'

But he isn't letting it go so easily.

'My God, I only wish I could have a chat with my old man again,' he says, shaking his head as tears fill his eyes once more. 'It sucks the guts from me every time I think of how stubborn we both were, when beneath it all, all we wanted to do was reach out and understand each other. Sometimes, the people we love most are the hardest to reach, but it's so worth finding their hand when you do.'

I sit here and try to imagine how I'd feel about my own father should he ever fall into ill health, which I know is inevitable as the years tick by and he grows older and slower on his feet. I try to think if that will change the way I feel about him.

I think about my fancy family home in all its splendour,

tucked away from the nearby town; I see my mother tiptoeing around inside it as she lives on the edge of her nerves and worries about her up-and-down health issues. I hear my father play from the pulpit the role of the great saviour and leader that everyone believes he is. I recall the good times before all that power and inheritance went to his head – times when he was just my dad who loved the simple things in life and not the great Reverend Bob Campbell who felt he had to rule the world.

I take a sip of my beer. As much as I respect and admire Peter's efforts and intentions, I think we'll have to agree to disagree on this one.

'Go and enjoy your cigarette, Peter,' I say, taking another gulp and enjoying the taste as it hits the back of my throat. 'I'm really enjoying your company today, so let's leave my dad out of it for now. He will always be my father, but he stopped being my dad a long time ago.'

MARCH 2012

20.

KATE

David has been on the phone to an estate agent for the past twenty minutes, and I can't help but laugh hysterically as he communicates with me via rather dodgy sign language to describe the conversation that is going on between them.

We have been in deep negotiations recently about a three-bedroom detached residence with its own garden that has had us salivating for weeks now since we first viewed it, and as I walked around the house with its modern decor and cool white interiors, I dreamed of how I'd put my own stamp on it with a more countryside feel, almost cottage like. I'd buy an Aga and a Belfast sink, and I'd insist on a free-standing bath with claw feet, just as I'd always dreamed of one day having since I saw one in a hotel in Donegal as a very young child.

David is talking numbers now, and although we've agreed to place an offer based on the budget we've spent weeks working out, the excitement of it all is something else as I listen in to him chatting to the estate agent about local amenities, future market value and a question about a plumbing issue that was flagged up the surveyor.

'OK, I think we're ready to make an offer,' he says, giving me a 'thumbs-up' sign as I nod like a giddy pup and do a silent crazy dance in the kitchen of our little apartment. 'Yes, we'd like to offer the asking price, please, and we'll keep that offer on for seven days.'

He hangs up the phone and swings me around in delight, and just as we're lost in celebration of taking this first big step, I get an awful sinking feeling that this is all too good to be true.

'What's wrong?' David asks as he pours us both a cold sauvignon blanc straight from the fridge. 'You look like you're having second thoughts?'

It's a bright spring Friday evening. We have a little balcony that shoots out of our kitchen, with just enough room for a round table and two chairs. I follow him out there to enjoy the sunshine.

'No, no, it's very much the opposite, David. I'm just so happy,' I tell him as I take in my surroundings. 'At last everything is going so well for us both. You are flying in your job and the students adore you, I've made some great friends here and I love the hospital and all the challenges it brings, and now it looks like we're a step closer to owning our very first home together. I'm so happy.'

He lifts his glass and we clink our drinks together, then he picks up a bridal magazine that sits on the balcony table.

'And then we have all this to look forward to,' he says, pulling a funny face.

'What's the face for? Is it all a bit déjà vu for you?' I ask him jokingly. 'I keep forgetting you've been through all this before.'

'Never with you,' he says, leaning over for a kiss.

His phone rings from the kitchen and he goes to pick it up, leaving me again with an awful fear of everything going wrong. This is not like me, but lately I feel as though I can sense something really bad is going to happen to tip our whole world on its axis again, just when we are getting on so well.

It's not like me to think like this, but for nights now I've been lying awake in bed or else letting thoughts cross my mind when I'm on a night shift that fill me with dread. I think of my mother and how I noticed when we were home a few weeks ago to check in on David's mum that there were a lot of empty wine bottles stashed away under a blanket in the garden shed, as though she'd been hiding them from us all. I've been trying to pluck up the courage to address it with her, but I'm too afraid of what I'm going to hear. And then there's Mo and the whole Sean McGee saga, as he sneaks around and bullies them all from both near and far yet still holds on to Mo with an iron grip. I know she's been spellbound by him again while I have been away. He creeps me out, reminding me of darker times when my mother was in prison and when he lorded it over our community, and I shudder to think of the hold he might have on them now.

'Why is he around so much?' I asked my mum, who rolled her eyes in despair. 'Is Mo seeing him again?'

'Don't mention it to her, for God's sake, Kate,' Mum had said to me. 'There's no talking to her and you'll only end up annoying yourself more. You know what Mo's like when it comes to him. He moulds her like putty and then leaves her out to dry, but it's the way it's always been. Without you here to keep her straight, she'll just do her own thing when it comes to him.'

Shannon, who had been so full of promise, looked a little bit unhealthier when I saw her, and Mo let it slip that she had been running around with an undesirable crowd. I'd tried to speak to her about it but she changed the subject and slammed the door on me, an act which I'm hoping and praying is just part of her teenage years and not something more concerning.

'I'm worried about her,' I told Mo, but it was like talking to a brick wall. 'I don't like where she's heading, and I need you to promise you'll keep a closer eye on her.'

'She's her daddy's girl,' said Mo, which made my skin crawl at the thought of Sean McGee influencing my beautiful niece in any way. 'You can't control that any more, Kate. It's up to Shannon now.'

And then there's my dad. My culpable, reflective, deep and sincere father, who wears his heart on his sleeve as he constantly fights with his own addictions and traumatic past, living alone and probably just about scraping by while I live here in a different country, in a totally different world, where I'm settled and happy and have enough love in my life to make me feel like I can move mountains.

'You'll come and visit us again soon?' I said to him on our last phone call. 'We loved having you here at Christmas, so why not come over again and stay a bit longer this time? I've some holidays to take before the tax year ends.'

'I'd love that,' he said, but I could hear fear in his voice. Something was going on over there and I didn't like it.

I wish I could take a leaf out of my own book and go easier on myself, as I used to tell David to do, but no matter how much I try, since the new year came around, I can't stop feeling like I've left my real life behind.

The sun begins to set in the distance and I close my eyes to breathe in the moment as I hear David's voice lilting up and down in the background. It might be the estate agent again, I think, feeling a flutter of excitement as I allow the prospect of our offer being accepted to be a possibility. I smile as I picture us in our first family home and let myself drift off in that much more positive thought. We've talked a lot about babies, and I just know my life will be complete when we have our own child. Then again, would I want to be here, so far away from my own family, when that happens?

'Kate, I just got great news!' David shouts, which clicks me out of my daydream immediately. I stand up and make my way through the balcony doors to where he stands there, his arms wide open in disbelief.

'What is it?' I ask as I walk towards him. It's the house. It has to be the house.

'Mum has got the all-clear at last,' he tells me, his voice shaking with delight. 'She is completely cancer free and is hoping to come and see us very soon.'

I run towards him, just like I did earlier, but this time he doesn't spin me round. This is a new kind of delight. It's a relief, it's the answer to our repeated prayers, and it's the perfect sign, just what I needed, that everything in our little world is beginning to make sense at last. Maybe, just maybe, everything is going to be all right.

DAVID

I wake up the next morning after hearing my mum's news to find Kate gone from the bedroom. When I call out her name, she is nowhere to be found. I check the kitchen and the tiny balcony where she so often spends her mornings off reading or meditating, and it's only when I look at the calendar on our fridge, which she marks so impeccably, that I notice she has in fact been at work since eight this morning. How could I have forgotten? I don't think that has ever happened before.

I crawl back into bed, glad of the silence now, and take comfort in knowing she is all right, and I drift off in a hungover daze as I ignore my phone, which bleeps through message after message. It's Saturday morning, so I'm betting it's some of my work colleagues who live locally, wanting to meet up for a pint later in the afternoon. The very thought of it is enough to make me feel queasy, especially as I remember knocking back the bottle of wine and a few beers last night to celebrate a great day of progress.

I sleep for at least an hour, get up and shower and, as I'm enjoying a coffee and slow coming round to the day ahead, my phone rings and demands an answer. It's Annie, Kate's mum, and I know the moment I hear her voice that something is terribly wrong.

'Is Kate with you?' she asks. I can tell her voice is slightly slurred and I recall how Kate told me she was concerned her mum might be drinking a bit on the quiet lately. 'I don't want to tell her over the phone. I need you to tell her, David.'

'Annie, love, I've absolutely no idea what you're talking about,' I say, flicking the switch on the coffee machine again to get my second cup of fuel. I rub my forehead. I don't think Annie Foley has ever had reason to call me before, and I didn't have her number saved, so to hear her voice has come as a bit of a surprise to say the least.

'We've been messaging you all morning,' she says, weeping now. 'Is Kate working?'

'Yes, what's wrong?' I ask, rubbing my pounding forehead.

'I'm sorry, I haven't even looked at my messages yet. What's happened?'

'I've got the most awful news,' she says, and I sit down at the table, ready to hear the worst even though I have no idea what to expect. 'I can't tell Kate myself, I'm sorry. I think it would be better coming from you.'

I curse and swear out loud as I try to find a parking space at the children's hospital. It is only less than ten miles from our home, but the journey feels as if it's taking years as I weave through the heavy Saturday afternoon traffic. My heart is in my mouth as I lock up the car, and I hear every footstep I take as I make my way towards the state-of-the-art children's wing where Kate has worked for almost two years now.

When I get to the door, I stop and take a deep breath, praying for the inner strength to carry out this most awful task and break the news to the person I love the most in the whole world – news that is going to smash her own world into pieces.

I've practised what I'm going to say so many times on the short journey, how I'll tell her, what I'll say, where I'll say it. I couldn't phone ahead to warn her as I have to give her the news in person, so I've turned up here at her place of work and now I have to find a way to break it to her.

I walk past reception, press the number on the elevator for the Savannah ward, where Kate works with children with cardiology problems. When I step out onto the ward, I'm immediately greeted by one of her colleagues.

'I'm so sorry, but it's parents only for visiting,' she tells me in apology. 'Oh hang on, you're Kate's partner? David, is it?'

She beams a smile in recognition, but then her face falls instantly when she realizes I'm hardly here on a social visit.

'I need to talk to Kate in private, please,' I tell her, my own voice barely recognizable as the words spill off my tongue. 'Is there somewhere I can take her? Maybe you have a room we could talk away from everyone? I'll have to take her home straight away, I'm sorry.'

The lady's face nods slowly in acknowledgement that I'm about to deliver some horrible news, and she leads me down the corridor to a little sea-green coloured room with two sofas and a low coffee table with just a box of tissues on it.

A quick glance at the posters on the walls and the leaflets in a holder that stands freely by one of the sofas tells me that this room has seen its fair share of bad news being delivered.

'Oh God,' I say, closing my eyes briefly.

I sit down and stare at the floor, trying to decide if this is real or not. It doesn't feel real. It doesn't feel right. The heavy door opens and Kate comes in, her beautiful face stunned and shocked already, before she's even heard what it is I have to tell her.

I go to her. I take her hand. I lead her to one of the small

319

sofas and we sit down in unison as I do my best to find the words. But there's no way round it. I just have to tell her straight, as much as I know it's going to destroy her.

'I'm so, so sorry, Kate,' I say, and she puts her hands over her eyes, closing them tight, then blocks her ears as if she can't bear to hear what I'm about to say. 'Your mum rang me earlier. She wanted me to tell you in person instead of you being told on the phone. It's your dad, Kate. I'm so sorry. He's gone.'

She crumples and folds into me and then she screams from the pit of her stomach, clutching at my T-shirt as tears pour from her eyes.

'No, not my daddy!' she says, pleading with me as she shakes her head in disbelief. 'No, David, please not my daddy!'

'I'm so sorry, baby,' I say to her, holding her tight as she fights to stay still, pulling and clawing at me to make it all go away. 'Come on, let's get you home as soon as possible. We'll get on a plane this evening and we'll get you home.'

21.

KATE

'There were signs of a break-in when we found him,' my mum tells us as she clutches onto a glass of red wine at the kitchen table when David and I get home. 'It looks like he'd been in bed but got up to confront the intruders and collapsed then called me during the night. At least that's what we think happened. There's so many blanks, so many questions. Oh Peter, you didn't deserve to dic like this! He must have been so afraid.'

I notice David swallowing and staring into nowhere as she speaks and I can tell that he too has a blaze of anger burning his insides, just like I still do.

'Had he expressed any concerns to you lately?' I ask Mum. 'Was there someone he was—'

But Mo chirps up for her. 'He wasn't being threatened if that's what you think!' she says quickly as Shannon chews gum beside her, playing with her thumbs. 'So if you're coming here to ask questions or point fingers in certain directions, don't bother!'

'I'm not pointing fingers,' I cry. 'But yes I *am* asking questions about what happened to my own father and I think it's very natural that I'd want to try to piece together why he is dead!'

'You're blaming my dad,' says Shannon. 'I just know you are! Everyone around here blames him for everything but it's nothing to do with him. If Peter was afraid of anyone, it's nothing to do with my dad so keep him out of it.'

I see David fidget, his mouth tighten, and he wrings his hands, a movement which I keep catching out of the side of my eye.

'No one is blaming anyone,' I say, as always being the peacemaker in my family, a family that has lost its foundation lately and now I can see why. Shannon and Mo are under Sean McGee's spell once more, my mother is hiding her own regret and fear in alcohol, and whatever has happened to my dad or whatever he has been going through lately has slipped through the net, eluding all of us who should have been looking out for him, including me.

'Kate is well within her right to ask as many questions as she pleases,' my mother says, topping up her glass. It hurts me so deeply to see her wash away her pain with a bottle or two of red wine, but it makes sense now why Mo has turned a blind eye to her drinking. She has been too preoccupied and besotted again with Sean McGee. 'And no one is suggesting Peter was afraid of anyone. She's just asking questions.'

The room falls silent and I feel so glad of my mother's support, even if I know she might not remember this conversation the next day. I can sense how everyone is scrambling to think of what to say next. David is sitting across from me at the far end of the table and, once more, his body language distracts me.

I look at him, willing him to say what's on his mind. He's the only one of us here who is fit to distinguish the wood from the trees right now in this awful riddle. Although he only knew my father in recent times, he is so far removed from any torrid history my dad might have had that I'm hoping he has some words of wisdom to share. I need him to settle my worry as images of my dad struggling against someone who had been making his life a misery flashed across my mind.

'Peter *was* afraid actually,' he says eventually, and we all turn quickly towards him. 'He was very afraid and knew he was being watched.'

'What?'

He stands up and paces the floor, rubbing his forehead as if he is trying to remember something.

'I don't know – it was a very brief conversation we had when he was with us at Christmas. We were having a drink at the pub, but he said there was darkness in the community of a new sort, not like before. He did mention Sean.

He said he felt there were eyes upon him, but he didn't say why. He didn't need to.'

Now, it's my turn to stand up and Mo does too.

'What are you trying to say, David?' she cries. 'Are you saying Sean had something to do with Peter's death? How dare you! Peter O'Neill died of a heart attack, so don't you dare come here recalling drunken conversations you can barely even remember from months ago! He died of a heart attack!'

'He died of a heart attack because perhaps someone had been threatening him and they broke into his house!' my mum shouts, but I'm no longer listening to them and their bickering. I have only one question that sits in my stomach as if I've swallowed lead.

'David, if my father was so afraid . . .' I whisper. 'If my father was so afraid of someone or something, how could you have known that and not told me?'

I stand on the kitchen floor, my face frozen in bewilderment.

'Because he made me promise not to tell you, Kate,' David pleads with me. He comes towards me but for the first time since I've known him, I turn away from his approach. My skin prickles in horror. I want to press rewind and help my dad. I feel like I'm drowning. 'He didn't want you to worry about him. He was afraid of you getting involved and getting into trouble!'

'Oh my God, no! He must have been terrified!' I say,

crying now with such regret that I didn't know and I didn't do anything to help him.

David looks wretched as he tries to find the right words to convey what he knew and, more importantly, why he didn't tell me.

'He told me it was a different way of life to how it used to be round here,' he says. 'He told me it's all about power; it's about drugs as well, and the power that some like to think they have around here, even stretching to their belief that you and I shouldn't be together, Kate. He called them thugs. He told me not to worry and not to tell you.'

I shake my head.

'But you should have told me, David!' I cry. 'You should have told me! We could have helped him! Did he owe them money? What did he say?'

'He said . . . he said they were making him pay in more ways than one.'

'Pay for what?' I plead, my eyes wild with panic. 'Pay for us? Was this to do with us? Was it Sean McGee?'

Mo storms out of the kitchen at that, almost taking the hinges from the doors, and Shannon follows, which stuns me and stings me almost as much as David's secret did. All I can do to numb the pain is fetch a wine glass and join my mother for a drink to try and block it all out, but no matter how much wine I sink, I can't sleep a wink when I go to bed, and I can't get what my father told David out of my head.

Why was my father so afraid? Why did this happen to him? Was it because of us? David and me? Was he threatened because of me seeing David or was there something else behind his fear? I don't know for sure, but I won't settle until I find out.

David reaches out for me in bed, but I turn my back on him and hug the pillow instead. I am numb to the core and I just wish I could turn back time. I knew there was something simmering here. I feared my dad was hiding something that was on his mind, but I never, ever thought it would come to this. Now I'm racked with guilt that I should have paid more attention.

A traditional Irish wake is a singular occasion. As I sit in my mother's tiny living room watching face after face – some familiar, some less well known, others complete strangers – come towards me, shake my hand, and offer words of sorrow and pray over my father's body where he lies in his open coffin, there's a strange comfort in it. Meanwhile I'm being washed along on a wave of grief that I know hasn't even fully hit me yet.

'He was a real character, a fine gentleman who thought the world of you, Kate.'

'He loved your mother till the day he died, even if they weren't together any more.'

'He was an intelligent man in his own way. He could hold an interesting conversation. We had many laughs.'

'You're the image of him. You have his eyes. He always said you had his eyes.'

Hearing how others recollect stories and sharing their memories of my dad makes me feel both happy and sad at the same time, but beneath the cloud of constant hand-shaking, never-ending tea drinking, hurried whispers and various stories of my father's life, I feel a simmer of anger ripple beneath my skin as I try to understand what exactly happened to him on the night he died.

There's a much bigger story involved, a much bigger issue than a natural heart attack, which will inevitably be listed as the cause on his death certificate, and I won't settle until I get to the bottom of it.

The funeral will be held in the local church where my father was baptised. As I sit here at his wake, numb with shock and pain, with streams of sympathizers expressing similar thoughts to me, I look at each of them wondering if they know what lies behind all this, and how much the sound of the underground is rattling behind their tears and words of sorrow.

As I look at them all for clues, I remember David's father's words of warning that day at the Old Rectory Manor when he made David choose between me or his parents.

'It's not the gossips or whispers, but the sound of the underground you should be more concerned about.'

And as much as I can't stand the man, his words or warning seem to have rung true. So with all of that in mind,

I ask David to go back to England and go back to work ahead of me.

'You mean, you don't want me to stay with you for the funeral?' he asks me, his face crestfallen and hurt in a way I never dreamed I could have caused.

'Stay for the funeral, yes, but after that I need to have some space to clean up all this mess and think things through,' I tell him, and then, when he isn't looking, I slip a note into his case before he goes saying 'Sorry'.

I'm so heartbroken on so many levels about my dad; I'm so confused and upset with everyone around me and I don't know if I can leave here after the funeral for a very long time. I've turned my back on everything I've ever known for a life that was so great, but I've neglected the people who needed me most. I need to fix my broken family, or at least what's left of it, and to do that I'll have to let David go back to England without me.

'I-I don't know what to say,' he tells me before he leaves to go back to the life we left behind before this tragedy. 'I can see how upset you are, Kate, and I know how much you're going to miss him, but your father wouldn't want you to punish yourself like this. I don't think he would want you to ruin everything we've worked so hard for.'

'My family needs me,' I whisper to him. 'I'm sorry, David, but right now my family needs me more than anyone else, even you, and I have to stay here to do what I have to do. You've no idea what it's like to live here in the shadows when just a few miles away you lived the most privileged life; sometimes that makes me bitter and angry.'

He looks away and shakes his head, then bites his lip.

'You're angry at me now for our different upbringings?'

'Not at you personally. God, I don't know, I suppose just at the cruelty of it all,' I try to explain. 'You only think you knew trouble, you had to live with your father's views, you knew which parts of town to avoid where you wouldn't feel welcome, but you never knew trouble like we did here.'

Even though we're standing so close right now, the distance between us has never felt greater. He takes a moment.

'So . . . will you come back?' he asks, his face crumpled in disbelief. 'Or is this it? Is this goodbye?'

I stare at him, my mind scrambled and my heart sore. He nods slowly at my silence, then clenches his fingers into the palm of his hands and breathes out long and slowly.

'It's what I have to do – at least for now, David,' I gasp, feeling my throat closing in. 'I'll have to stay here for as long as it takes to put my family back together.'

We stand there face to face on the pavement outside my family home as life goes on around us – children race past us on bikes, an ice-cream van rings out in the distance – while both our hearts break over the differences I feared would always catch up with us.

The truth is I don't know if I'll ever be able to go back to where we left off and pretend my father's death was nothing to do with us.

'I just need some space and time to fix things here, so I'm going to have to take some compassionate leave from work and try to do just that,' I say to David. 'For now, that's as much as I can plan ahead. I'm sorry.'

DAVID

It's been three weeks since Kate's father died and, as I go through each day on autopilot, not knowing if or when she is ever going to come back here, I slip deeper and deeper into a place where I never wanted to go in my mind.

It's a place where darkness rules and old thoughts of negativity come back to haunt me and it feels as if it's taking control, pulling me downwards with its mighty grip.

The apartment is a mess as I live off takeaways and beer, disguising the smell of alcohol on my breath as much as I can to my fellow staff and students every day at school but, of course, young people are intuitive, and one of them has already copped on that something has changed within me.

'You look like shit,' he tells me when he comes back after class to pick up some books he'd left behind. 'Hope you're all right, sir. You could sure do with a wash and a shave, just saying, and you smell like a brewery.'

After that, it isn't before long until Andrew Spence, the principal who boosted my career wholeheartedly when he promoted me to head of department only two years into the job, realizes too that things are totally off kilter with my teaching, not to mention my appearance, and he calls me in for a chat.

'I'm not here to lecture you, David. That's not my style and you know it,' he says to me across the table. 'In fact, as you know, I've always run this school with empathy at its core. You've been a huge part of its success, so if you're in any sort of emotional or even financial trouble I'd prefer you came to me instead of trying to hide it like you've been doing.'

I blow out a deep breath. My throat is dry and my head is banging as it is constantly these days. Three weeks have felt like three years and so much has happened in that time, so much that it feels as though everything is out of control.

I try to find the words. I can't.

'What's going on?' he asks me. 'Forget I'm the school principal and talk to me, man to man. My God, we spend days drumming that into our students, so I'm asking you to spit it out and get it off your chest. You might feel better just by doing that?'

I can feel my lip tremble in a way it hasn't done since I was a child. I look around the room, my face in a deep frown as I try to find the words to explain how I'm feeling. Yes, I'm heartbroken about Kate and I'm petrified of a future without her, but this is bigger than all that. It's like a moment I've been expecting, a moment I've dreaded, an inevitable crash I always knew wasn't too far away has swallowed me whole and I don't know how to get out of it.

'I think . . . oh God . . . I think I'm having some sort of belated breakdown, Andrew,' I tell the man in front of me, as I contemplate the fallout from years of built-up trauma – my relationship with my father, the bomb and how it haunted me, Aaron's untimely and cruel death, the miscarriage with Lesley and the cancellation of the wedding, my mother's long illness, my injury in Haiti and the trauma I witnessed there, and now Kate's father's death and the fact that I did know something was wrong with him but I kept it to myself.

'Keep going.'

'I feel like I'm falling apart,' I say as my voice changes. 'I need to get off this damn carousel once and for all. I'm so dizzy I feel as if I'm going to fall off and never get up again.'

And at that I break down into tears – huge, sobbing, ugly tears that distort my face and run into my overgrown beard and sting my tired eyes.

I forget that I'm in school, in my principal's office, here in a place where I'm held in such high esteem. A place where I'm the one everyone goes to for advice, where I'm a leader and a tower of strength. I've crumbled at last. It was only a matter of time but I've totally crumbled.

'I should have told Kate that her dad was afraid,' I say to Andrew, who listens and watches as I fold in front of him. 'I didn't want her to worry, nor did he, but Kate isn't a worrier, she's a doer – she would have helped him. I just feel like I've messed up by keeping that from her and I don't know where to start to fix it.'

Mr Spence sits forward in his chair and clasps his hands together.

'Every upset in our lives is like a drip in a cup, David,' he tells me softly when I get a grip of my emotions and quieten down at last. 'It can only take one drip to make your cup overflow and it seems that's what's happening to you now. It's your relationship that has caused this overflow now, but you also have to deal with all the drips from before. I'm here to help. I'm telling you I can help you. You don't have to suffer through this alone.'

I shake my head.

'She's . . . she's gone,' I say to him, holding my head in my hands. 'I just know that Kate's gone and that she won't be back. We were meant to be buying our first proper home. We were meant to be planning a wedding and a family but it's all ruined now. She isn't coming back, Andrew, I know it. I can't believe I've lost her and even though I understand her upset at what happened, I thought we were so much more than that. I thought she'd be back by now.'

I realize Andrew is probably struggling to keep up with my incoherent ramblings, but he was right to get me to talk about it. It feels good already to have been able to get it all out and tell someone the truth of what has been going on, instead of picking up a bottle to drown my sorrows – sorrows that are very quickly learning how to duck and dive and keep up with me now.

'I would usually suggest some time out of work to any

staff who have a bit too much going on, but I think you need to try and stay focused, David. So I'm going to ask you to do this,' he says to me. 'Put the damn bottle down for a start, eh? Clean yourself up and try to show Kate that you are worth coming back here for.'

'I don't know if I've any more fight in me left,' I tell him.

'Of course you do!' he says. 'You might not feel it now but you will. My goodness, David, fight for her. Prove to her that you are the man she fell in love with. It might take some time but I believe in you. I always have. The students here adore you. Try and remember who you are inside and why you are so loved. You are needed and you are loved.'

I look up at the older man and my eyes widen at his compliment. His very few, simple but effective words mean more to me right now than anything I've heard before; words that I've longed to hear from my father all my life.

I swallow and absorb what he has just said.

'*I believe in you.*'

The only other person who ever believed in me was Kate, but now I know it's time I started to believe in myself. I will have to do my best to get a grip and I will do just as Andrew Spence has advised me to.

I'm going to deal with my shit, mop up all the drips from my overflowing cup once and for all and, when the time is right, I'm going to prove to Kate that, no matter what, I won't let anything else destroy what we have, even if it takes time on my part too.

NOVEMBER 2012

22.

KATE

My father's death eight months ago choked me, and it has changed me in ways I could never have predicted.

I returned home back in March with the intention of seeing the funeral through in a respectable manner like he deserved, but instead I was met with a hornet's nest, a tangled-up mess in a world that I'd turned my back on for far too long. I had always been the fixer in my family, the glue who kept us together through hard times and good times, but being away meant I hadn't noticed the many cracks that had been appearing.

My mum was verging on deep depression and alcoholism as the stresses and trauma of her time in prison haunted her deeply, Mo had been sucked in to becoming the lapdog my mother had once been to Sean McGee and his posse, believing everything he told her and taking her on a road to nowhere, but the biggest shock of all was Shannon, who had gone from being an ambitious, focused teenager to an unruly, rebellious young adult who had moved into a flat on her own and was throwing her life down the gutter in a way that broke my heart.

And then there was David. I was stumped when I heard he had known of my father's inner fears and kept them from me. I was horrified that he had a secret that could have saved my father's life if I had been able to step in and pull him out of danger, just like I've spent the past few months doing with my sister, my niece and my mother.

'You don't have to be everyone's guardian angel,' he told me in one of our earlier conversations, when I decided to take a twelve-month career break from nursing and spend some time at home to try and pick up the pieces of my family's very broken life, using up all the money I'd saved to put down as a deposit on my first property I'd planned to buy with David.

'You have no idea of any type of life outside your own pampered privilege,' I spat at him, knowing I was taking out most of my anger and grief on the person I loved the most. 'I can't just turn my back on them and pretend it isn't happening. This is real shit and it's my shit and you should have told me!'

Gradually my family began to pick itself up. My mother grew stronger by attending AA meetings and taking up some new voluntary work at the community centre, which gave her a purpose and a sense of belonging; Mo slowly began to see sense, recognizing Sean McGee's true colours when he was imprisoned for his part in the break-in to my father's house that had triggered his fatal heart attack. Shannon too, thankfully, straightened herself out and moved to Belfast to begin a course at art college for which I'd helped her apply. Meanwhile I focused on building up my charity work again, and Silent Steps began to gain a higher profile on both a local and national level.

I've worked hard at becoming the voice of trauma, where I use my experience as an example of how to turn hard real-life issues into positives. I'm invited to speak in schools, to community groups, and even to the media, where I've secured a weekly column on a local newspaper. I'm fast becoming recognized and admired for the hard work I do to improve lives on so many levels.

But no matter how much I bandage over my heart with work, and in my daily efforts to keep my mum, sister and niece on the straight and narrow, I just can't shake off the knowledge that a huge part of my life is missing. And that part is David.

I cry for him every single night, I yearn for the strength of his arms, I long for our life in England again where we'd go to work, greet each other afterwards like we hadn't seen each other in weeks, and where we'd cook and cosy up on the sofa, dream and plan our future, and believe that the world stopped at our front door as soon as we closed it.

I want to go back to the day before my dad died when we were planning on buying our first house, and when we were browsing through bridal magazines and doing our financial homework on how and what we could afford in order to make our immediate future the best it could be. I want to stop punishing myself and David for my father's death, but I can't forgive myself for not listening to my inner voice, which warned me there'd be trouble if we insisted on being together.

For eight months we've talked, we've argued, we've cried, we've given each other space, we've acknowledged the huge hurdles we've had along the way and we've both said we're not quite ready yet to try again as we accept that us being together played a part in my father's death.

The wounds are weeping still, but I can't stop loving him, and I miss him so much.

The simple everyday things are what made what we had so special. God knows I'd love to get those simple times back again.

'I'm seeing a therapist,' he told me on a phone call a few months ago. Those calls, though very infrequent, are heart-wrenching and desperately painful, but have strangely helped me stay grounded and focused and not totally derail when the tug and pain of missing him becomes unbearable and I want to jump on a plane and forget everything else, only us. 'I'm trying to be the best I can be, Kate. I need to be sure I can be as emotionally strong as I possibly can be before I see you again.'

And that's exactly what he has been doing. He spent the

summer on a retreat abroad to heal from all the darkness he has had going on in his head. I admire that and, from afar, I don't think I have ever loved him more, even if our last conversation was challenging and almost ripped me apart.

'You can't put your life on hold for other people for ever,' he told me before he left for India. 'Maybe you need to accept that you don't need to change the whole world, Kate. Maybe you should work on yourself a bit more. While you're fighting to save everyone around you, there's someone right here who is the only one who would ever fight for you. That person is me.'

His words hit me hard as I know them to be true. I know I always feel I'm the one who holds my family together, and when I'm away they all fall apart, but can I – should I – babysit them for ever? I'm missing David. I'm missing all we had and I'm scared now I might have left it too long.

'I'm so tired of fighting, David,' I told him, rubbing my forehead. 'I honestly don't think I can take any more grief or upset, but when I'm here I feel I'm in control.'

'Well, maybe I need time now too,' he said, which pierced me right in the heart.

'What?'

'You heard me,' he said. 'Maybe I need time too. I'm going on this retreat to really think things through. Have a nice summer with your family, Kate.'

Now, as autumn has passed and winter and the dark

nights draw in, I don't know how much longer I can go on without him, but I must respect his decision. Just as I needed time and space to help out my own family here, he needs time out to help and heal himself.

It's been almost eight months since my father died, eight months since I packed a case at our apartment in Bromley and pledged to David that my family needed me more than he did; eight months since he had an emotional breakdown that knocked him to the floor but never, ever broke him fully.

But time is beginning to chip away at me and I need him so badly. I forgive him and I need him, but I have to know we are both ready before we can ever try to be together again. I may be ready now, but it turns out he isn't and that's something I just have to live with.

'Are you all set?' my mother asks me as I put my make-up on for a talk I'm giving today in Belfast, the biggest speech I've given to date on trauma and its aftermath.

I've bared my soul to my listeners many times at a local level, where I've talked about the effect of the bomb and how I promised myself I would follow my dream to be a nurse. I've spoken of the night terrors and the emotional pain that haunted me for years and how I used it to promote awareness of topics that mean something to me. I've told of the horror of my father's death at the hands of lowlife gangs and how I've taken a career break, moved my family out of a crippled and damaged estate into a home in a much more beautiful part of the neighbourhood where they can all make a fresh start in life. Every penny I'd saved since I left university, every penny I saved for a future with David, I've invested in them and I feel better for it.

I've told many people my story, but today is the biggest audience I will face to date, and to say I'm nervous is an understatement.

'I'm as ready as I'll ever be,' I tell my mother, noticing how she looks at me with such pride.

'I'm so proud of you,' she whispers, and I look in the mirror to see the tears well up in her eyes. She is wearing a spectacular black trouser suit that shows off her enviable figure, her hair is styled and curled, and she is wearing the gold necklace I've always meant to ask her about. She has made such an effort to be by my side today.

'Did Dad buy you that?' I ask, my eyes diverting to the fine gold chain around her neck. 'I notice you wear it every day.'

She touches the delicate necklace tenderly and smiles.

'He bought this for me the day you were born,' she tells me with a smile. 'I remember his face when he gave it to me. You'd have thought he was presenting me with the most precious jewels. It meant the world to him and it meant the world to me too.'

'Ah, that's special,' I whisper. 'I always knew it was special.'

'As are you, my precious girl. You know, Kate, your dad and I were crazy about each other behind all our trouble,' she continues, 'but I pushed him away so many times until he decided never to come back again. You'll never know regret like I do now, I hope, my darling. My heart is broken since he died and I realize that, although I thought I'd loved before, everyone and everything else I loved before him just left a scratch in there. Now, since he has gone, my heart, when it comes to romantic love, is broken for real. A heart can be scratched many times, but it can only be broken by a romantic love once in a lifetime.'

I stare at the necklace and my own heart aches when I imagine my dad picking it out for her on the day I came into the world.

She puts her hand on my shoulder.

'You paused your own life with David to come and help us,' she says to me. 'You sacrificed your own wonderful life and I only hope you can pick up where you left off with him. He's a great man, Kate. He's the only man I can ever imagine you being with. Please don't let him go. Don't break your own heart for the sake of honouring things that are way out of your control. We used always to ask what we would do without you, but now we have to learn for ourselves. You can't stay here with us for ever.'

'I know that now, Mum,' I reply, feeling a sinking sensation of guilt grip my insides. 'I was angry at David for reasons that were so unfair to him. I was angry that he didn't know the life I'd lived here, the threats we suffered, the trauma we faced so often. The differences in our backgrounds werc always simmering beneath our happiness, and then – just like I'd feared – they came to a head and boiled over. I hope he will forgive me soon. I'll never stop waiting for him.'

She pats my hair and fixes it at the back. I'm wearing an emerald green dress that shows off my eyes and, when I look in the mirror and tuck my hair behind my ears, I feel a pull inside me and a longing for him that's physical, emotional, and so overpowering I don't know if I can get through this day without him.

I wish he was here. I want him back but I just hope we haven't left it too late, because now that I've fixed my family, all I want to do is fix us.

DAVID

I don't tell either of my parents that I'm paying them a visit today.

Instead I just rock up to the house in a taxi, having bussed it from the airport to my home town, and as I stand at the front door I know that today is the first day of the rest of my life. It's the day I grab everything by the horns, after months of therapy, self-help and rebuilding myself into the person I want to be from now on.

I feel taller in stature, I'm stronger physically than I've ever been and my mind is crystal clear.

Every step I've taken on my journey out of the darkness has taught me something that I'll always hold dear. I've learned that sad times will only ever make us appreciate happy times more, that absence from those we love will only make us love them even more, and that when life gets too noisy or busy, it's teaching us how much we should appreciate the quiet, more peaceful times, or vice versa.

A summer at a Buddhist retreat in India plunged me to deeper parts of my existence that I never knew I could reach. I realized that – although Kate and I were so strong and she is always going to be the best thing that ever happened to me – I was like those swans we saw on the lake that day. I was masking my inner turmoil; I was gliding along on the surface and paddling so frantically underneath that I finally crashed. It took Kate leaving to make me see it all for what it was – she had been propping me up all along, and without her I was unsteady; but I needed to learn to stand strong on my own and I'm so glad to say I can do that now.

My mother opens the door and her hands clasp her face when she sees me.

'David!' she exclaims. 'Look at you! So handsome! Come in! It's so good to see you!'

I step inside my family home and allow myself to remember for only a second the scenes that occurred on my last visit here with Kate on the day of our engagement. Those days are gone now. I'm no longer the fist-clenching, blame-giving, hostile person I used to be when it comes to my father. I've come to accept my part in our troubled relationship and also acknowledge our vast differences with understanding that yes he did change, but he also gave me many precious years as a child that I can only look back on with love. He hasn't aged well, he has suffered with his own health lately, while ironically my mother has gone from strength to strength.

But it's also in memory of Kate's father, Peter O'Neill, that I come here today. He planted the seed in me to never leave what we have to say until it's too late. His words have never left me and I want to do this not only for me and my father, but also to acknowledge his strong advice. I can then rest in the knowledge that I tried my best.

'Does your dad know you were coming here today?' my mother asks as she does what she usually does when I come home. She makes me take off my winter coat, she sits me down on the comfy chair which was always my favourite as a child and she puts on the kettle for a cuppa.

'I only decided to make the trip last night,' I tell her. 'I've been filling my weekends with all sorts of activity since Kate left, but this is the first Saturday I've had nothing in my diary so I made the decision last night and got a last-minute flight.'

'Oh,' she says, stirring the cup of tea before she hands it to me. 'He's in bed most days now for a nap around this time, but I told you that on the phone already. He doesn't have the same energy to be as bitter and angry any more. Even his congregation, who used to hang on his every word, have noticed how much he has mellowed. He isn't, let's say, as forceful and energetic as he once was.'

I blow on the tea in my mug and go over in my head what it is I want to say to him, but the truth is I have no script.

'How is Kate?' Mum asks, making my heart leap when I hear her name.

'She's – she's doing OK, I suppose,' I reply, feeling my heart break all over again as I think of how geographically we are now so close, closer than we've been for most of this year. 'I rode in a taxi through town from the bus station to get here and imagined I saw her in every shop doorway, just as I used to when I looked for her after the bomb.'

'Does she know you're home?' she asks me. I shake my head.

'I think I'll go up and see Dad now.'

'That's OK, honey,' Mum says to me. 'I'll just go and let him know you're on your way. I think he'll be very glad to see you.'

I go into my father's bedroom, now in a different room to where my mother sleeps. It was always known as the spare room when I was growing up, and has hosted many famous names from the world's clergy, but its majestic decor is now faded and old, a bit like the man who lies beneath the covers.

'I wasn't expecting you,' he says to me. His voice is low

and fragile, his face is thinner and the redness from before has gone, but it's his hands that catch my eye the most. They are the hands that once held a bike for me as I tried to ride it without stabilizers for the first time. They are the hands that many times threw a ball in my direction so I could score a goal between the posts he made with wood that left his fingers splintered. They are the hands that once helped me roll a snowball into a snowman so large that I was the envy of all my friends when I was only seven years old.

'I wanted to . . . I wanted to come here and make peace with you once and for all,' I say to him, and I see a tiny smile climb onto his face. It's not a smile of happiness entirely, but more like one of intense relief. 'I know we're both stubborn fools, but one of us had to make the first move and I'm stepping it up right now to say I'm sorry for any trouble I've ever caused you and that I forgive you for the hurt that you, intentionally or not, have caused me.'

He licks his lips which are dry and flaky and takes a deep breath.

'You know, David, our time apart has not been entirely pain-free on my part either. I've had a lot of time to think and ponder over a lot of what I said to you down the years,' he says to me. He pats the bed and I sit down at the bottom of it, the familiarity of the satin throw bringing me right back to my childhood.

I almost lose my breath.

'I had a visitor here one day,' he continues slowly. 'A very unexpected visitor, and since we spoke and cleared the air it made me realize that perhaps I've been a hypocrite in many ways and that my expectations of others, especially you, were sometimes out of reach.'

'A visitor? Who?'

I await his answer as he pauses in thought.

'Peter O'Neill,' he whispers eventually. 'Kate Foley's father.'

My eyebrows rise and my mouth opens in disbelief.

'We talked in depth about everything – from love and regrets to fatherhood and religion – and we aired our very different opinions on life. He asked me to pray for his safety,' he tells me, clasping his hands so his knuckles are white as he does so. 'He seemed afraid and desperate, but he wanted to meet me and he asked me to pray for his soul and for you and Kate, to give you strength.'

'Oh Peter.'

'He died shortly afterwards.'

I shake my head slowly, trying to take this in.

'Since that day I've written you letters and thrown them in the wastepaper basket as I lacked the courage to send them to you, but as time has worn on, I've realized that I was at risk of leaving it too late. I was being a coward, David. I was preaching to others about forgiveness, and all the time I was turning my back on my own son simply because he loved a woman whom I stubbornly chose not to understand.'

I'm deeply shocked at all of this, and at the same time overwhelmed that a conversation with my father for once might just be going in a direction in which we can both find peace.

'I'm glad Peter reached out to you,' I whisper, picturing the man, so frail and worried, yet who took the time to come and try to help Kate and me in any way he could. 'He may have held the most opposite political beliefs to yours, Dad, but his heart was the size of a lion,' I tell my father.

'I could see that, once we put our own bigotries to the side,' he agrees. 'We have had very different lives in the very same tiny little part of the world, and we had very similar regrets.'

I gulp back tears as I imagine the efforts both men must have gone to, all for the love of Kate and me, and to give us a chance.

'When Peter died,' I explain to my father, 'the love and outpouring of grief from his family – who had had many differences with him – taught me that his words to me were true. We are all just people, trying to do our best in life as we face very similar battles on a daily basis. We all want to be the best father, the best son, the best husband and the best friend. If you peel back the layers of religion or race or politics, you'll find that we are all craving the same things, and most of that comes down to a very basic human desire, which is to be wanted and to be loved. Sometimes, the people we love most are the hardest to reach, but it's so worth finding their hand when you do.'

He nods in agreement with a smile.

'Maybe I should have had you or Peter O'Neill write some of my sermons,' he says with a chuckle. 'You might have made a better job of them than I did sometimes.'

I shrug.

'I've been doing a lot of work on myself lately,' I explain to him. I'm not sure if the bedroom where he lies is warm and sticky, or if I'm hot because of the conversation, but I loosen my jacket to cool down a bit. 'I don't think I'd have been so worldly or wise before this year took everything I loved the most away from me. Losing everything has made me reassess my actions and the direction I want to go in.'

He looks across towards the window, closes his eyes for a moment and then looks back in my direction.

'You loved Kate Foley deeply and still do, I know that now,' he says to me. 'And I was a fool to believe I could ever stop that.'

I feel my eyes sting as he says her name with dignity for the first time.

This was not what I expected to hear from my father and, although I never needed his permission to be with Kate, to have his blessing is a lot more than I could ever have imagined.

'She's making a speech today in Belfast's Waterfront Hall, you know,' he says, nodding towards a newspaper that lies on his bedside table. 'Why don't you go and support her?'

I lift up the newspaper quickly and scan the pages until I find Kate's face in a smiling photo. I feel butterflies in my stomach as I touch her face in the picture.

'I'm not sure I can make it to Belfast in time,' I say when I check the clock on the wall. 'The event starts in just over an hour and Kate might be one of the first speakers in the line-up listed.'

Now it's my father's turn to raise an eyebrow.

'Take my car.'

'Really?' I ask him.

'Really,' he whispers.

I look at him, trying to absorb this almighty change of heart.

'"Even if the opposition to love is only merely *time* itself,"' my father reminds me of a sermon he used to give, '"it will only fan its flames." Take it from a sorry old fool who is admitting he was wrong before his clock stops ticking, David. Please don't waste another second. Go and find her. Go and find Kate, just as you both promised you would one day. Take the car. Go and find the woman you love and who loves you.'

23.

KATE

There are 2,250 people in this packed auditorium, and the lights are so bright I can't see any of them from the wings of the stage when I peep out waiting on my turn to speak, which is probably a good thing as I'm sweating buckets at the very thought of so many faces sitting in the darkness.

I know the first row has been assigned to the Press, and there's a family and friends section to my right where my mum, Mo and Shannon sit along with my old friend Sinead who has travelled up to Belfast from Dublin to support me, along with a couple of our colleagues from the hospital where I worked, but there's still an emptiness in my heart as I address the crowd and a deep regret that I didn't contact David to invite him here.

I should have told him how much today means to me, and how it would make it even more special if he was here, but I promised I'd give him the space he needed, so he can do what he needs to do. I swore to myself I wouldn't push him into seeing me or any regular contact, knowing that if it were meant to be then love would find a way, and I prayed that he might forgive me for lashing out my blame on him over my father's death.

I step out onto the stage and the silence is deafening, then a trickle of applause turns into something louder and I do my best to stay focused on the job at hand. I'm the third speaker in an event that was designed to inspire young people to be the best they can be, no matter what life throws at them, and the audience is mostly young people in school uniform and their teachers, who hope to become inspired in some way by what I have to say.

The biggest element to my own story of overcoming adversity is of course my bomb-survival story, which I've told so many times, but this time I want to pay credit to David and the part he played that day in not only helping Shannon and me stay calm, but also to the person who taught me that love knows no boundaries, love has no rules and love has no religion.

'We called him the ice-cream shop boy for years in our house,' I tell the audience in my off-the-cuff speech, which I've decided doesn't need a script or visuals of any sort. I've learned that the best way at such events is to deliver from the heart and let the story speak for itself. 'That name stuck. The ice-cream shop boy.'

The audience seem to find that both endearing and

amusing, and as I go on to say how we then met again ten years later and began a relationship which saw so many ups and downs, including the worst of times when David was injured once more in faraway Haiti, and then our parting this year after the passing of my loved and adored father.

I speak about inner grit, about the importance of asking for help when it's needed, about leaning on good friends and about surrounding yourself with goals, milestones. I talk about never saying no to new opportunities.

'We were the last generation to remember what was known as The Troubles,' I say as I move towards my conclusion. 'That three-decade conflict saw those of nationalist and unionist beliefs tear each other apart in a bloody campaign of horror. We can be grateful that we were the last to experience soldiers on our streets, we were the last to experience bomb threats and bullets as part of our daily lives, and we can be grateful that our children and that you, the next generation, will never see what we saw. Along with that gratitude, on a more personal level, David and I wanted to prove to the world that our love was bigger than all the differences imposed on us by others. We wanted to show the world there still could be a wonderful life, full of love, after trauma.'

I've slightly changed direction in my talk perhaps, but it's what is on my mind now and I know I've got their attention.

'It's an age-old saying that love is blind, and I believe that now more than ever, because I've learned that true love doesn't see colour or class, race or religion, age or occupation,' I conclude. 'True love doesn't see scars or illness as a barrier, or money or poverty as a threat, nor does it recognize jealousy or pain as a weapon. True love is everything that is warm and good, and tough and strong, and determined and righteous. Most of all, true love never comes to an end. It can't. It's always there because it doesn't know how to leave. It has nowhere else to go.'

I see his tear-stained face in that doorway now in my mind, I feel his hand so strong in mine; I see his beautiful smile as he reminded me of our brief and innocent flirtation, I sense the power and strength of how it feels when he holds me. I close my eyes and I feel his lips on mine. I want him now so badly.

Oh God, how I miss him so.

'True love is so blind that it doesn't recognize time,' I continue, fighting back tears. 'It doesn't . . . it doesn't recognize distance, and it doesn't even recognize death. True love lasts for ever, no matter what comes in between.'

The audience begin a light trickle of applause as I finish.

'I'm so lucky to have had true love in my life,' I conclude, 'and no matter what trauma I still face ahead, that's something I will hold in my heart for ever, because nothing can take it away from me. Our love story isn't over yet. It will never be, no matter what. Our love has nowhere else to go.'

I take a deep breath and I can feel my palms sweating

and my hands shaking as the house lights go up ever so slightly for questions, but the audience are already on their feet. The compère, a friendly lady called Jackie who is much more glamorous and confident than I am in front of such a crowd, takes the podium at the far end of the stage.

I purse my lips together and fight with my eyes not to cry. I'd promised myself I wouldn't cry today. I just wish he was here. This is a milestone of celebration, a moment in time that I'll never forget, and I should be proud enough of myself to hold my head up and take questions without breaking down.

'We'll have questions now,' Jackie says as the applause fades and the audience takes their seats again. 'Just a few. I'm sure Kate is exhausted after her most inspirational story, so a couple of questions from the front, please?'

I gather myself, and when I look into the crowd of unfamiliar faces all staring back at me, I think I see him for a moment, but I blink away his image to the back of my tortured mind. It can't be him, of course it can't. When I was getting ready earlier I thought I heard my father's voice in my ear, and now I'm make-believing I'm seeing David in the midst of over two thousand people at an event he knows nothing about.

'I'm so sorry, could you repeat that, please?' I ask the journalist who asked a question that I didn't even hear one word of.

I compose myself and answer the lady, who wants to

358

know what professional help I can recommend for victims of trauma, and I spend probably far too long touching on my own training as a nurse and how I specialized in that area. I'm rambling but my head is mangled. I was sure I saw him.

The next question is from my own local newspaper at home and it's a friendly compliment at first more than a question, but he asks me to explain what my darkest moment was and how I got myself through it. Again, I stumble over words to answer as best I can, and to my relief he seems satisfied with my answer.

But it's the third question that takes me most my surprise, and I realize that it doesn't come from the front row where the Press sits, but from the area that my eye was drawn to a few moments ago when I was sure I was seeing things.

'Do you miss the ice-cream shop boy?' the man says, and the whole audience cranes their necks in his direction. 'And more importantly, would you like to see him again soon?'

The question stops me in my tracks, and I feel my heart thump in my chest as I search for exactly where the voice is coming from. I step forward to try and get a better look as more than two thousand other faces all look towards me now for an answer. I see a journalist shift in her seat at the front with her pen poised.

'I miss him so, so much every day,' I whisper, and the room begins to spin. 'I've been looking for him in my mind since we last said goodbye and I feel totally lost without him. I can't wait to see him again, but until that moment comes, I love him still.'

The room goes completely silent.

'He misses you too,' says the voice, and I feel my heart suddenly glowing strongly inside. 'He has never stopped missing you and he has never stopped loving you either.'

The crowd gasps and I gulp as tears prick my eyes.

'Oh David,' I say, and when I glance across at Jackie on the other podium, she is dabbing her eyes, but it's David who has got everyone's attention as he gets up from his seat and walks down through the auditorium towards the stage.

I shake my head in disbelief at the sight of him and all his gorgeousness, with his dark hair neatly cut, a light, shadowed stubble on his face just as I like it, and wearing a long coat over jeans and a white shirt. I can barely breathe and I'm sure my face is a picture of so many emotions – shock, relief, disbelief, delight, but most of all love.

He climbs up the steps to the side and wraps his arms around me.

'Please come home,' he whispers into my ear. 'I'm ready for this. Are you?'

'I'm ready, David,' I tell him, and when we head off the stage into the wings, I know now that I want to be with him for ever, and nothing can or will ever come between us again.

DAVID

After celebratory drinks with Kate's family and friends, during which we pose for photos and we toast her amazing speech, which is rumoured to be all set for some front-page news stories tomorrow, we are both on the crest of a wave. But our night is only just beginning.

Her heels click alongside me as we walk up the cobbled streets of Belfast in search of the hotel we booked on a whim. It's so good to be alone at last.

'So, how does it feel to be front-page news?' she asks me, and I know immediately what she is getting at.

The photographers at the event wanted pictures of Kate and her 'ice-cream shop boy' as a story of hope and survival; it was a far cry from the times when we were too afraid to be seen together, never mind photographed for the country's media.

'I tried to pose using my best side,' I joke, and then she huddles me into a corner on the street as the rain falls down on us and we share a tender moment that sums up all our hunger, pain and regret about the months we spent apart. Her kisses are soft and meaningful, yet so full of passion. We've so much to catch up on I don't know where to start, yet I'm settled in the knowledge that we have our whole future to make up for it.

'How did you know I was speaking this evening?' she asks. 'I didn't even get to ask you that amidst all the madness of tonight. How did you know?'

'My dad told me.'

'Your dad?'

'Well, yes, and that's a story in itself,' I explain to her. 'He even let me take his precious car.'

'No way.'

'I know! Look, this is our hotel now. Let's go in and relax with a drink and I'll tell you all about it.'

Kate and I wake up the next morning in a luxurious king-size bed, wrapped in soft white sheets with our bodies entangled, and I can't help but take a moment to watch her in admiration as she sleeps. She is smiling, a picture of pure contentment, and I yearn to touch her but don't want to wake her from her deep slumber, a well-earned rest after a year that is bound to have exhausted her on so many levels.

I've never met anyone who cares for others like she does. She is fiercely loyal, she is unconditional and imperfect, she is passionate and raw, and she is the only person I know who sees right into my soul as I do into hers.

We are soulmates and we will never be apart again, no matter what happens from here on in. Of that I'm sure.

I go to the shower as she snoozes and make a coffee, then I smile in disbelief when the porter delivers a continental breakfast to our room with the morning papers.

'I forgot we ordered breakfast,' says Kate as she stretches her arms and wakes up at last. 'Oh God, are we really in the newspaper? I don't think I'm mentally prepared to see that. I hate seeing myself or reading back the words I said.'

I find the page and hold it up while munching on a croissant, and she covers her mouth in mock awe.

We can't wait to be wed, says the main headline and then it reads: *The love story of two young people from opposing communities who survived a bomb, and of community resilience.*

'Please don't read it out, I'm cringing!' says Kate, which of course makes me want to read it out loud all the more.

'Kate Foley, a nurse and charitable campaigner, and David Campbell, a science teacher, first met when their paths crossed on the day of a tragic bomb that ripped the hearts out of their community, but brought theirs together.'

Kate pretends to block her ears so I stop and instead scan the rest of the article to myself.

'They don't know about how I spotted you at the bowling alley when you had purple hair,' she says as she comes to where I'm sitting at a round breakfast table by the window in the hotel room. 'Or how you flirted with me when I came into the ice-cream shop!'

'You mean, *you* flirted with me!' I protest.

'Yeah, but you stood there staring with your mouth open,' she says, sitting on my knee and draping her arms around my neck. 'You were love-struck. You couldn't even speak.'

'You said you liked my T-shirt,' I remind her as I nuzzle

her neck. She lifts a croissant and tries to nibble on it as she laughs.

'It was a plain white T-shirt,' she says sarcastically. 'Like how much more obvious could I have been? Who on earth could say they liked a plain white T-shirt? Oh, the innocence! It was the best I could think of at the time!'

The cool November rain batters the windows outside our fifth-floor hotel room and, just as I've felt so many times before, when we are together it's as though time stands still and the rest of the world doesn't matter. I've learned however that it does matter, and I'm strong enough inside now to play my part in a bigger world for us both; a world that will see us grow in love and extend it to others who need us both, be that her family or mine.

'It's so good to be together again,' she says to me, kissing my forehead and then wiping off crumbs that come from her lips. 'I've missed you like my heart had been smashed and stood upon. I'm not myself without you.'

'Yes, you are,' I tell her, and I really mean it. 'You are everything to me and I'm everything to you, but you are complete in yourself and that's why I love you so much. You're strong, you're compassionate, you're beautiful, and that will never, ever change.'

'How come you always know the right words to say?' she asks me, echoing a question I used to ask her so many times.

'I was taught by the best,' I reply, looking into her eyes with sincerity.

Kate lifts her phone and checks the time.

'We don't have to check out for another hour,' she says with a cheeky glint in her eye. 'So, David Campbell, how about we make good use of this room while we still have it? It's about time we started practising really hard to make a Kate or David junior, isn't it?'

I race her to the bed and we bounce onto it, and then wrap ourselves in each other's arms.

'You haven't lost your touch either,' I tell her as my hands wander on her velvet skin. 'You *still* know all the right words to say.'

JANUARY 2013

24.

KATE

I stand in the toilet cubicle on the Savannah ward of the children's hospital where I've been working again since after Christmas, and my jaw drops open in a mixture of shock and utter disbelief.

'Kate, are you all right in there, love?' shouts Molly, one of my fellow nurses in her friendly, rounded Yorkshire accent. 'You've been in a while. Just checking you're still alive.'

She chuckles as she says it, which makes me wonder what she would do if I didn't answer, but this is no time for jokes or silliness. It's the third anniversary this week of David's return from Haiti and, after giving him a present in appreciation for all he has done for me with Silent Steps (a pair of white and green Nike trainers he's been harping on about for weeks since he spotted them before Christmas), we enjoyed a delicious dinner prepared by my own fair hands. Now, I can't believe that when I get home later I will be able to give him another present that will most certainly be the icing on the cake.

I'm pregnant.

I'm *actually* pregnant.

I stare at the two blue lines, I shake the stick and blink my eyes three times, but no matter how many times I look away and then look back again, the two lines glare up at me. I put my hand on my tummy and breathe as I imagine the very tiny life that flutters inside me.

'I'll just be a second,' I shout to Molly, resisting the urge to blurt out my most wonderful news, but there's no way I'm telling anyone, as difficult as it might be to keep secret, until I tell David first. I've two more hours left on this shift and, as the snow falls outside, I know it's going to take every ounce of patience I have in my body to resist the urge to phone him before I get home and spit out the news.

Christmas was truly wonderful, if very surreal, as we sat around the huge dining table at Old Rectory Manor, just as my father had hoped would happen one day, and enjoyed a magnificent dinner prepared by Martha. I couldn't help but think of him every step of the way.

'It's a bloody mansion!' Mo said when the old reverend was just about out of earshot. 'I've never been in a house like this! Do you think you and David will inherit it?'

'Mo!' I exclaimed to her. 'Thank goodness he is hard of hearing and not as sharp as he used to be! If he heard you swearing within these walls, he'd crock it!'

'He looks like he might crock at any given moment,' whispered Shannon. 'He doesn't say much, does he?'

'You've no idea,' I said, rolling my eyes. 'Don't knock it.'

The whole afternoon passed by without any hiccups, and I was delighted to hear my mum and Martha laugh and plan to meet up in the New Year when they discovered a shared passion for reading, even pledging to start up a book club for some of their friends.

'I can feel your dad is here with us in some way,' David said to me as we washed up after dinner. 'Do you? Or am I becoming spiritual in my old age, now that my father isn't fit to tell me I should be?'

'I feel him, yes, for sure,' I told him, and now as I put the lid on the pregnancy test, wrap it in tissue paper, put it back in the box and into my handbag so I can show David later as proof of our impending parenthood, I can't help but think of my dad again and how he'd have loved to have been a grandfather.

'Are you happy, my girl?' I hear him saying, and before I leave this cubicle, I close my eyes for a moment and imagine myself replying.

'I'm happy, Daddy,' I say to him in my mind. 'I'm happy in here and in here.'

I point to my head and then to my heart.

'Then I'm happy too,' he says, and his image disappears back into my memory.

I pull myself together, wash my hands, and go back out onto the ward where a 10-year-old congenital heart disease patient called Missy is ruling the roost on the ward and keeping us all entertained with her rendition of 'Gangnam Style'. There's never a dull moment on this ward, through smiles and tears, and that's how I like it.

DAVID

I take my time to set the table for dinner, placing everything perfectly as the smell of roast beef wafts from the oven. It's Sunday, my favourite day of the week believe it or not, because it's the day that Kate and I have learned to kick back and relax, eat a hearty lunch at leisure, drink some wine, watch some old movies and spend time loving each other. Since she moved back here to England a few weeks ago to start her job, having tied up all her loose ends back home, we've had so much to make up for and also so much to plan for.

'You'll have to propose to me all over again,' she joked one day when she put her engagement ring in her jewellery box before she left for her shift at the hospital.

'That's no problem at all,' I told her. 'I might take my time on that one.'

She playfully rolled her eyes, but the cogs of my mind were already spinning and now today, which I've calculated as three years to the day when I returned home from Haiti, is a good day for us to officially start all over again.

If I can time it properly and leave the apartment now, I'll be able to meet her after her shift at the hospital, where I plan to surprise her with the ring in its original box and a chocolate-box proposal in the snow followed by a delicious lunch at home, just the two of us.

I check the oven as the roast beef cooks low and slow, put on my coat, and set out into the chilly January afternoon.

KATE

'Molly, I can't stand it any longer,' I say to my colleague. 'Sarah is here early to take over from me, so is there any way I can leave just twenty minutes early? I'm mad to get home. You see, I've just found out – actually, no, I'm not telling anyone. I need to tell David first. Molly, can I slip on home just a little bit early? Please?'

Molly's smile beams over her face and her eyes light up as she reads between the lines.

'I will say nothing,' she replies. 'Mum's the word, quite literally I have guessed, my love. But it's treacherous out there, Kate, so take your time. The roads are crazy in the snow.'

'You guessed right! I'll be careful, I promise,' I say, giving her a hug. She's the eldest on our team and her words of wisdom are legendary around our ward. 'Thanks, Moll! I'll see you tomorrow!'

I put on my navy coat, a present my dad bought me when I graduated and one that is still as good as new, and make my way down the corridor and into the elevator. When I step outside the hospital and walk towards the car park, the chill hits me. After my eight-hour shift I'm exhausted but too full of adrenaline to let the tiredness kill my mood.

I can't wait to get home. My car isn't great in the snow, though, and I'll have to take it very easy. I just hope I can stay awake long enough to get there safely.

DAVID

The windscreen wipers swish back wet snowflakes and I blow into my hands as I begin the eight-mile journey to the hospital.

It's absolutely freezing, minus three according to the car's thermometer, but I'm smiling inside imagining Kate's face when she sees me outside her place of work. I know exactly where I'm going to stand, just beside a little wooden bench that has a holly tree still in bloom with berries. This is the year of new beginnings for us. It's the time to start again and the time to move things forward.

I double-check my inside pocket for the engagement ring box, and swear when I realize I've left it on the kitchen table.

'Ah, shit, come on!'

How could I be so stupid? I should turn back, but an announcement on the radio gives me another idea.

'Traffic is slow and heavy city-bound today, with

motorists advised to display extra caution when travelling,' says the radio news. 'With more snow predicted for the afternoon, the Met Office are strongly advising against any unnecessary travel.'

I look at the clock on the dashboard. It's ten minutes until Kate's shift finishes and I wish I'd messaged her in advance and told her to leave the car at the hospital. It's best I pick her up. I don't want her driving in this weather. I'll text her to stay put. So much for my romantic proposal in the snow!

I lift the phone, glancing back and forth between it and the windscreen as I text her. The radio station is playing some classics and I crank it up between texting when I hear one of our favourites, 'Sweet Baby James' by the legendary James Taylor, come on. What a song.

KATE

My phone bleeps as I'm pulling out of the car park but I don't dare try to check it in this weather.

I'm driving like a snail as it is and the tiredness I felt earlier is creeping up on me fast. I wish I could wave a magic wand and be home safe and sound, lying up on the sofa with David as we stare into space in each other's arms and plan our future with our new arrival. Of course my head is buzzing with names already, and we need to start house-hunting all over again. There's no way we'll be bringing our baby home to our tiny apartment. We have so much to get organized and I'm guessing that if the baby was conceived in Belfast back in November, we'll be looking at an August birth.

Wow. August – the same month as the bomb when we first properly met. A shiver runs through me, then I turn up the radio when I realize that they are playing one of our all-time favourites, 'Sweet Baby James'. So many signs!

Maybe the baby will be a boy and we could call him James? David's face is going to be priceless. I might record him and send it home so the whole family can see his reaction. This is going to be the best day ever.

DAVID

I sing along to the song on the radio and check my phone to see if Kate has replied, but she hasn't yet. I put my car lights on full beam, and then flick them back as the traffic swirls past.

I lift the phone again.

I glance up quickly towards the road but my blood turns into hot lava in the blink of an eye when I realize I've swerved slightly onto the wrong side of the road.

'Jesus! No!'

I swerve in the opposite direction as quickly as I can but the low droning sound of a lorry's horn blasts out of nowhere and his lights flash a warning to me.

'*No!*'

It's too late. The lorry clips the wing mirror on my car, sending it into a whirl, and as the car turns round and round like a spinning top, the whole world goes into slow motion.

I hear a loud blast, like an explosion, and then everything goes silent as a thick smog fills the air, billowing outside as I blink and blink and blink it away, my head slamming against the window, against the steering wheel, against the window again . . .

I see Kate in the doorway all those years ago. I see Shannon; she is a child again, covered in dust, holding a balloon, but when I look at her face it's not Shannon at all. It's a different child.

I hear sirens, I smell smoke, I see dust, I see black.

I see a baby's face. It's a little girl. She looks like me. No, she looks like Shannon. She cries.

I see nothing. I feel nothing.

I see Kate. I will forever want to see Kate.

KATE

The traffic slows down to a stop and I push my head back onto the headrest and let out a deep sigh.

'Come on!' I say in frustration as I wait, the car in front of me barely visible in the flurry of snow. Its tail-lights are about as much as I can make out, and it looks as if we're going nowhere, so I yank on the handbrake and check my phone, remembering I've a message from earlier, plus I want to message David and let him know I'm stuck in traffic.

I can picture him dancing around the kitchen like he does on a Sunday afternoon, the radio playing his favourite classics from the 1970s, the smell of roast beef in the air. He'll be wearing my apron thinking it's absolutely hilarious that he is doing so.

'Stay put, babe,' the message says. 'I'm coming to pick you up. Don't dare drive in the snow.'

I scrunch my face and curse myself for not checking this earlier. He'll be on his way now. I crane my neck to see if I can tell what's going on ahead but an ambulance screaming past makes me sit up straight and my blood curdles.

There's been an accident, which is hardly surprising in this crazy weather.

I know it's not safe to do so and I know it's mental in these conditions, but I can tell now the scene must be less than half a mile away, so I open the car door and walk along the far side of the traffic, ignoring the pelting snow on my face. As I wipe away the snowflakes I convince myself I'm doing the right thing.

Of course, I'm doing the right thing. It's my instinct. I'm a nurse. I need to help. I can't just sit in the car and wait for more emergency services to arrive in this weather. Someone needs my help and I'm going to give it.

I keep walking through the blizzard until I see the commotion in the near distance. A lorry sits tight against the left lane and there's a mangled car, turned on its roof, where an ambulance crew work as two police cars tape off the scene.

This is bad.

Any sense of exhaustion or exhilaration has left me now as I turn into full-blown work mode, switched off from everything, only my duty at hand.

Maybe I'm in shock. Maybe I already know what's ahead of me, but when I come on the scene eventually and am told I can go no further by a police officer, I see the number plate on the car, I see a white and green trainer lying on the roadside and I fold into the police officer's arms.

'You can't go any further, lady!'

'David!' I scream into the snow. '*No!* Please God, no!'

'I'm sorry, miss, you can't come closer,' she says as I push and claw at her.

'David!' I scream. 'We're having a baby! Don't leave me! *David!*'

'Can someone get a blanket for this lady,' I hear the police officer shout. 'She's pregnant and I believe she knows the victim. Quickly!'

My whole world goes dark.

'Is there someone we can call for you? A family member? A friend? Anyone?'

I shake my head.

'I'll call my mum. Just take me home, please.'

* * *

The police have brought me home and I enter the flat to the smell of our burnt Sunday dinner.

The radio is still on; the apron he wore to prepare our meal lies strewn over the back of the chair and the table is set to perfection. He was planning something, I can tell, and when I see the engagement ring in its box beside my place mat I realize that it was the proposal I'd been waiting for.

I howl and scream and kick and beg for this all to be just a terrible nightmare.

'*This is not true!*' I scream into the empty walls of our apartment. 'Please tell me it's not true. David, come home. We need you. Please, David, please come home. *Please!*'

My mother answers my call in the middle of my meltdown but I can hardly speak. I can only scream out his name and I just cry and sob and scream at the injustice of it all.

'We're coming to you right now, baby,' my mother tells me, her voice crippled with sorrow. 'We'll get there as soon as we can. It's our turn to look after you now, Kate. Stay strong! We're on our way, my love.'

I slide onto the floor and clutch my belly, screaming for mercy from this nightmare that has unfolded on what should have been our happiest day so far and the beginning of so much joy as a proper family.

'I can't do this without you, David,' I whisper as I lean my head against the kitchen cupboard, cradling my stomach. 'Please don't leave me. Please don't go.'

FIVE YEARS LATER

August 2018

25.

'Which do you think is nicer, ice cream or ice lollies?' We approach the awaiting crowd in the town centre for the twentieth anniversary of the bomb, a very modest gathering compared to the scenes ten years previously, and the questions keep coming.

'Which should I get for my birthday, a puppy or a kitten?'

'Who does she remind you of?' Shannon asks me with her eyes wide open in wonder. 'I swear, she even looks the same as I did. Was I really that annoying?'

'Don't say that, Shannon!' says Mo. 'She isn't annoying. She is adorable. Will I take you for some ice cream, darling?'

My 5-year-old daughter, Hope Foley-Campbell, grins and takes her aunt's hand and, as they walk towards a corner shop, I watch the scene in front of me with a sense of déjà vu.

'How you coping?' asks Shannon. She's 26 now and I'm approaching the grand old age of 40; they say that life begins then, but to be honest my life has been pretty full up until now and I'm ready for it to stay quiet for a while.

'Pretty tough, to be honest,' I tell her. 'You?'

'I hardly remember it now.'

'Lucky you,' I whisper. 'Do you mind if I take a walk?'

She smiles knowingly.

'I'll come with you if you want?'

I shake my head.

'I'd rather do this alone if that's OK,' I say, swallowing back a huge lump of emotion. 'I need to do it. It's like my own little ceremony and, as hard as it will be, I'll feel better for doing it before we all go back to England tomorrow.'

'Sure,' says Shannon, and I can sense her watch me as I head off up the hill, feeling the sun on my face. I get there and brace myself, and then I peel off my jacket as I approach the doorway of the shop where our story first began.

I find the little doorway, our shelter from the world, and I stand there and close my eyes as flashbacks of our life together so far flood my mind.

It's good to look back on our lives before and after all the events that have shaped us to get us where we are today. It reminds me of how far I've come – of how far we've all come since that day.

I watch as the townsfolk go about their daily business, I listen as a church bell chimes in the distance, I look on as children skip along and as couples go in and out of shops chatting and bickering, laughing and smiling in the sunshine. Life really does go on, and I can almost hear my dad saying it. I miss him so much, I really do.

'I thought I'd find you here,' says Mo, shaking her head

in surrender. 'Sorry, but she wanted to follow you. I put her off for as long as I could but she just wants her mummy.'

Hope flashes me a cheeky smile. She holds a balloon in her hand and I do a double take when I see it.

'Was the balloon your idea, or hers?' I ask, just a little bit freaked out at the sight, transported back to the day of the bomb again. She is like a mirror image of Shannon and my skin rises into goose bumps at the similarities between this day and the one twenty whole years ago.

'I wanted it and Shannon said I could have it if I stop asking so many questions,' Hope tells me, her little fist clasped around the string as if her life depends on it.

'What can I say? I bribed her. Sorry.'

I smile at my niece's efforts. Having another little lady in our lives has been the most wonderful gift and she's given us all a brand-new focus and direction in our lives.

'Why are you sad, Mummy?' she asks me. 'Were you crying? What is making you sad? It wasn't an expensive balloon.'

I gently pull my little daughter towards me and sit her on my knee as Mo folds her arms and looks away with tears glistening in her eyes.

I take a deep breath, feeling the warmth of her soft skin on my face as we sit cheek to cheek.

'I'm just sitting here waiting on you and I was thinking about how proud I am of you,' I tell my daughter. I push her hair behind her ears and smile at how it's sticky with ice cream. 'You can have all the balloons in the whole wide world, no matter how expensive they are, and you can ask as many questions as you want to all day every day.'

'Really?' she asks, looking up at the sky.

And at that, she lets go of the balloon, and it drifts away from us before any of us can scramble to catch it.

'Oh no!' Mo exclaims, and we wait for the inevitable meltdown.

'It's OK, Aunty Mo,' says Hope, licking her ice cream. 'I did that on purpose so I'm not going to cry. I'm giving my balloon to Granda Peter up in heaven.'

My mouth drops open in wonder, as does Mo's, and as Shannon joins us the four of us girls watch as the balloon floats up into the bright blue August sky.

'I swear it's like she can read my mind sometimes,' I say in disbelief. 'My daughter has this crazy sixth sense and sometimes it really does freak me out.'

'What's a sixth sense?' Hope asks, and Shannon shakes her head at the idea of answering another question, but my phone ringing lets me off the hook this time.

It's David, just as I hoped it would be. I take a deep breath and thank the heavens that I'm still able to hear his voice every day of my life.

It was almost, in the blink of an eye, so very different.

'I was just thinking of my dad,' I say to him when I answer the phone. I look at the clock and smile at how he promised he would ring me to mark this date and time and my grand arrival at our doorway, the very spot where our survival story first began. Mo and Shannon discreetly distract Hope to give us our moment together.

'Your dad's watching over you, Kate,' he whispers. 'He's watching over every single one of us, every step of the way. I totally believe that.'

And I know that's true.

David might frequently be bedridden with chronic pain from the serious injuries he sustained; he may suffer horrific flashbacks and post-traumatic stress after all he's been through; he may never be able to travel back and forth to our childhood home town like we once loved to, but he is a living, walking miracle and I thank God that he's still with us every single day.

'I'll see you tomorrow,' I tell him as I tuck my hair behind my ear and watch him on my phone screen. 'You look tired.'

'You look amazing,' he says.

I roll my eyes but they fill up when I predict what's coming next.

'Ask me a question,' I whisper, gulping back tears.

'Why are you so beautiful?' he says, which makes me beam into a smile.

'Charmer,' I whisper, touching his face from afar.

We both take a second to drink in this precious milestone and be grateful to be still alive and, more importantly, still together.

'The last person who asked you that question also asked you to marry him, didn't he?'

I feel a warmth in my belly just by seeing his handsome face and by hearing his familiar voice, especially as I sit here in this doorway again and think of all we have been through since the horror that brought us together twenty years ago on this very day, at this very time.

'He did,' I say, remembering our wedding day fondly. It wasn't as we'd planned but it was immensely beautiful and special, with Hope in our arms and love in our hearts. 'And I promised that man I'd be there for him always, just as I promised to find him again after we first met.'

His face wrinkles around the eyes as his mind goes back in time.

'You're good at keeping promises, I'll give you that,' he says with a teary smile. He is physically frail in comparison to the man I first fell in love with, but with every year that passes he is becoming stronger, and with every day that passes I love him even more. 'I love you, David, I'll see you when I get home tomorrow.'

'I love you too, Kate,' he whispers, and blows a kiss to the camera. 'Give everyone over there a big hug from me.'

We say our goodbyes and immediately I feel I can't wait to get home to him. It's lovely to be here with my family and important to take time to grieve on this anniversary day, and to reminisce, to laugh and share stories and plans for the future, but my real home will always be where David is, and that will never change.

'It's my birthday soon,' says Hope, who skips over to me bringing me right back to reality. 'I want a really good present but I don't know what it is yet.'

'It's my birthday *today*,' says Shannon, as if in competition with her 5-year-old cousin.

Mo catches my eye and we laugh at the simmering rivalry between our two daughters, despite a twenty-one-year age difference.

'Come on, let's get out of here and plan some birthday celebrations,' I say, pulling myself up from the doorway. 'For both of you, of course!'

As we walk hand in hand back down the hill towards the town I love and where I grew up, the knot in my stomach loosens a little, and when I hear Hope giggle as Shannon tickles her playfully, I acknowledge that we are all survivors in so many senses of the word – me, Mo, Shannon, Hope and David.

I may be complete in myself, but I know that he made me the person I am today and I will never stop loving him..

'Are we going to see Nanny Martha later?' asks Hope, and Shannon rolls her eyes.

'Yes, we can go see Nanny Martha now,' I reply, ignoring my niece's reaction. 'And Granda Bob too, of course.'

'How on earth is that man still alive?' asks Shannon, which makes me chuckle. 'Jesus, he must have the constitution of an ox.'

Mo and I laugh heartily together as Hope demands we swing her along as we walk.

'Life goes on, eh sis?' she says to me, patting me on the arm. 'You're amazing, you know that.'

I nod and blink back tears.

'As are you, Mo. Yes, life goes on,' I tell her. 'It really does, even when we know it's never going to be the same again.'

'Nothing ever stays the same,' Mo says to me. 'But you and David – you've got this.'

We walk down the hill towards the car park and I feel I can take another step away from the bomb that threatened our lives and took the lives of so many precious others, even if the scars are still within me somewhere. So much else has happened since, so many hurdles, so many traumas, but together we are strong and we have learned to appreciate the good times and cherish every precious moment of our lives.

Life can be devastating, it can be unfair and cruel, it can deal us the most almighty blows, but beneath the fog and the storms it can still be beautiful; behind the clouds there is always a blue sky waiting to bring us better days.

Our lives might have changed for ever but, for David and me, our love story isn't over yet. Not even distance, not even illness, not even time itself will change that.

Our love will never come to an end. It can't. It will always be there because it doesn't know how to leave.

This love of ours has nowhere else to go.

THE END

Author's Note &
Acknowledgements

Dear Reader,

While the story of David Campbell and Kate Foley in *The Promise* is entirely a work of fiction, the incident described in chapter three and thereafter is based on the real-life bomb in my home county town of Omagh on Saturday 15th August 1998 which claimed the lives of 29 people, including unborn twins and injured hundreds more.

The Omagh bombing was the biggest single atrocity in over thirty years of The Troubles and as most of us who live in Northern Ireland do, I remember distinctly as the horror unfolded on the TV news. Later that evening, first-hand stories of eye-witness accounts rippled through our wider community, causing grief and trauma that still feels fresh to this day.

I'd like to convey my utmost respect to all those who suffered so horrifically on that Saturday afternoon, to all of those families who still bear scars both emotionally and physically to this day, and also to those who have worked so hard to make sure that new generations grow up in more peaceful times.

I opened this story with a quote from the late John Hume, one of the biggest advocates for such peace, who sadly passed away in August 2020 when I was writing the first draft of *The Promise*. I feel it's important to acknowledge the immense work of John and all those who worked with him, before him, and after him to pave the way for future generations in our society to live in a more integrated way where one day difference will not be a threat, where equality will be for all sections of the community, and where diversity will be respected. There is still some work to be done, but thank goodness we now live in much more peaceful times.

Like all my books, *The Promise* began with a very small seed of an idea. As it grew into the story it eventually became, I had the best team around me to bounce ideas off and brainstorm with. Thank you as always to my agent, Sarah Hornsley, from The Bent Agency. Thanks also to my editorial team Kim Young, Kate Bradley, Lara Stevenson, Emily Ruston, and Charlotte Ledger (with whom this seed was planted during a conversation at the HarperCollins Christmas party – see, we are working all the time even when off duty!).

A huge thank you to all the promotions team, cover designers, and foreign rights teams at HarperCollins UK and Ireland who help get my books out there. Thanks to all of you I'm thrilled to be able to say that my stories have been read in Germany, Italy, Holland, Hungary, USA, and Canada to date!

Thank you to all the amazing booksellers who have worked with us in such challenging times to make sure readers can still access great stories in a variety of ways. Especially to my local bookshop, Sheehy's in Cookstown County Tyrone, who continue to champion my work and have done since the very beginning of my writing career – thank you to TP, Madeline, Una, Carol, Emma, Bridie, and Mia for making sure shelves are full and signed copies are always at hand for those who would like one.

Thank you to all my social media friends, influencers, and bloggers who help shout about my books the minute they hit the shelves – there are so many of you wonderful advocates out there and I'm so, so grateful. I must give a personal shout out to local ladies Annette

Kelly (Little Penny Thoughts), Caroline O'Neill (DiggMama), Patricia McVeigh (Walking Updates), Olivia McVeigh (OMcV), Cliodhna Fullen, Emma McPhillips (EnjoyEverythingEmma), Michelle Donnelly (SweetMommaSimons), Seána McCrory (The Syngle Girl), Charlene Greensword (The Hyp Midwife), Siobhan Murphy (Shivonstyle), Caroline Slane (WrappedUpLuxuryGifts), Sharon McKeown (BabySensorySharon) and to all the ladies at The Belle of Mid Ulster who support me every year in so many ways.

2020 was a quiet year for events, but it was also the year we discovered Zoom and we had great fun with our virtual conversations! A big thank you to The Book Club Biddies and the Soul Book Club for having me as a guest member, and for lots of chat and craic along the way!

Despite the silence on the socialising and events front, I did have brilliant fun at a photoshoot in Belfast (every author needs a good profile pic) with Catriona Corrigan from Divine Photography and Aisling O'Connor of Dream Beauty. They worked their magic and came up with some new photos for my portfolio. The results as always were fantastic – a perfect treat in a year where we could get still dressed up even if we'd nowhere to go!

Thank you to all at Libraries NI, especially Peter Hughes, for including me in virtual events and for making sure my books are well stocked for local readers. A big thanks to all the librarians across the UK and Ireland for bringing books to readers against all odds, and to the PLR people who make sure we authors get a royalty when are books are picked up and read.

I am appreciative for the support of the press and broadcasting media at home and afar – especially Cameron Mitchell, Lynette Fay and Connor Phillips of BBC Radio Ulster, Ronan McSherry at *Ulster Herald*, Jenny Lee at the *Irish News*, Ian Greer at *Tyrone Courier*, Gail Walker at the *Belfast Telegraph*, Mags McGagh

(Salford City Radio), Keely Ryan (Her.ie), and Martin Breen at *Sunday Life*.

On a personal note, thank you to my wonderful family and friends for being by my side every step of the way. To my fiancé Jim, our children Jordyn, Jade, Adam, Dualta, and Sonny James; to my dad Hugh and my siblings Vanessa, David, Rachel, Lynne, Rebecca, Niamh and to all my beautiful nieces and nephews, my in-laws and my mum-in-law, Irene.

A special mention goes out to my 6-year-old niece, Juno Molloy, who inspired the line 'which do you like best, babies or horses?' I hope you don't mind me using your very important question in my book!

Lastly, I can't express enough how much gratitude I have for you, my readers, whose messages of love and support never fail to put a smile on my face. One of the joys of social media is that we can all keep in touch from near and far, so please do continue to drop me a line or two at any time and I'll do my best to respond as soon as I can. I have covered many topics in my books over the past few years, and it means so much to hear that these themes may resonate to your own life experiences even in the smallest way. 2020 was a tough, tough year for everyone but I'm humbled and honoured to have 'met' so many new readers who have not only enjoyed my stories, but who also trust me enough to share their own with me. I'm so grateful. Thank you.

Until the next time, take care and stay safe.

Emma x